FAIR GAME

FAIR GAME

Paul Daugherty

ORANGE FRAZER *PRESS*
Wilmington, Ohio
1999

ISBN 1-882203-58-5

Additional copies of *Fair Game* or other Orange Frazer Press publications may be ordered directly from:

Orange Frazer Press, Inc.
Box 214
37 ½ West Main Street
Wilmington, Ohio 45177

Telephone 1.800.852.9332 for price and shipping information
Web Site: www.orangefrazer.com

Library of Congress Cataloging-in-Publication Data

Daugherty, Paul, 1957-
        Fair game / by Paul Daugherty
        p. cm.
    ISBN 1-882203-58-5
        1. Sports--United States. 2. Newspapers--Sections, columns,
etc.--Sports. I. Title.
        GV583 .D38 1999
        796'.0973- -dc21
                                        99-35770
                                        CIP

To Jillian, truly God's child, and Kelly,
who can be whoever he wants.

ACKNOWLEDGEMENTS

Thanks to John Baskin, who thought this was a good idea. Thanks to my wife, who typed most of the columns into book form. Thanks to the *Cincinnati Enquirer*, the *Cincinnati Post*, *Cincinnati Magazine* and *Ohio Magazine*, who published the stories the first time, and paid me to write them.

Thanks to Mark Tomasik for his easy demeanor and to Julie Engebrecht, who pushed me to be better.

Thanks mostly to you, for reading.

Contents

Down and out

A Rose by any other name

Politically indecent

UNCOMMON VALOR

HOME PLATE

PREFACE

At a party once, a woman asked me what I did for a living.
"I'm a sportswriter," I said.

"No," she said, smiling. "What do you really do?"

There is an expression: "Find a job you love and you'll never work a day in your life." I worked once, as a waiter at a country club, where rich matrons snapped their fingers and called me honey. That was 25 years ago. I haven't worked a day since. Only Marge Schott calls me honey now.

This book is a distillation of my last 12 years of not working, first as a sports columnist at the *Cincinnati Post* then, beginning in 1994, at the *Cincinnati Enquirer*. It is a book of stories about people who play games for a living. That is, people who work less than I do.

I like heroic people, so there are lots of stories about heroes. I like people with courage and people who understand there is a world beyond the arena. Their stories are here, too.

I like writing about ridiculous thinking and pompous thinkers.

I'm a bad golfer. I like writing about that. I write better than I play.

There is room here for sentiment, so you will meet my dad. There's room for remembering. What is sports if you can't remember? There is a bleacher seat reserved for The Kid Down The Hall, who has taught me much about the beauty of youth, even today, in the dark age of Backward Baseball Hat Wearing Nation.

There are good people in this book, and good people gone bad. The common thread is that they've played the games and I've had the privilege of watching them.

Some make it easier than others: Boomer Esiason, Joe Nuxhall.

Some make it a pleasure: Eric Davis, Anthony Munoz, Pete Rose Jr.

Some don't.

It's as close to the truth as I can make it. It's as close to personal as the subjects would allow.

I'm not a big sports fan, not in the radio talk-show sense. I couldn't tell you who's in the Cleveland Indians starting lineup, or who Ohio State's quarterback will be next year. I'm amazed at those who can,

When I'm away from the games, I rarely watch them. I have teams I follow, but not so much anymore. There are things more urgent now than how many hits Clemente had last night.

I love sports, though. I love the games. In the people who play them, I still find truth and beauty that made me watch in the first place.

Boomer Esiason, playing a last season for his son. John Kapoor, running for his life. The grace of Eric Davis, the dirt on Chris Sabo's shirt. In deepest January, I think of Joe Nuxhall's voice.

I still go to work every day armed with the child-like notion that I'll see something I've never seen before.

I'd like to think I could write about other things. People are people, with or without headfirst slides. But the truth is, sports writing is fun. The woman at the party had it right. The next day I work for a living will be the first.

—Paul Daugherty, July, 1999

This ball—this symbol; is it worth a man's whole life?
—Branch Rickey

FAIR GAME

2

All-Stars

"Greatness comes and goes like streetcars."
—*Paul Daugherty*

Farewell, Mr. Football

August 8, 1991

*M*assillon, Ohio—At seven minutes to 11 it was all over, precisely 23 minutes after it began, and the little church on Third Street spilled its people onto the lawn. Paul Brown's burial service was short and to the point. Just like one of his practices, someone had said.

He would have liked it. Not the attention, so much—there were coaches and front-office people there who should have been getting on with their life's work, he'd have said—but Brown would have appreciated the crowd. It was a football bunch, and football was his whole life.

Paul Brown portraits painted themselves into soft hues of a pretty summer morning, and there was no one present who could say Brown hadn't touched their lives for the good in some way.

Shortly after 10, the current team of Massillon Tigers marched two-by-two up the block and onto the grass in front of 158-year-old St. Timothy's Episcopal Church. They looked like football players. They wore white shirts and orange Massillon Tiger ties that shimmered in the sunshine, and their necks were too big for their collars.

The night before, 100 freshmen and sophomores at Washington High School had collected for a football workout on the artificial turf at Paul Brown Tiger Stadium. They were 14 and 15 years old, shiny new keepers of Brown's gift. Odds are favorable that each was newly born with a football in his crib.

That's how it works in Massillon. It's a front-porch place, built on steel mills and football and the faith that each will endure. Brown, the winningest coach they ever had, owned half the monopoly. They'll never let him forget it.

2

They passed by Third Street in their cars. The Massillon Tiger pennants were attached to their radio antennas, singing in the breeze.

They stood across the avenue, in shirt-sleeves and Sunday dress. Others made their way up the short hill to the church lawn. They lingered beneath the oaks and the maples, arms folded, shuffling their feet a bit, stuck in the strange place between reverence and despair.

They were old and young, black and white, fathers and sons and young mothers with babies. Some cried.

"We'd be a ghost town without football," one said. His name was Al Drobney and he wore a white shirt with a black tie that had an orange Massillon Tigers emblem on it. Drobney last wore the tie in 1970, as a trainer on the last Massillon team to win a state title.

"It's been hanging in my closet for 21 years," Drobney said. "And I'll probably never wear it again."

Bill Walsh was there, and Pete Rozelle and Tex Schramm and Paul Tagliabue and Al Davis. The black limousines pulled up to the curb and the Hall of Fame poured out. Brown was about loyalty and respect and family. This was his extended family, collected once more to honor all that he had been.

Inside, a pipe organ sang odes to joy and peace. Ten candles flickered at the altar, their flames mixing with the sunlight streaming through the stained glass windows and beaming down upon Brown's casket, covered in white.

The Rev. Henry G. Harris read from the Episcopal Book of Common Prayer, the 23rd Psalm. "The Lord is my shepherd." There was more prayer, and a hymn and a short tribute to Brown. That was all.

An appropriate measure of a man is not what he takes with him, but what he leaves behind. The night before, on a satiny evening soft as first love, a Massillon Tigers coach named Jim Letcavits was in the meeting room of Tiger Stadium.

"If you could just be here when we have the McKinley parade," he was saying. Each year, Massillon's big game is with Canton-McKinley, and the night before, the town breaks out in lusty celebration of itself.

It has been tough times in Massillon. The mills are mostly silent, their workers scattered to other jobs in other places, their lives irretrievably changed. The soot that stains black the white granite of St. Timothy's is from a different time, when things were more secure.

The football endured. Brown built it to last. It was the way he built all things, from his beloved Browns to the Bengals to his family and his friendships.

The football is forever. It is what he left behind.

Jim Letcavits said 170 boys will try out for the Massillon football team this fall. They will be watched by 18,000 people at every home game, some of whom will have inherited their tickets.

Every boy in town still grows up wanting to play football for Massillon. When they do, the first picture they see in the team meeting room is Brown's.

By noon, they were mostly gone. Otto Graham, Brown's greatest player, lingered to breathe in some memory, but the rest had said good-bye.

Fair enough. Brown would have passed on the glory. Upstairs now, he was surely wondering what all the fuss was about.

The friends were good, though. And they were all there. He'd have liked that.

Mr. Shortstop

*B*arry Larkin doesn't do praise well. His brother says Barry hits a golf ball farther than anyone he has ever seen. His former football coaches at Moeller say he was one of the hardest-hitting safeties the school has ever had. His mother says he was the most calm of her four sons.

Nobody has a bad thing to say about Barry Larkin.

Here's one. Here's a bad thing:

He's lousy at taking compliments.

Barry Larkin couldn't hit a high, hard compliment with an aluminum two-by-four.

If you want to torture Larkin, lock him in an 8-by-12 room and tell him how great he is.

I've sauntered to his cubicle at Riverfront frequently. In the last eight years, I have made this trip maybe 500 times, occasionally with the intent of reminding Larkin of his many skills. It's always the same.

This time, I tell him his brother Byron has suggested Barry, at age 31, is faster than he has ever been. "Faster than I've been in the past?" Larkin asks.

Yes.

"No."

Quicker, then. You're quicker.

"I don't know if that's the case, either," Larkin says.

Well, OK, then. You belong in a rocking chair.

"Maybe more aggressive on the bases," Larkin offers, before catching himself and making base-running aggression a team concept. Founded, of course, by someone else. "It's just our attitude this year. I think Deion (Sanders) brought that here."

It goes on like this for a while. Larkin reacts to praise as he might a fastball to the earlobe.

What's the nicest thing another player could say about you?

"That whoever it is you're speaking of gives his all every time out there," Larkin says.

That would be you. You that "I'm speaking of."

"Right," Larkin says. "That would be the ultimate compliment."

He is different, in the age of self-promoters, instant superstars and guys who do music videos and list their occupation as "entertainer." He is unique, almost, in this time when players change teams as often as socks, when loyalty is as thin as a dollar bill.

How many players in the National League have been with the same team 10 years? How many started with that team, a decade ago? Tony Gwynn, right? Robby Thompson, the second baseman of the San Francisco Giants. Anyone else?

Four years ago, Larkin could have left here. The choice was this: Stay in sleepy Cincinnati, an easy place with a recent history of fielding competitive teams; or move to a bigger market, where the lights are brighter, even if the achievements aren't.

Larkin signed a five-year deal to stay. "It wasn't a big decision. I'm comfortable here, and we always have had a chance to win," he says.

Now, it is more than that. Larkin is the best player on the best Reds team since 1976. He is the unquestioned leader of a team that has assumed his quiet, determined personality. You can't praise anyone else in this group, either.

Larkin leads the league in steals, is second in fielding percentage, has hit better than .300 all year. No shortstop has better range. In the summer of '95, no player has had a more profound impact on his team than Larkin.

If the vote were taken today, Larkin would deserve to be the Most Valuable Player in the National League, the first shortstop to win the honor in 33 years. There's nothing he can do about it.

"I think Barry has set a goal for himself," says his mother, Shirley. "To be the best shortstop there ever was. He wants to be recognized for that. He feels now is the time to make that move."

Did he say that to you? He couldn't have said that to you.

"Well, no," says Shirley Larkin.

A mother's intuition?

"There you go," she says.

I'd never get him to say that. Not in a million years.

"No," Shirley says, "you wouldn't."

Larkin doesn't let strangers get too close. We knew more of Deion in 12 months than we'll ever know of Larkin, who has lived here his whole life. Larkin is graceful in all things. Grace is an acquired trait, one that does not lend itself to screaming headlines or CNN's Play of the Day. It is best admired from a distance, over a long period of time. This is how we have come to know Barry Larkin.

To know Larkin, we must watch him play. Banging a knee on a steal attempt, and playing the next day. Going deep into the hole, beyond the white, painted line that passes for the outer edge of the infield at Riverfront Stadium. Back-handing a two-hopper. Making the throw to first. Bang-bang.

Taking an extra base on a bloop single. Stealing a base when a run is desperately needed. Playing. Day after night after bruise.

Playing. That's Barry Larkin.

"He's good at the little things," says second baseman Bret Boone. "I'm not a base stealer, so it's fun for me to watch him do that. His first two steps are quicker than anyone I've ever seen. It's not that his speed is overwhelming. If you put him up against Reggie (Sanders), Reggie's faster.

"But Barry knows how to play. He just knows. Like the tight situations. Two strikes on him. Runner on third. One out. He'll get the runner in. Base hit, fly ball, whatever."

Says Hal Morris, "If I needed a hit to win the seventh game of the World Series, I'd want Barry at the plate."

Larkin doesn't hit home runs, mainly because he hasn't been asked. If the Reds needed him to hit 25 homers, he'd lengthen his stroke, pull the ball and hit 25 homers. He bats leadoff, second and third. Each spot requires completely different skills. Larkin has handled each well.

He is the MVP of the league.

"No, I'm not," Larkin says. "I don't consider myself a candidate. I don't hit home runs. I don't drive in 130 runs. I don't take over games offensively. Maybe I do intangibles."

Intangible means, "not able to touch."

"Sports writers around the country (who pick the MVP) see on ESPN (Ken) Griffey or Barry Bonds hitting home runs. That's the item that gets attention, and that's fine."

They see you play defense, though, I suggest. Defensive highlights.

"No, they don't. They see Ozzie (Smith). They see (Cal) Ripken go in the hole. You still got the Wizard of Oz. A 40-year-old guy who does backflips. That's what people want to see. That's what I see on ESPN when I look at it. That's OK.

"The player that got the most attention here was Chris Sabo," Larkin says. "And Eric Davis. Spuds McKenzie and Eric the Red."

So Barry is just Barry. What you see deep in the hole, making grace even Ozzie would love, is what you get.

The MVP is a slippery award, never so obvious as home runs or runs batted in. Kirk Gibson won it in 1988, compiling so-so statistics for the Los Angeles Dodgers. Two years later, Atlanta's Terry Pendleton was the MVP, even though Pittsburgh's Barry Bonds had 30 more RBI, and 33 more stolen bases.

Voters credited Gibson and Pendleton for their leadership, for the subtle ways each bent his team to his personality. The '95 Reds have assumed Barry Larkin's personality.

Larkin would agree. As only Larkin can.

"My role as whatever-you-want-to-call-me on this team is like what Ken Griffey Sr.'s was. I get along with everybody. I can communicate with everybody. It's not something anyone planned. It just evolved."

You could say it is Larkin's singular burden to work in the era of Ozzie and Cal, in a town that wears its anonymity like a badge. You could. He wouldn't.

"You've got to understand," says Byron Larkin. "He doesn't need the recognition. He's doing a good job, he's respected by his teammates, he's making good money." Says Shirley, "The notoriety he's getting now. That's the burden to him."

That, and compliments. They're worse than curveballs.

Munoz' Greatest Hits

December 19, 1992

*U*p on the little movie screen on the wall, Dexter Manley is getting pounded. Play after play, the Washington Redskins' All-Pro defensive end takes the wide turn toward Bengals quarterback Boomer Esiason, then finds himself on his face. Anthony Munoz is always there, somewhere above him, looking as great as they all say he is.

"Anthony kinda just absorbed him. You know what I mean?"

Jim McNally, the Bengals' offensive line coach, has a remote control in his hand. You've come to ask him about Anthony Munoz, and to see the greatness. For so long, Munoz has been a consensus great. You want the definitive version of why.

You ask McNally to pick a tape from the shelf on his office wall, any tape at all, put it in the machine and talk about Munoz. Out of the serious blue, McNally pulls a video of Cincinnati's last game of the 1988 regular season, the sweet Super Bowl ride that lifted off with this game, a win over the Redskins that clinched for the Bengals the home-field playoff advantage.

For the previous hour, McNally has been rummaging his tape library for Munoz bits. Pittsburgh in 1987. "Look at that surge," McNally says. Houston in 1985. "There he is, laying big Jesse Baker on his butt." The Cowboys in '85. The Colts in '89. The L.A. Raiders, this year. "Look at that," McNally says. His eyes are wide, like a kid's. "Look at that agility. He's still got some pretty good niftiness."

The movies show Munoz flattening pass rushers, shoving linemen from the path of James Brooks and Ickey Woods and Pete Johnson. They show Munoz literally blocking people off the screen. Mostly, the pictures are about Munoz controlling his man to such an extent, it's like Munoz is 290 pounds of Velcro.

But this Redskins tape, McNally plays all the way through.

"The first play of the game. Look at that. First and 10, 14:53 to go. First quarter. Playing the Redskins. Look at Manley," says Jim McNally. (Manley is on the sod.) "Look at that. That was Dexter in his prime. Basically, Anthony eliminated him."

We have Munoz for two more weeks, it seems. Munoz will start Sunday at the left tackle spot he has pretty much re-invented. If he's healthy, he'll do it again next weekend, and you have to believe that will be it. Munoz hasn't said if he'll play next year, but his contract runs out this season, he has been hurting and the Bengals want to get young in a hurry.

The point is to watch him while you can, watch him the way Brooklyn watched the Dodgers in 1957. We may not see his like again, here or anywhere else.

McNally punches a button to stop the tape. "Generally, you just knew that if Anthony was playing, we'd erase his guy," McNally says. "The guy he was blocking that day, we'd just call him The Eraserman. We'd just X that guy out."

That was it. For the past decade, at least, the Bengals have designed offensive game plans knowing that nothing would go wrong at left tackle. Munoz was there, erasing people.

McNally goes back to the movie, where Dexter Manley is face-first in trouble. "Look at that. The guy was an All-Pro. Anthony buried him." McNally has one of those John Madden clicker gizmos. He waves it like a wand. We see the same play 10 times. Esiason back to pass, Manley swinging wide on his pass rush, windmilling his meat-hook arms, arcing like a floodgate. Munoz crushing him like a grape. To McNally, this is like seeing *Gone With The Wind* for the first time.

"Who knows if Anthony's the best ever?" McNally says. "I mean, there was Jim Parker, and all those guys. But in his era, Anthony is top 1, 2 or 3." With runners and catchers and throwers, and even with tacklers, greatness is always posing for pictures. It's easy to see, easy to define, easy to pick. The basic truths are out there. But with offensive linemen...what?

Blocking well can be an invisible thing, so what you do is go to the movies. It's where eternal truths are revealed. Or maybe it's just where you see Anthony Munoz's opponents on the ground a lot.

"Mostly it's his quickness," McNally is saying. "His agility, his balance. He's strong, but not muscle-strong like those old Pittsburgh linemen in the '70s. But he's just such an athlete."

Cue the videotape.

"Here he comes in on the linebacker," McNally says. "*Boom.*"

"Here he knocks the whole pile back. Here he gets his hands on Manley. *Bang-bang-bang.*"

It's 90 minutes of Anthony Munoz's greatest hits. Literally.

Only the thing is, this was just Jim McNally, pulling tapes at random off the wall. This was Munoz, doing what he does.

Take a good look Sunday and next week. Greatness doesn't drop by often.

11

Golden Boy's Sweet Ride

September 5, 1989

*T*he thing was, Cris Collinsworth was just a guy. Through the money, the glory, the women—such women!—the hype, the pressure, the temptations, through all of it, he was who he was. Just a guy.

The trick in athletics is to be both great and good. Cris Collinsworth waded through traffic to make a painful 15-yard catch across the middle. But no more often, maybe, than he waded through autograph hunters in Wilmington, scribbling good will on scraps of paper.

In eight years, he caught 417 passes and the city's imagination. He was our most enduring and endearing football presence.

Bengals offensive coordinator Bruce Coslet once said of Collinsworth, "He's just a good guy, enjoying life from on top of the world," and that's about right.

Collinsworth never took his talent or his station in life for granted. He liked the attention it brought, even courted it, but he resisted fame's down side. He was who he was. After eight years, still the good ol' boy from Florida.

The Bengals cut him Monday. To those who had watched him closely this summer, it was no big surprise. Time waits for no one, and it was passing 30-year-old Cris Collinsworth by.

He stayed too long on a team with too many capable wide receivers. He made too much money ($550,000) simply to be an insurance policy. Collinsworth was competitive and, like most competitors, he had to be shown the reality of his situation.

Nine years of crossing patterns tend to stomp the spring from your step. Cris was the last to know.

His Bengals epitaph was standard football scripting.

"Cris has taken a lot of licks. The hits...are catching up to him," Sam Wyche said. "He made a lot of big catches here (but) the other guys (have) a little bit more speed, and we think they are going to withstand the season a little bit more.

"He's a great guy, a friend. There's no embarrassment. It's just that another era of his life is beginning."

He almost left here after the '84 season. John Bassett, the owner of the USFL's Tampa Bay Bandits, was throwing $3 million at Collinsworth, spread across five years. That was big money back then.

Collinsworth agreed to the deal. Any other Bengal would have been viewed here as a turncoat, with loyalties as thin as a dollar bill.

Anyone else would have been escorted out of town by the toe of a boot. In the Bengals' last home game in 1984, the fans at Riverfront Stadium cheered Collinsworth's every move, then lamented his imminent departure. It was, and is, impossible to dislike him.

He could have been mad Monday, at the unceremonious way he was dumped. The Bengal-Brown trust is lots of things. Sentimental isn't one of them.

Collinsworth chose to laugh.

"My future?" he said. "My future right now is I've got to get some homework done or I'm going to be embarrassed in class. Then I'm going to see if I can get my handicap under 10."

He is two years into law school at the University of Cincinnati. In a year, he'll own a law degree. The legal profession may never be the same.

"He ought to be feeling good about where he is right now," says Wyche. And where he has been.

Collinsworth was the stereotypical white wideout, only faster. He had good hands, ran precise patterns and was fearless across the middle.

Max Montoya: "His rookie year, we were playing Buffalo. He came across the middle, took a shot and held onto the ball. He got up bleeding with his chin wide open. I looked at him then and said, 'This guy's a player.'"

"I didn't think I was ever the greatest player here," Collinsworth said Monday. "I wasn't even the best receiver. But I'm not sure they ever had anybody here who enjoyed playing more than I did."

Cris Collinsworth had it all. He still does. Only now, the pieces are different.

It could be that some team will sign him. After he clears waivers, Collinsworth can deal with anyone, for whatever salary. Maybe some team is interested in having Collinsworth's knowledge and glad presence on its roster. Maybe not. As Wyche said, "At some point, you just have to say, 'It's time.'"

In November 1981, during his rookie season, Cris Collinsworth said this: "It's been kind of dreamland so far. It's almost like I'm stealing something, like sooner or later somebody's going to catch on that I'm just an ol' boy from Florida and kick me out of here."

After eight years, they finally caught on. Meantime, it's been one sweet ride. For Cris. And us.

That $550,000 the Bengals are saving now can be plowed back into the contract offer to holdout Eddie Brown. The football business marches on.

Without Cris Collinsworth, who made the business a pleasure for us all. So long, Golden Boy.

The Best Story of Them All

July 30, 1991

*W*ilmington, Ohio—All the running backs go before their time. They die at the hand of a fork, or their knees wither or their bodies simply fill up with hits from the blind side. They aren't machines, even the great ones.

Then there is Bengals halfback James Brooks, who is 32 and runs like you just drove him off the showroom floor. This spring, Brooks turned a 40-yard dash in 4.4 seconds. It's the same time he ran 10 years ago. "Still faster than any back we got," he said Monday.

This is Brooks' 11th year as an NFL running back, a position with the average lifespan of a gypsy moth. Brooks has thrown his 180-pound body around the arena for a decade and still looks like a new penny, and if you don't think that's unusual, check out a list of great running backs whose supply of hits to the body ran out well before they made it to 10 years.

How about Earl Campbell? Eight years, 9,407 yards, a new Hall of Famer. Campbell's body needed a tow by the time he was finished. He was done when he was 30.

Last year, Brooks ran for 1,004 yards. The last three years have been the best of his career. At his current pace, Brooks will need three more years to pass Campbell on the all-time rushing list.

A man's mind wanders across the NFL, seeking names of current backs who have started every season for the past decade. The mind stops at two, Ottis Anderson of the New York Giants and Marcus Allen of the Los Angeles Raiders. That's it.

Allen, a sure future Hall of Famer, is fading. Anderson, a Hall possibility, will be a bit player this fall if he sticks with New York. Brooks is the center of Cincinnati's offense.

15

So there is this notion now that a dozen years hence, James Brooks will be giving his acceptance speech in Canton, and everyone will be wondering what they were doing when Brooks was playing the game.

Brooks is the best athlete this town has never appreciated. We've responded to the hype and glory of Boomer and Ickey and Eric Davis and skipped right past the best story of them all.

Maybe it's because Brooks is just 5-9. Or because he does something awfully unconventional these days, like keep his mouth shut and show up every week ready to bump heads.

What we've missed is the career of one incredible jock. "He's the most remarkably conditioned athlete I've ever seen, in any sport," says Bengals defensive coordinator Dick LeBeau.

There are reasons for this, of course, and they start at the base of the red seats at Riverfront Stadium. The red seats are where you go if you want to catch a ballgame and incur cardiac arrest at the same time.

Brooks runs them. Thirty-six sections, 26 rows each, straight up, straight down, several days a week between the start of February and the end of June. It takes him 35 minutes.

"When I start, I don't stop until I'm finished," he said.

Brooks does other drills, equally demanding, the point being that nothing occurring in training camp or during a season can be any worse than what he puts himself through in his free time.

"My body always asks me for a vacation," he said. "I always tell it no."

Some years, the Bengals draft halfbacks. It's more their fascination with "skill position" players than a snub at Brooks, but Brooks adds it to the chip on his shoulder nevertheless.

That's another thing about him. Brooks remembers slights. It could be something major, such as a Pro Bowl snub, or minuscule. Brooks is still angry that he has never been invited to take part in the Superstars competition.

"They asked that fullback from Pittsburgh, (Merrill) Hoge,"

Brooks said. "Who's he?"

Brooks broke his left thumb in the opening round of the playoffs last year, a compound fracture in which the splintered bone punctured the skin. The next week, before the Bengals played the Raiders, he walked around Spinney Field with the thumb in a splint.

Coach Sam Wyche spent the week lying to the local media, saying Brooks wouldn't play. Anybody who knew Brooks more than five minutes knew he would play, and he did.

Age only matters when the body tells it to. To now, Brooks has gotten no such messages. "It's not the age, it's what your body is doing," he said. "Your body can do anything you want it to do.

"Once they've been in the game for a while, players think they've got it made. They don't work. It's like they get paid, and they get full. They're not hungry. I'm always hungry."

We hadn't noticed, at least not enough. Maybe it's time we did. "I haven't lost a step, or anything like that," Brooks said.

The Return of Eric the Red

May 12, 1996

*E*ric Davis returns to Cincinnati in a different light because that is the way celebrity works. When Davis was the next Willie Mays, we rushed to find his faults. Won't play hurt. Won't fix the damned hitch in his swing. Won't smile for the cameras. Won't play the Cincinnati shut-up-and-play game.

We dwelled in a Chris Sabo space in time. Our heroes wore humility and dirty shirts. Davis was an L.A. guy and that said it all.

17

"It had a lot to do with expectations. No matter what I did, it was never enough," he says. "I don't care how strong a person is, those things will wear on you. It wore on me."

He is past that now. So are we. Those quick to disparage Davis in his prime are now singing the praises of a prideful old man. "Elder statesman," he says.

Revisionist history is often kinder than the first draft. What we are seeing with Davis is the coda to a fine major league career. It is a pleasure to behold. Davis is attempting to paint a pretty twilight. The early strokes look good.

Here's a sports story for you, kids, one your parents can read you beginning to end, without a V-chip. We were beginning to wonder. Money, strikes, domestic violence and Marge. Are we having fun yet?

Here is fun: Eric Davis, hitching, coiling, raising his front leg, swinging his black bat like a snake, hitting an opposite field home run with only his wrists.

Here is the best kind of story: Davis the ballplayer, bad neck, tired legs, a baseball prodigy done at 33, coming back. Davis the man, living the values we treasure in our athletes: perseverance, determination, dedication, striving. The whole character catalog.

Striving? In the past three months, Davis has traversed the Himalayas. Nearly cut in March. Platooning in left field in April. Centerfielder, cleanup hitter and essential piece in May.

"To succeed, you have to fail," Davis is saying. He knows a lot about each. Davis was the best player in baseball in May 1987. In May '94 he was among the worst.

"They were talking about his bat speed," Reds hitting coach Hal McRae is saying. "He always had bat speed. It was the timing. That was the first thing I told him."

As recently as mid-March, Davis was not catching up to major-league fastballs. The Hitch was generally assumed to be the problem. Davis' familiar batting slouch—hands held low, below his waist—had not changed, but his reflexes had slowed.

Davis had heard this for years, and always resisted the advice to bring his hands up, closer to the hitting position. His stance was how he hit. Also, who he was: Cocky-confident, arrogant, cool. Unique. Nobody else did it that way. Maybe nobody else could.

"I don't think a hitter can be effective if you get rid of the mechanism he has used his whole career," McRae says.

Instead, McRae worked on Davis' timing. "When the timing is late, he gets caught down here," says McRae, holding his hands below his waist. "You can't hit from down there. Nobody has bat speed down there."

McRae introduced the front-leg kick. The leg kick gets Davis' swing started early enough that low hands are not an issue. The kick creates a rhythm to the swing.

Credit Davis, too. In his old age, he has become a hitter, not just a swinger. Three of his first seven homers were to right field. "When I was young, I was real pull-conscious," he explains. Now, he lines RBI singles to centerfield.

As striking as his hitting is Davis' demeanor. He left here proud and angry and unhappy. He returns with only the pride.

"You get older, you learn things," Davis says. Time rounds a man's edges and softens his suspicions. It doesn't dim his resolve.

In Cincinnati, he was disenchanted with the burdens of his potential, in L.A., by the hype that came with a return home and his reunion with boyhood friend Darryl Strawberry. In Detroit in 1994, he was a physical mess.

Last year, it all became too much. So Davis left, to run his businesses and do good works for the kids of Los Angeles. It was enough. "I didn't think about baseball," he says. "I made decisions. I stuck by them. I wasn't forced out of the game, I wasn't told I couldn't play any more. I did it on my terms."

He was happy with that, but not fulfilled. Nobody wants to leave the game batting .183 in his last year. Still, when Reds General Manager Jim Bowden approached Davis' agent, Eric

Goldschmidt, about a possible return, Davis did not immediately agree.

"I worked out," Davis says. "I swung the bat. I ran. I threw. I wanted to see how my body would react. I didn't want to return and embarrass myself. I didn't want people to say, Why did he come back?"

Having satisfied himself, Davis signed for $500,000. Judging from today's salaries, he has already earned all of it. Yet McRae says, "I think he can have an Eric Davis-type year."

Says Davis, "I wasn't supposed to be here, you know. Just by making an appearance in that uniform, I've won. In my eyes, I've won. I'm not saying I'll hit 30 home runs. But I can still hit the ball out of the ballpark. I can still run. I can still catch. I can still throw."

Says Barry Larkin, "He just goes about the job the right way. Eric is a man, you know? He takes on responsibility, he accepts what comes his way. I've never seen him hide from anything. He's a straight shooter, he's accountable. And he can hit a fastball."

For so long, the only thing Reds fans knew about Davis was that he could, indeed, hit a fastball. Maybe now, in his twilight, they are seeing the rest. It has always been there.

"If the young guys can learn anything about this game, it's perseverance," Davis says. "Constantly working hard. Never letting people tell you what you can't do."

Davis has carried the Reds recently, smashing grand slam homers on consecutive days in San Francisco, winning another game with a 12th-inning homer. But we're not watching a tribute to May 1987, any more than in May 1987, we were watching a tribute to Willie Mays.

We are watching Eric Davis. Finally, that seems to be good enough for everyone.

A Winner's Arrogance

August 22, 1988

*F*ew men are the best ever. Even fewer redefine our notion of greatness. Johnny Bench was one of those.

There always was an undefeatable look of success about Johnny Bench. He owned a winner's arrogance. From the first, he wanted to be the best catcher who ever lived. Eventually, he was.

They will honor him Sunday in Cooperstown, N.Y., where he and Carl Yastrzemski will become the 158th and 159th former major leaguers enshrined in the baseball Hall of Fame.

They will testify to Bench's wonderful athletic ability. They will praise his throwing arm, his durability, his power, his knack for hitting in the clutch. They will forget his arrogance. In honoring Johnny Bench, no one will emphasize his "inner conceit," as Bench calls it. Ultimately, it was his greatest gift.

Reaching for greatness is one thing; expecting it is something else altogether. John Bench expected greatness, and pursued it with a cocky, hot-blooded eagerness that would have looked foolish in a lesser man.

He predicted he would be the rookie of the year in 1968. He was. He wanted to play until he was 35. He did. He wanted to be a millionaire by the time he was 30. He was.

In October 1972, from the front row at Riverfront Stadium, his mother asked him to hit a home run. It was the bottom of the ninth in the fifth game of the National league Championship Series. The Reds trailed the Pittsburgh Pirates by a run.

"Hit me a home run," Katy Bench said. John Bench did.

He played 17 years. He won all there was to win. Home run titles, RBI titles, Gold Gloves, Most Valuable Player trophies, World Series rings.

21

His were the tools of elegance. Bench reinvented catching, from the one-handed way he caught pitches to the iron-handed way he handled pitchers. Arguably, he had the best throwing arm ever.

George Culver, a Reds pitcher who won 11 games and threw a no-hitter in 1968, Bench's rookie season, said in the spring of 1969, "I wish I had his arm."

And his arrogance. At 22, Bench said, "I can throw out any runner alive." He was right, of course. The fact that Bench was barely of voting age when he said this didn't matter. An essential part of being the best in anything is the haughty notion that where others fail, you succeed.

Bench was the best. He knew it. He was comfortable with it. No brag, just fact. The best.

I don't think Bench ever believed he would be anything but the best catcher ever. I don't think he ever considered the possibility.

Even before he was the best, he knew he would be. To John Bench, it was an honor waiting for him, a trophy waiting for a space in his case. It was a foregone conclusion.

In 1966, when he was 18 and nursing a bad thumb, Bench leaned over a railing at Crosley Field and yelled into the Reds bullpen: "If any of you guys are catchers, you better remember me. I'm going to take one of your jobs."

In 1969, Bench was catching a pitcher named Gerry Arrigo. Already, Bench had shown he was adept at handling pitchers, even those a decade older than he.

In his second full season, Bench let the Reds' pitching staff know it was he who called the shots. On this day, Arrigo wasn't listening.

"He thought he had a fastball," Bench said, "but he was pitching against a hitter I knew he couldn't possibly throw it by."

"I called for a curve and he shook it off. I called for a curve again, and he shook it off. I called for a curve again. He shook it off. He finally threw a fastball."

Bench caught it.

Bare-handed.

Arrogant.

But the message was clear, and it took hold very quickly: Don't shake off the best. Even in his second big-league season.

You wonder if there will ever be another as good as Bench. Catching has always been the quickest ticket to the majors, yet there is a perpetual dearth of good catchers.

Certainly, there will never be another story as good as Bench's. Now that America is a nation of malls linked loosely by highways, Burger Kings and Pizza Huts, no kid will ever again rise from someplace like Binger, Okla., population 600, to make the Hall of Fame.

In America now, you can be 2,000 miles from home, but you're never more than two blocks from a hamburger. In the 1960s, if Johnny Bench didn't play professional baseball, he could have picked cotton for two cents a pound. His was the old-time, newsreel version of the American Dream. We won't see it again, and maybe that's just as well.

Bench's arrogance set him apart; today it would make him one of the crowd. It wasn't pretentious or loud or boastful. It was only Bench's way of letting us know he was a winner. The best.

In Cooperstown on Sunday, they will celebrate John Bench's skill. Some of us will remember the winner's arrogance that brought it all out.

Boomer at the Wall

I never figured Boomer Esiason would get old. He was too cocky, too hip. Publicly, he looked too free from worry or fear or anger or anything that tends to put miles on a man.

He was too blond, you know? Besides, who could be old that calls himself Boomer?

Esiason turned 36 last month. Into middle age he goes, with the rest of us.

Somehow, I never thought I'd see the quarterback who sat in front of the replacement players' bus 10 years ago—has it really been that long?—return to Spinney Field and say, "This is a chance for me to go out gracefully."

That was Boomer on Monday. So was this:

"I'd like to make sure the young guys know how to appreciate what they have. It's prestigious. You're lucky to be here. You're making money that 99 percent of the population doesn't make. You're working for six months."

This is not a view shared by many of his younger brethren. Probably, it wasn't in Esiason's thoughts as he blocked that bus. But a decade will do that to you.

Now, you can almost hear Esiason saying, "When I was your age...." Soon, we'll be calling him Norman.

You hang your years on certain memories. After awhile, you realize the memories don't get older. You do.

I remember talking to Esiason in 1981, when he was a sophomore at Maryland. He sat out the previous year, as a redshirt. He spent that season enjoying his team's games from the upper deck, with his girlfriend and a flask of Jack Daniel's.

"That's exactly right," Esiason said Monday.

Well, not exactly.

"Girlfriends," he said.

While working in New York in '87, I remember watching Esiason's sit-in on TV. "It was a bus that had nobody on it," Esiason said Monday. "A bus that was parked. It was symbolic more than anything."

I asked Esiason where that guy is now. A memory, maybe.

"I think there's still a part of me like that, but also a part of me that's grown up (and) understands what his actions mean to everybody else. Your actions speak for your teammates and your organization. When you're younger, you're not sensitive to that," he said.

Over the years, I counted on Esiason throwing TD passes at Maryland. I counted on Esiason to be outspoken, as he was the day after the '84 draft, when he suggested everyone who allowed him to slide into the second round had made a huge mistake.

I counted on him play-faking to Stanley Wilson, before dropping bombs on defenses that could never quite catch Eddie Brown.

But Boomer, aging? I never counted on that.

"I don't have the arm strength I once did," said Esiason. "But I have the experience. (Defenses) can't do anything to me I haven't seen."

Other things have occurred. Esiason's son Gunnar, 6 now, was born with cystic fibrosis. Sick kids age a man, in ways only he can know.

"Every time he coughs, I think, 'What's another wind sprint?'" Esiason said. Gunnar was due for his six-month physical Monday, routine for CF patients.

"He's anxious. He knows he gets needles," Esiason said. "He knows he gets X-rays. It's a six-hour deal. I let him sleep with me last night."

The Bengals are full of young, prosperous players now, who think the world will always be theirs. Immortality is a privilege of youth. But it's a shame they can't know what Boomer Esiason knows.

25

"I never took for granted being an NFL quarterback," he said. "If it didn't mean anything to me, I could have retired a couple years ago."

I told him I never pictured him as an old player.

"We all get older," he said.

Yes, we do. I wrote about Esiason's wife, the former Cheryl Hyde, when she played field hockey in high school.

It was a long time ago.

The Voice

March 4, 1999

*I*f you are of a certain age somewhere between infant and timeless, you have spent the better part of your life listening to Joe Nuxhall on the radio. He is the voice of summer. He is the sound of muggy nights wrapped around a can of cold beer sweating in your hand as you sit on the deck of your house and look at the moon. Joe is the calliope music of Cincinnati's best season. You can't remember when he wasn't.

Sometime around 2 this afternoon, he'll take the microphone from Marty Brennaman and call the third inning of the Reds first exhibition game, against the Minnesota Twins.

"And now with the play-by-play, here is Joe Nuxhall," Brennaman will say.

"Thank you, Marty," Joe will say, and you will feel free to dream of springtime.

It's Year 33 in the booth for the Old Left-Hander, the last year of his current contract. Cincinnati might disappear if he doesn't sign a new one. But Joe is 70 years old, 56 years in the game. He needs surgery on both knees. One of his hips isn't the greatest. He smokes too much. He could stand to lose some pounds.

Sometimes Joe will be on an airplane, looking out the window, and he will lament what he has missed. Baseball has given him every summer; it has also taken them all away. "I've seen the entire country," he says, "from 35,000 feet."

He'd like to go to the Grand Canyon in the summer. He went once, long ago, in the winter, but that wasn't much. "Yosemite," Joe says. "I'd like to go there."

He hates the travel, the late nights and early mornings, the sameness of the hotels. "You travel the best there is, but the hotels still have four walls," he says.

Golf keeps him going. Golf, and the game. Joe does love the game.

It took me a few years to figure Joe out. Joe is an acquired taste. When I was young and knew everything, I thought Joe was slow. Seasons changed quicker than Joe called a close play. Robins would blast springtime before Joe would criticize the Reds. After 12 years here, I'm still waiting for Joe's first question on the Star of the Game or the Nuxhall Report or whatever they call it.

Silly me. Joe's secret is he has no secret. In an age of media phonies and sound-bite overload, Joe is Joe. The boys in marketing will never mess with him. Joe sounds like the game.

Joe lolls. Joe pauses. Joe ambles and strolls. He takes his time. The game is not on the clock. Neither is he.

We do enough running around. We sprint across our days, sure in the notion that if we work longer, achieve more and wring every second from every day, our lives will be better and fuller with meaning. They're not, of course. They're just more tiring.

Joe is a hot bath. He's a cold beer. He's there at the end of the day. Listening to him makes you want to prop up your feet. It's a damned fine night when the stars are out and the air is warm and soft as down and you're sitting outside and the game is on and

27

there's nothing to do but listen. It's the time of your life.

"You feel like you're a fan, talking to a fan," Nuxhall says. He very rarely decorates himself with the word "I." It's presumptuous and immodest and really, we all know what he means, anyway. "You want them to feel like they're sitting there with you and they're seeing the same thing.

"You try to be as fair as you can. You try not to be flowery unless something special comes up. You have to be critical in some instances. But you try not to dwell on it."

Does anyone who knows Nuxhall dislike him? Does anyone dislike him at all? Twelve years here, I've never heard a bad word about him. He doesn't even cheat at golf. It's an amazing thing to live your life with no one disparaging you. Nuxhall does it without trying.

"The real good feeling I get out of the whole deal is shut-ins," he says. He likes bringing the game to those who can't get out. He gets lots of letters from people like that, who tell him the games are the best part of their day. "To do something for them is very special," Nuxhall says.

He thinks about retiring, but what would he do with that? He could play more golf, but he already plays his full. He could celebrate some holidays without worrying about leaving home at 3 to get to the ballpark by 4. Easter. Memorial Day. The Fourth of July. He could make some of those trips he talks about. But would they be better than the game?

"I know I'd miss the game," he says.

So Joe is likely to re-up after this year. One more time. "I'm going to think real hard about it," he says, "but probably so. I'd like to hang around long enough to get into the new stadium." That would give him seven decades in baseball. Maybe he would rest then.

I don't want to think of the games on the radio without him, so I won't. I'll think of working in the yard instead, or helping kids with homework or sitting on the deck in the thick of a starry summer night, all the time listening to the radio. Nuxhall will be there, his cadence somewhere between 33 rpm and molasses. It'll be slow and drowsy, and it will sound like baseball. It'll be just right.

Spuds in the Limelight

July 8, 1988

*H*e's your mechanic. Your electrician, your mason, the phone company guy. Maybe he's your plumber. He's schlepping U-joints in the boiler room and cursing the single guy in 3G who stuffed banana peels down the Dispose-All. Only single guys stuff banana peels down the Dispose-All.

He needs a union card.

He's no artisan. He isn't Eric Davis. But he makes the most of what he has. He says this daily. There is no greater triumph.

For that, he's an All-Star. Chris Sabo is a bomber, a kamikaze, a baseball primitive. A dirty shirt. If you and I could hit .310 with 31 doubles in 84 games, we could be Chris Sabo. Right now. A blue collar to anyone coming up with another All-Star matching that description.

Only in Cincinnati, in this summer of baseball torment, could Chris Sabo be one of the Reds' two best everyday players.

This was supposed to be the year of youthful arrogance and elegance, an Eric Davis-Kal Daniels flashdance through the West. Davis, wristing 400-foot home runs! Dancing up outfield walls! Daniels, spraying line drives to wide open spaces! Silky power! What a feeling!

The Reds almost won the West on talent and style points last year. This summer would bring redemption.

Redemption, such as it is, isn't Davis or Daniels. In this blue Reds' summer of '88, it is a dirty shirt.

Nothing comes easily for this team this year. Nothing ever has come easily for its third baseman. In July 1988, five days from the All-Star Game, the Reds 9^1/$_2$ games behind the first-place Dodgers, it fits that Sabo will suit up in Riverfront Tuesday night.

In a moment of clarity, Marge Schott recently said her team could use a shot of "Saboism."

He is everything the Reds haven't been. Too often, they have lacked Sabo's joy for the game, his basic pride in his workmanship. They've lacked dirty shirts.

It's no coincidence that Cincinnati's other All-Stars, Barry Larkin and Danny Jackson, are equipped with temperaments similar to Sabo's.

No one is tougher on Larkin than Larkin. Jackson's left arm and high-strung leadership are indispensable to the Reds, a young team begging for direction.

And Sabo is Sabo. An original. It's nice, he is saying. It's better than nice. OK? I'm excited. "Don't make it sound like I'm not excited," he says. Do we hit yet?

As recently as early March, Sabo was ticketed for another year in Triple-A, another season of dirty shirts in Nashville.

He came north mainly because Buddy Bell had a bad knee and the immortal Angel Salazar couldn't hit water if you threw him from a boat.

Now, Sabo is an All-Star. What does it mean, someone asks. "You can look back and say you had a good two or three months, if nothing else," Sabo says. "I didn't think I was one of the top two third basemen in the league. But I'll take it."

Someone tells him that Cardinals' manager Whitey Herzog selected him. Sabo doesn't know that. It doesn't matter. "I thought it was a committee of managers or something."

He tried to have included in his contract incentives for making the All-Star team and for winning rookie of the year honors, but the club said no. Sabo, a 26-year-old rookie wanting mainly to play every day and get his shirt dirty, didn't have much leverage.

He's making $62,500, the major league minimum. It doesn't matter. "You can't complain when you're making sixty-two five," he says.

Sixty-two five is high elegance in Detroit, where he's from. Sixty-two five is a big Ford at the curb and dinner out once a week.

The game is what matters. Put me in coach, I'm ready to play. Today. Put me in the game. The best thing anyone can ever do for Chris Sabo is to write his name on a lineup card. For more than a week, he has had back spasms. He has a deep chest cold. "Pneumonia or something. A real pain," he says. For spasms, he takes "a couple aspirin."

"You gotta play hurt. That's the name of the game. If you're only going to play healthy, you're not going to play many games. I've had back spasms for the last week and a half. So what?"

He never dreamed about being an All-Star, only about making the major leagues. Just working hard, every day. Like punching a clock, only with room service. "If you give 100 percent, you can never second-guess yourself," he says.

He gets a little impatient with all the cameras, the lights, the questions. The answers. It's just a game. I play the game hard. It's what I do. Anything else? I gotta go shag balls.

He should have his name in lights. He should also have it stitched in script above the breast pocket of his bowling shirt.

That's his charm, his credit, his triumph. I hope he has the time of his life Tuesday.

The Last Action Hero

December 2, 1994

*H*e was the picture of a Sunday afternoon. The way we remembered it, before the agents and the networks took over. The nobility of a football player is forged in dirt and cast in blood. None was nobler than Tim Krumrie. We will not see his like again.

"Blood running down his pants leg." Bengals offensive lineman Bruce Kozerski is talking about his teammate of 11 years. Someone asks him: Paint a picture fit for a Sunday afternoon.

"Fingers mangled," Kozerski says. "Blood everywhere. That gash on his nose he's had since he was born."

"He's here early. He stays late. Last guy in the weight room. Last guy off the field." Dave Shula didn't know it, but he was delivering Krumrie's epitaph as a football player. Krumrie announced his retirement Thursday, after 12 seasons, proving everything is inevitable.

Time waits for no one. Not even for Tim Krumrie, who would be the first person to run it down from behind.

"I think back to '88, when we were good," says punter Lee Johnson. "We were playing that 3-4 defense with guys averaging 255 on the defensive line, winning with a defense people thought we shouldn't be winning with. That makes me think of him."

It does, doesn't it? Winning, when people thought he shouldn't. That describes Krumrie's whole professional life. A runt, a stowaway, a survivor. A real pain in the ass.

He loved it when the Bengals picked a center first in the 1983 draft. He thought it was ironic that he, a 10th-round pick, would be lining up nose to nose with an instant millionaire poster-boy like Dave Rimington. Ironic, and funny as hell.

Between plays that first summer, Krumrie would spit on the

football. When Rimington bent over to snap it, Krumrie would toss dirt in his face. "This is war, fat boy," he would say. And it was.

For 12 years. Through 161 starts in 162 games. Through hamstring pull, twisted knees, hyperextended knees, internal bleeding and busted fingers. Through a broken leg that would have crippled a lesser man. Krumrie's leg snapped in four places in the 23rd Super Bowl.

The doctors tried to take him to a hospital. Like hell they would.

"How are we going to tape this sucker?" Krumrie asked them.

"You're going to pass out," the doctors told him. "You're going to go into shock."

"Give me a beer," Krumrie said. They did. He watched the game on TV, from a table in the dressing room.

He never missed a game for an injury. He never had an agent. He never held out. He never complained about any of it.

"He loved coming here," Kozerski says. "Every single day. Every team says they have one like that. He is our version. If you ask me, he's an original." The last original.

He has the shoes he wore when he came into the league. He has the socks they cut off him at the Super Bowl. He has the gash in the bridge of his nose, from his too-loose helmet banging around for 12 years. Every summer, Krumrie fought equipment man Tom Gray over the fit of his headgear. It's supposed to be tight. His never was.

"I need the blood from the gash," he explained, "to really feel like I'm into it." The nose has been stitched. "Hundreds of stitches," Krumrie said gleefully to me a few years ago. "Ten a crack."

"He loved the gash," says Lee Johnson.

He loved it all. He really did.

"I never gave up. I never stopped trying. I never stopped proving myself," Krumrie says.

What can you say? The man has owned three bulldogs. He works out with an anvil. As a kid on a Wisconsin farm, he drove a

33

truck in the summertime fields, killing time doing bicep curls with cinderblocks.

Now, he's done. In three weeks, the hitting will be over. The Gash gets a permanent rest. Regrets? None. "I don't regret one damn day. I busted my ass every single day," says Krumrie. No argument about that. Or this:

"Tough bastard," says team strength coach Kim Wood. "Warrior."

2

Golf And Other Tragedies

"Golfers are not jocks exactly. There's a spiritual element to their quest. They seek the impossible shot. The unimaginable putt. And while everything they see and know tells them these things are not possible in this life, they play on, ever believing."
—*Michael Heaton, Cleveland golfer*

The Ultimate Addiction

July, 1990

*T*his is the story of an addict. My friend Ray. Good guy. Family guy, house in the 'burbs, 2.2 kids, good job, loving wife, minivan. The works.

Ray threw it all away at 14. He picked up his father's wedge and a lump of X-outs, went to the schoolyard and began taking divots.

Now he's 32. He plays golf three, four, five, hey, why not six times a week. He plays at 6 in the morning, he plays at dusk.

He plays in bad weather. In hurricanes, he plays a low-trajectory ball. He plays mostly at Crooked Tree, where his golf hat bears the club's logo and the words "Twisted Mind" because, face it, that's what it takes to play as much golf as Ray does.

Ray makes his own clubs, Ray watches golf on TV. Occasionally, Ray will remember the names of his wife and children.

The happiest moment of Ray's life? "The day I tied the course record at Hickory Woods," he says.

This is his story. And yours, big guy. And yours and yours. Whether you're a hacker or a 2-handicapper, there's a little bit of Ray in all of you. Because the truth is, any man who is married *and* serious about his golf game knows that bigamy is not illegal.

Summer is in full bloom, and a man's mind turns to...golf. Golf is in the air. Golf makes the world go 'round. What the world needs now, of course, is golf, sweet golf.

Ray is not alone. Last year, 393,389 rounds of golf were played on Cincinnati's seven public courses, this according to the Cincinnati Recreation Commission's golf division. Several of those rounds may have been played by women but, for our purposes here, they are a blip on the radar.

Women do not play thirty-six holes of golf, come home and watch a taped golf tournament for three hours, then spend a fun-filled evening in the basement golf shop, making golf clubs, before cozying up with the latest issue of *Golf Digest*.

Men do this. Why do men do this? What is it about golf that makes men forget everything in their lives except what to hit off the fourth tee at Maketewah? (Driver or 2-iron.)

Men miss anniversaries, birthdays, Mother's Days, wedding days. Men are in a daze a good bit of the time, but not when they're playing golf.

There are no statistics on golf-related divorce, but there ought to be. Golf ruins more marriages than wallpapering. Golf, in fact, is a major, major reason women think men are scum. Isn't it?

"Top three," says Kevin O'Sullivan, the golf professional at Crooked Tree, a public course in Mason. "Golf is probably second, right behind sex and ahead of Monday Night Football."

Some men play golf for the fun of it, but the truth is, most play to avoid doing things that aren't in the least bit fun. Men would rather play golf than do whatever it is they're really supposed to be doing.

It is July. It is a Saturday morning in July, or maybe a Tuesday afternoon. The lawn needs cut, the fence painted, the messages are waiting, there is a 3 o'clock meeting with a buyer from New York and the phone is ringing.

Our other friend, we'll call him Fred, is playing golf. His wife, Ethel, is calling the pro shop, the snack bar and the front desk, but she can't find Fred. She never finds Fred, and that is the point.

Fred called for a tee time and used an assumed name. He does this often when he plays golf. "We have a lot of Mr. Smiths and Mr. Johnsons playing here," says Kevin O'Sullivan.

At the turn, Fred will use the pay phone in the clubhouse. If it is after 5, he will call Ethel and tell her something came up at the office. If it is before 5, he will call the office and tell them he got hung up with a client in Columbus.

It's always Columbus, because Fred does, in fact, have clients in Columbus. But also because he knows that, in the two hours it would take him to drive from Columbus to Cincinnati, he can tour the back side in a leisurely manner.

He will make these calls with a beer in one hand and a driver in the other. He will be smiling. This is his golf game on the line, and he has no shame.

"He can remember holes he played three years ago, but he can't remember my birthday." This is Gayle, Ray's wife. When Ray and Gayle were dating, Ray was not playing golf. "He played basketball more than he played golf," Gayle says. The addiction "was dormant," Ray says.

Then in 1983, their first year in Cincinnati, Ray was asked to substitute for a neighbor who played regularly in a foursome. The following year, Ray was organizing a league.

I'll just have one little drink....

"Here's something I've always contended," says Kevin O'Sullivan. "Have you seen those anti-cocaine ads on TV? It's like, 'I first started doing coke once in awhile with friends, then I did it every day.' Golf's like that, too."

O'Sullivan tells this story: "A guy was playing out here, and his work was calling for him all day long. He came in at the turn and ran around for several minutes. Got all out of breath.

"He called his office and said, 'I'm not playing golf. My car broke down. I pushed it from I-71 to the Kenwood Shell.'"

It would take two hours, at least, to fix, he said. Two hours. Back nine. Of course.

When Ray and Gayle take vacations, it's generally to golf places. When Ray hits practice balls, he takes the family along. "Laura (their 3-year-old) plays in the sand trap," he says.

Ray calls himself a "seasonal" hard worker, meaning he works less, much less, in the summer. "I'm at the course at 6," he says. "I'm pulling into the parking lot when it's still dark and slipping on my golf shoes as the first rays come out."

This is a fraternity to which Ray belongs, and the ties run deep. I'll tell you truly that they sometimes lie.

"I cover for them," says Dave Tieman, the pro at Sharon Woods, "because they'd cover for me."

The men playing at Sharon Woods who should be doing something else usually park their cars at the maintenance compound. Or in the park, or a mile away or just about anywhere but the parking lot.

They play nine holes, call their wives/girlfriends/bosses and say that tee times are running late, and that they haven't even started yet. They have to sign to rent a cart, so they ask to use assumed names.

Once at Crooked Tree, a wife who was in the process of divorcing her husband couldn't find the lout anywhere. She called the club but, of course, no-o-body had seen him. The wife gathered all his clothes, drove to the club and dumped them in the pro shop. The husband picked them up after his round.

Ray's not that way. "It's a tough balancing act," he says, which causes Gayle's eyes to roll only a little.

Ray is a 3-handicap, and has been as low as a 1. He has thought seriously of trying to make it on the pro tour, but realizes that, with a wife and two children, you can be married to two loves, but you can only be completely faithful to one.

However...

"Most of our major disagreements have been over golf," Gayle says to Ray. "Maybe you never noticed."

"Must've been during the commercials" of a televised tournament, Ray says.

Ever want to take his 9-iron and plant it in his skull?

"Oh, yeah," Gayle says.

Says Ray, "Then I'd just go make another 9-iron."

Instant Golf

August 27, 1995

*R*on Curran said he could teach me to play golf in three hours. "Solid, respectable golf," he said. Someone who could do that could also get me to the moon the day after tomorrow. Fine, I said. Let's do it. I've never been to the moon.

"Do you play?" Curran said to me.

"No," I said. "I commit. I commit golf, the way Jerry Seinfeld commits acts of unspeakable comedy. When I play golf, the birds fly south and the gophers dig to china, just to escape the wrath of my ill-smote Titleist X-Outs."

"Golf is not rocket science," Curran said.

"Nope, it's applied torture and quantum abuse," I said. "Golf is God's way of telling us we have too much time on our hands."

"I can show you how to play golf without embarrassing yourself," Curran persisted.

"I doubt it," I said. "I'm in the rough so often, I'm thinking of going into horticulture. When I'm in Palm Springs, I play winter rules."

I read all the golf magazines. They offer quick and easy instructions, helpful articles like "Tom Kite's 49 Easy Steps to a Better Swing Plane" and "The Fred Couples Method For Ultimate Spinal Agony." I have concluded that you really do have to be a scientist to figure these lessons out. And a contortionist to put them into practice.

In golf, as in other sports, the instant you begin thinking about what you're doing as you're doing it, you are dead. As the great catcher-philosopher Crash Davis said to the pitcher Nuke LaLoosh in the movie *Bull Durham*: "Don't think, Meat. You'll hurt the ballclub."

If you read the magazines or take lessons from the pros, they will have you thinking about every fiber of your being, every time you pull back the club. Thusly paralyzed, you will whack a clump of sod several feet. Happens every time.

"I call my method Instant Golf," said Ron Curran.

"Great oxymoron," I said.

"What the pros are teaching isn't working," said Curran. "Golf is not about the golf swing. If you work at it long enough, you'll find a swing that gets the ball where you want it to go. Golf is about the short game. Golf is putting and chipping."

Curran spent three hours with me. I went into it playing like Bill Murray in *Caddyshack*. I came out of it bolder, wiser, more handsome, swinging like a topsail in a fair wind and...playing like Bill Murray in *Caddyshack*.

Actually, two hours in the classroom and an hour on the range later, I saw some improvement. As Ben Hogan is my witness.

Here is who Ron Curran is, and here is how he does it:

In 1982, Curran played in a company outing at Western Hills Country Club. Stroke play. He shot a 102. "After that, I decided to work on my game. I was tired of embarrassing myself."

Curran spent the next year taking lessons from club pros, attending golf school, watching instructional tapes and scanning magazines for tips from the PGA's finest. "I really worked at it," Curran said.

In 1983, at the company outing, he shot a 101. "I called it the $2,000 stroke," Curran said. He continued to analyze the game, with a wiser, more jaundiced eye toward "expert" advice.

He discovered what the rest of us have suspected: The golf swing can be understood without an advanced degree from MIT. Curran took the next step.

He boiled what he'd learned down to its essence.

What he discovered was:

(1) Golf swings do not require many moving parts

(2) Sweep, don't stab

(3) Follow through

(4) Do not hit and lift

(5) Solid and accurate is more important than fast and hard

(6) Don't use a 9-iron in a sand trap

(7) Buy clubs with big faces

(8) Don't buy one piece golf balls

(9) You don't need spikes

(10) Never play a Nassau with a man named Bear.

Curran doesn't care about grip or stance or cocked wrists or hip explosion or any of the other 99 million helpful tips your local pro will suggest to help your game and drive you insane.

"All I want to know is that the club face is aimed at the target, and that you keep your head down and your body behind the ball," Curran said.

It's more that that, of course. Curran favors a slightly open stance, to promote hip turn, and a shorter backswing because it provides less chance for you to screw up before the club meets the ball.

He teaches that the stroke for chipping and putting is identical, up to 60 yards; the only differences are the lengths of the backswing and follow through. He suggests that, in the short game, distance is more important than direction. He admonishes you never to try to lift your ball when you hit it. That is the club's job, Curran says.

And so forth. All this took barely three hours. After the two hours in the classroom, I was ready to take my used Wilsons and assault Pebble Beach.

What Curran has done is take the Dead Sea scrolls and reduce them to *My Weekly Reader*. He has turned chess into checkers. He does not promise to make the beginner into a scratch player. He does promise to make even the halt and the lame into bogey players who won't embarrass themselves.

As a player who frequently turns 6,000 yards of golf course into a mini-marathon, I am all for that.

Curran is not a pro. He is an 11-handicapper, a salesman who is almost 60 years old. He lives in West Chester with his wife and his dream. "My claim to fame is not that I'm a great golfer. But I know something a lot of people don't know, and I know they want to know," he said.

He knows he has a good idea. He's trying to figure how to market it. I got his number from his classified ad in *The Enquirer* about six weeks ago. About 30 others have called. Curran has the manuscript for a book; he is planning a cassette tape. If everything works out, he will offer lessons.

Instant Golf. Why not? Nobody says you have to be Greg Norman. You'd just like to play 18 without causing trains to wreck.

In the meantime, let's be careful out there.

The Putter

May, 1991

*G*olf is a game favored by the masochistic and the insane. Anybody who plays golf for fun deserves what he gets. What he gets, generally, is three putts from five feet.

Putting belongs in golf, and nowhere else. Putting is God's way of telling you that you belong in the office at 2 on a weekday afternoon.

To putt requires a putter, though Curtis Strange did win a tournament once while putting with a sand wedge. And various pros have tried rakes, drain pipes, pool cues, Coke bottles, and sixteen-inch shells from the battleship *Missouri*. In their spare time, of course.

Metaphorically speaking, the putter is the rope bridge between the mountain of reason and the valley of the irrational. And damned if it doesn't break every time.

Chi Chi Rodriguez once said, "Putting isn't golf" but unfortunately, putting is a lot of golf. The putter is only one of fifteen clubs in the bag. But if you play professionally, you look at your putter thirty-five or thirty-six times a round. If you play like everyone else, you look at it more than your wife.

"I've used every putter ever made," the pro David Graham once told me, "and they're all hopeless."

You have to like your putter. The way it looks, the way it feels, the way it flies into the cornfield when you miss from two feet.

It's as simple as this: if a man likes his putter, he will make more putts. If he looks at his putter and sees the little girl from *The Exorcist*, it may not be a fun afternoon.

Pros spend entire careers seeking putting truth. Arnold Palmer once won The Masters using a different putter every round. Lee Trevino won the 1974 PGA Championship with a putter he found in the attic of the house where he was staying that week.

Trevino's story, which he told me several years ago:

"I was staying in the house with a lady whose husband had recently passed away. The attic was this little room over the garage. As I was walking to my bedroom, I could see the attic door was open a crack.

"I could see a set of clubs on the floor. The putter was sticking out, and it looked like the one I used. A Wilson-Arnold Palmer model. It still had the original shaft and grip on it.

"I asked the lady if she would sell it, and she said no. So I said, 'Do you mind if I use it?' I never missed a putt the whole week."

It's not always so simple as this. Putting makes men do strange things. Just this past January, for example, you could turn on your TV on a Sunday afternoon and see Rocco Mediate winning the Doral-Ryder Open by putting with a length of tailpipe.

Mediate's putter was almost as tall as Mediate. It was, in fact, 25 percent longer than a normal putter. Mediate looked ridiculous. But he won lots of money, which means that very soon, many professionals will putt with lengths of tailpipe.

Or, maybe, with Putterscopes. Putterscope is one of those 800-number inventions you see advertised on obscure cable shows very late at night. For $19.95, you get a mirror that attaches to the bottom of you putter's shaft.

The maker says this mirror, which looks even dumber than the tailpipe, "teaches the player to view the cut of the green, and reminds him to check the break of the green." Have your Visa or Mastercard number ready.

My friend Ray was interested in this Putterscope. Of course, my friend Ray would putt with a stop sign if it would improve his short game.

Ray knows that golf is elective self-torture, and that the putter is the sporting answer to a cattle prod. In his spare time, Ray stores data in his home computer on every putt he attempts, how long it is, and where it stops.

Ray also makes his own clubs, subscribes to many golf publications and watches all the televised tournaments. Ray is a sick man.

He has had five sets of irons in his 33-year-old life, but "at least a dozen" putters. Late last year, Ray found his latest putter—where else?—broken in half near the 18th green at Hickory Woods.

He took it home, gave it a new shaft, sandblasted the head (to take the shine off and eliminate sun glare) and away he went.

Ray will use this putter until it fails him miserably, at which point he will look for a length of tailpipe.

Men forge intimate relationships with their putters, and when's the last time you said that about a seven-iron?

Men name their putters. Ben Crenshaw has a Wilson 8802 his father gave him twenty-four years ago, for his 15th birthday. Crenshaw calls it Little Ben, and in his bag, Little Ben is starting to look less like a club than a teddy bear.

Gary Player had a putter he called Sweet Charity. Bobby Jones's putter went through its diabolical little life as Calamity Jane, Fuzzy Zoeller knew his putter as Betsy. An old, old Scot named Ky Laffoon had a name for his that just cut very close to the heart of things. My Son of a Bitch, he called it.

Men abuse their putters because it's a heck of a lot less life threatening than abusing themselves.

Plus, men are genetically incapable of admitting inadequacy, and putting tends to reinforce that emotion fairly strongly.

I once knew a guy, Tommy Valentine, who, when he was an amateur, threw a putter out of a moving car and into a swamp. This was only after he had held it out the window for several minutes and chanted scatologically. "I wanted it to suffer a little before I killed it," he said.

Zoeller goes for the mental anguish. He carries two putters in his bag, "just to let them know they can be replaced."

There is nothing remotely equitable or democratic about driving a ball 300 yards, pitching it to five feet, then three-whacking it for bogey. In that respect, putting is un-American, but at least putting doesn't discriminate.

As Ray says, "Putting shows off the pros' weaknesses. It shows they have all the afflictions of the common hack."

Golf is one of the few sports you can watch and say, "Hey, I can do that." Nicklaus lips a five-footer on the 72nd hole, then misses the gimme coming back, and it's not at all like Bo Jackson fumbling on the goal line. Not unless you play 11-on-11 tackle football in full pads for relaxation.

But three-bumping from five feet? Who can't do that?

"When you're putting well, everything falls into place. When you're not, the world is ending tomorrow," says pro John Cook.

Amazingly, the sun always rises the next day. And it sure looks great in the mirror of my Putterscope.

We leave you with this pleasantness, from former pro Dave Hill, who knows more things about putting:

"From five feet into the hole," Hill says, "you're in the throw-up zone."

Hey, have some fun out there, okay?

It Ain't Me, Babe

August 4, 1998

I blame Kincaid for everything. Except the blown two-footer at No. 13. I blame my putter for that. If Kincaid hadn't signed me up for the Hickory Woods club tournament, I wouldn't have spent Sunday afternoon digging post holes with my pitching wedge.

Not that that was my fault, either. I made great swings. The ground got in the way.

You learn lots of things playing amateur golf. Lying, cheating, bribing the beer guy. Mostly, you develop a keen sense of denial. It ain't me, babe.

To blame yourself is to admit you stink and to admit you stink is to entertain the thought you'll always stink, which is just too depressing. You go buy a new driver instead.

Club manufacturers count on your denial. They thrive on it. They sell drivers with heads bigger than Sierra Leone because of it. They know what you think, which is:

It ain't me babe. No, no, no.

Wait until I spend several mortgage payments on the Biggest, Baddest Bertha Of All Time. I will never lose a match to anyone ever again. My tee shots will fly like silk on the wings of angels, and they will always land gently in the fairway and roll another 50 yards, perfectly straight. I will be something.

If I'm not, I'll just buy another club. Because it ain't me.

The pros are the same way. Watch a guy who's not putting well. Watch what he does with his putter after he misses another 3-footer. I once saw Bruce Lietzke miss a short one, then drag his putter, head first, down the cart path, to the next tee.

I asked him about it later. Why'd you do that?

"I wanted to show it who was boss," Lietzke said.

I'm chunking along Sunday, down three holes after 10 holes, playing great as usual, yet getting the typical bad breaks and lousy performance from my rotten clubs, when I drill a pure tee shot on No.11. It's a par-3, downhill about 160 yards. I swing a 7-wood softly. The ball rolls through to the back bank. Not my fault. The green couldn't handle the delicate backspin I put on the ball.

The ball lodges in a chunk of hardpan (bad break, not my fault) with a ledge of turf squarely behind it. I can't bring my wedge back and through the ball. Instead, I hack down on it, like I'm splitting wood.

The ball sprints across the green like its dimples are on fire. A 15-foot pitch becomes a 60-foot putt, and I'm thinking there is no fairness in the world. Who do I look like, Paul Bunyan?

I lose the hole to Price, my playing partner. Price is a 14-handicapper who says he plays "every other day." Every other day? What's your first name, Price? Nick?

Price waxed me after that. He won, 5 and 4. I couldn't overcome the injustice of it all. Because it wasn't me. It never is.

It was the course. It was bad luck. The tee shot at No. 4 that faded into the swing set? I didn't aim it that way. I made a great swing. It was the club. Time for a new 3-wood.

The approach from the parking lot? Planned. I needed the sunscreen from my trunk.

The near-whiff at 18? Somebody sneezed on my backswing.

It's lots of things. Lots of things can happen in four hours of golf. One thing it ain't, though:

Me.

It's the club, the lie, the wind, the noise, the heat, the cold, the rain, the shoes, the people in front of me, the people behind me, the people who scheduled the people in front of and behind me, the flies, the mosquitoes, the flock of geese caw-ing during my routinely fabulous hip turn.

It ain't me.

After I finished excavating the back nine and offering phony best-wishes to Nick Price in the next round of the championship, I seethed for awhile. But not at me. The clubs, the greens, the condition of the course, etc.

I know the drill. To acknowledge I stink would kill my self esteem. Better to hole up in denial. Next week, new clubs.

Jimmy's Last Nine

May 14, 1996

"*Y*ou be needin' your oxygen, Jimmy?"

No. Jimmy would not. Not today. The air is clean at Hyde Park Country Club. Clean and sweet. Jimmy Woods is 76 now, a diabetic with emphysema clutching his lungs, occasioned by too many cigarettes long ago.

On this Monday, Jimmy waves off the oxygen from his stepson, Jim. Today, Jimmy peels back some years. About 70.

"My daddy worked at a country club in Nashville, Tennessee," he says. Jimmy's voice emerges rough-'n-tumble, one last Camel non-filtered at 3 a.m. "We lived in a house behind the 4th green."

"I growed up right there. I would sneak up on the golf course 'round 7 o'clock, when it started getting dark. Every day. I'd play Number 4 and Number 12. There was a hill there, so's nobody could see me. I'd play 'til 10, 11 o'clock. Mom used to come out there, make me come in. I was 'bout 6 year old."

You couldn't see at 10 o'clock, I say.

Jimmy says, "I knew where the greens was."

His first clubs were sticks. "My father would cut limbs out of trees. They were golf sticks, as far as I was concerned," Jimmy says.

49

His father made the clubs left-handed. This is how Jimmy played, until a club pro told him he'd never be any good playing southpaw. Jimmy switched. Across the years, he hustled lots of suckers who didn't believe he could beat them playing left-handed.

"I got my first real set of clubs from a Cincinnati pawn shop at the age of 30. Before that, I never had a set of my own sticks, never had my own golf shoes, never had a place to play. But I could play. I could beat anybody that would play me."

He is sitting in a golf cart. Jimmy Woods is wearing an alligator sweater and a fine, blue golf shirt. He has a gold wristwatch, two gold teeth and a mustache validated by occasional gray sprouts. He is being honored as a 1996 Cincinnati Legend of Golf. It is time.

Jimmy tees off at 1 o'clock. The last time he played at Hyde Park, he shot a 69. This is what he recalls. "It's been some time ago," he says. Off the first tee Monday, Jimmy lets loose a drive we will politely call a fade.

"I'm gonna try to make five holes" is what he says after that. "Can't hardly breathe."

It would be enough to be the best black golfer ever to live in Cincinnati. Jimmy Woods won the Avon Fields club championship at age 72. He shot a 64 at Sharon Woods in, he thinks, 1970, a course record that still stands. At 55, he finished second in the Met.

That's enough. But it's his grace that makes his picture a portrait. His grace clings to him like leaves to the trees.

The old and the young are our best teachers. The rest of us are too busy running at vague dreams. Jimmy Woods has taught some young, black kids to play golf. A few of them, he has helped to become men.

Friend Danny Dell says, "Jimmy showed them how to play golf. He showed them how to be gentlemen. Some of 'em were about as tall as a golf club. What a wonderful inspiration."

Jimmy sits in the cart on this lovely spring day. One by one, the players come to him. They shake his hand, laugh, remember when.

A friend named Ron Garrett is there. Once, Jimmy hustled Garrett for $12. Garrett ran a grocery store in Corryville. To pay his debt,

50

Garrett sent Jimmy $12 worth of returnable empty pop bottles. Jimmy brought them in to Garrett's store, all 240 of them. A nickle apiece. He got his money.

"We used to have some good times. Didn't we, buddy?" Garrett says.

"Yes, we did," says Jimmy.

Sometime in 1997, they will open the Jimmy Woods Driving Range and Learning Center at Avon Fields. Kids will learn golf and the fine art of growing up wise. Jimmy plans to be around.

"They said to go as far as I can, and that's what I'm going to do," Jimmy Woods says. He is talking about Monday's round. Jimmy disappears down a hill in his cart, to the third tee. No oxygen is required. The air is new.

Bench Takes His Hacks

May 23, 1995

*F*rom the tee at the 483-yard fourth hole, Johnny Bench drove his ball 75 yards through the grass. Great shoulder turn, straight left arm, hips out in front and, *whammo*, a grounder to short. If Bench had hit baseballs that way, he'd have been Mackey Sasser.

It is maddening to know that a Hall of Fame catcher, who also has been playing golf for 27 years, is still capable of topping a tee shot and dribbling it 75 yards. Also, comforting.

Golf is an evil little pastime. Golf does not care that you are Johnny Bench, playing a qualifying round for the United States Open. Golf exists to torture. After a hard day's work perfecting thumb screws, the Marquis de Sade relaxed by inventing golf.

51

We love golf. But it is a cruel, inscrutable game. Don't try to figure it out.

"It's exhilarating," says Johnny Bench, who is, without a doubt, the best former major league catcher ever to try to make the U.S. Open field. Bench first picked up clubs when he was 20 years old. Twenty-seven years later, he has found no cure.

Bench also says golf is "terrifying. There is no reason or rhyme why this game mentally owns you."

Bench frets about his golf game. This is funny, because you could never picture him saying after a baseball game, "I don't get it. I was in perfect position. I had the proper release point on the throw. I had great follow through. And I still don't nail Lou Brock at second."

In baseball, Bench knew what he knew. "I owned it. I owned the game. I knew what I could do," he says. In golf, Bench is a scratch player who is a blind man. "Out here, it comes and goes and you're never sure why. You can't understand how your body and mind can betray you.

"It's like someone is saying, 'OK, I'm going to let you go out and have a few pars. Then you will hit it over here and over there, and then into these trees.'"

Or off this tee, 75 yards through the sod. "Then my next shot, I hit a 4-wood as good as anyone could hit it," says Bench. He played well Monday. Bench shot a 74 across the 6,665-yard Maketewah Country Club course. He played the back nine in 1-under par, the last 12 holes in 2-under.

At the ninth, his birdie attempt died an inch from the hole. The same thing happened at No. 16. At 17, his birdie effort was too strong. It rolled 2 feet past the hole. Cruel.

Still, take away the double-bogey and Bench shoots 72, good enough to advance to sectional Open qualifying next month. As it is, he leaves feeling good about the game. But not good enough. That is another thing about golf: Nothing is ever good enough.

"What happens with athletes is, you go from a 15 (handicap) to a 7 or 8 real quick," says Bench. "And you think, 'I got it now.' Fifteen to seven took me about three months." And then?

Torture, cruelty and near-death experiences.

Twelve years ago, Bench retired from baseball as a three-handicapper. Since then, he has shaved exactly three strokes from his average. A stroke every four years. At this rate, Bench will be Jack Nicklaus when he is 117 years old.

"It makes you want to beat yourself up," Bench says.

Last year, Bench played 200 rounds of golf. His handicap didn't budge.

It makes you wonder.

"Who was the best base-stealer you ever faced?" I ask.

"Joe Morgan," says Bench.

"What's tougher: Throwing out Joe Morgan? Or making the Senior Tour?"

"Making the Senior Tour."

"Who was the toughest pitcher for you?"

"Bill Singer."

"What's tougher: Hitting Singer? Or making the Senior Tour?"

"Making the Senior Tour."

"Has there ever been anything more thrilling and exasperating for you than golf?" I ask.

Bench thinks on this a bit. "Women," he says.

The Eternal Jack

June 16, 1989

*R*ochester, N.Y.—The trick is to ease out gracefully, to find the shadows before they come looking for you. You dance with grace before the music dies, and you get out.

You know where the door is. That's the trick.

Jack Nicklaus, 49, shot a 67 Thursday in the first round of his 33rd U.S. Open. The Eternal Jack, golf's longest-running sunset, three-under par, one shot off the lead, knows the trick.

Between strokes, a group of young men in the gallery chanted to him softly. Each looked about 25 years old. "Twenty-one," they said. "Twenty-one."

Twenty-one major championships. If Nicklaus somehow wins this Open on the East Course at Oak Hill Country Club, it will be his 21st major tournament win, eight more than anyone else. He won his first in 1962. His fans were a lot younger then.

Nicklaus doesn't dwell on his age. He confronts it. Probably, he hasn't done an interview in the last five years in which he didn't mention how deeply his business concerns have cut into his playing schedule.

He even calls himself a "ceremonial golfer" now, someone who tees off early, gives the galleries a quick legend fix, then hustles back to the office. "My work is more important than my golf," he says.

He arrived at the Oak Hill clubhouse Thursday morning just 40 minutes ahead of his 9:02 tee time. No time to putt.

No time for the range. Forty minutes before the start of the year's most prestigious tournament; no time for the ceremonial golfer to do much but change his shoes and play. Playing partner Lee Trevino had been there since 7:30.

"Sometimes," Nicklaus says, "I get to the tournament and say,

54

why didn't I spend more time on my game?'

"The problem is, I can't get motivated six, eight weeks in advance. I'm doing too many other things. I'm never as prepared as I used to be."

Rare is the great, aging athlete who looks in the mirror and sees the truth. Rarer still is the one who does something about it. Nicklaus has chosen business over golf because at 49, he knows golf isn't forever. It's a simple notion, one lots of jocks miss.

Nicklaus hasn't persevered so much as evolved. He hasn't raged against the dying light so much as he has turned on a different bulb. He spends more time designing courses than playing them.

You imagine him spending his mornings not on the range but on the telephone, maybe two telephones, grilling his top hirelings. He's reading the *Wall Street Journal*. He is wearing a tie and putting Titleists into a Dixie cup. He is giving dictation.

"If the U.S. Open was the most important thing in my life at age 49, I'd find time to do what I need to do to get ready to play," he says.

Nicklaus worked 10 days for this Open. Before that, he spent two weeks fishing in New Brunswick. He took with him a driver and a 5-iron, to hit an occasional golf ball across the Restigouche River.

Nicklaus still wants badly to win. On the back nine Thursday, he noticed every leader board. But it just isn't that important now. Nicklaus is making the switch from sports to real life as smoothly as anyone ever has.

Nicklaus is in his golf dotage, at least until he decides to play the Senior Tour. Probably, he is closer to a rocking chair than another major. Nicklaus' 67 was remarkable mainly because it was Nicklaus who shot it.

Several days of rain have pounded Oak Hill into passivity. Unknowns such as Jay Don Blake and Tom Pernice spray-painted the leaderboard in red graffiti. The early leader was someone named Emlyn Aubrey—or was it Aubrey Emlyn?—a qualifier who spent the last two springs avoiding snakes on the Asian Tour.

By dusk, 34 players were at par or better. Nicklaus' round was good enough only for five-way tie for second place.

No matter. Nicklaus has already won. Someone asks him about Kareem Abdul-Jabbar. Nicklaus, being kind, says Abdul-Jabbar was "just a kid."

At 42, Abdul-Jabbar trudged into retirement Tuesday night, after his Los Angeles Lakers were swept by the Detroit Pistons in the NBA Finals. Kareem left basketball an old man. He found the door too late.

It won't happen that way for Nicklaus, no matter what he does this weekend. "I'm either gullible enough or dumb enough to believe I can have fun for three more days," he says.

Only once in his 33 Opens has Nicklaus played a better first round than he did Thursday. That was in 1980. He shot a 63 at Baltusrol. He won the Open that year. He was 40. Just a kid.

Re-Inventing Augusta

*H*e played alone all day, unless you count the intangibles. Tiger Woods had ended the game Saturday; Sunday was for history and perceptions and predictions.

And for Charlie Sifford and Ted Rhodes and all those of color who had been denied a chance at this day.

And for Lee Elder, the first African-American to play the Masters, 22 years ago. "I said a little prayer" coming up the 18th fairway Sunday, Woods said, "of thanks to those guys."

And for Earl Woods and Tida Woods, whose mixed marriage—he predominantly black, she Asian—produced a son whose rich ethnic background could make all of us feel good about Tiger's first Masters championship.

And for the guys in the scoreboard tower bestride the 18th fairway, who were getting nervous the closer Tiger edged to Masters immortality.

"What's the biggest red number you got?" a man wondered from below.

"Twenty-three," the scorekeeper said, and he damned near needed it.

And for the game of golf, too long derided for its mercenaries and "clones", and forever waiting for its next Nicklaus. Do we have him now?

Who else was this for? What else could be served? This was not just about winning a sporting championship. The best ones never are. They're a little more complicated than that, a little richer experience.

Tiger Woods shot 18 under par, a record, to win the Masters at age 21, also a record, needing just 200 strokes to finish the last 54 holes, another record.

This puts cold, hard testimony to what occurred at Augusta National Golf Club Thursday to Sunday. The rest is yet to be judged. It was a good, amazing and sweet thing Woods did here. For every reason you could imagine.

At some point this weekend, Woods stopped chasing history and started inventing it.

Maybe it was the back-nine 30 on Thursday that did it, a stone-cold tribute to Woods' courage. Maybe it was his 65 Saturday, when his lead was just three shots.

Who knows?

Woods brought to this Masters a pedigreed game, having won three of his first nine pro events. What showed more was a steel will. Someone asked Woods his thoughts as he climbed the 18th green Sunday, floated by cheers.

"Boy, do I have a tough putt," Woods said. "My focus never left me. That's what I'm trying to say."

He had a plan to win Sunday. It sounded like Jack Nicklaus'

time-honored plan. Nicklaus has won six Masters. Good plan.

"Never make a bogey, execute, be patient, make birdies when I have a chance," Woods said.

He sweated Amen Corner (holes 11–13) even with a nine-shot lead. "I had to get through at even par. You never know what can happen on water holes."

Woods birdied 11 and 13. By then, his gallery stretched from tee to green.

Up next to the putting green, halfway between the clubhouse, the 18th green and history, Earl Woods sat watching his son on a TV monitor. Two months ago, he had bypass surgery.

I remember talking to him here two years ago, along the 9th fairway. Tiger was 19, in his first Masters, and very far away from who he is now.

"He'll win this thing soon enough," Earl said then.

After Tiger left the 17th Sunday, Earl rose slowly and made the walk to the scorer's tent behind No. 18, to participate in history.

Twenty years from now, or 30, this is how we'll recall this most significant of all Masters. History.

All week, we groped for superlatives, for comparisons.

Nicklaus in 1965? In 1972? Lee Elder in 1975? Sometimes, an accomplishment is so singular, it needs no partners.

Here is all that needs to be said: There has never been another Masters like this one. And there never will be.

3

Splendid Pleasures

"They came for the evening, dreamy and blue."
—*Paul Daugherty*

Opening Day

April 5, 1993

*I*t is the first and last day to trust the fantasy. The one and only day that baseball makes good on its promise. Opening Day is the only day that baseball is the game your father told you about. That is its singular blessing.

On Opening Day, you believe whatever you want, and all of it is true. This is the day to believe the Findlay Market parade is grander than a traffic jam with marching bands and that Marge Schott really is a great humanitarian.

It is the day to look at Kevin Mitchell and see Adonis. It is the day to be thankful for the new retro-uniforms, which will hide Mitchell's porkbelly a whole lot better than the old polyesters.

On Opening Day, you can be 35 years old and wake up thinking about your first glove and your first Reds game, and not feel like a sentimental simp. One of baseball's problems is that it has too many would-be Hemingways, too many fathers playing catch with sons, who would seek literary truth amid the locker room jock-straps. Dear Sirs: It ain't here.

But on Opening Day, baseball-as-life is OK. It is, in fact, preferred.

The game could use some dolling up. Lately, the people who run it have conspired to run it into the ground. They haven't succeeded yet. Baseball is proving very hard to kill. Give them time.

Baseball is too rich for lots of fans. The tickets cost too much. So does the beer, when you can get it. The games are too late and too long. On the mistaken theory that more is better, we have more teams and, coming soon, more playoffs.

More players earning major-league meal money who should be getting bus tickets. More reasons for a major network to complain about its post-season baseball ratings. If more people prefer to watch a regular-season NFL game than a baseball playoff game (as happened last fall) what makes baseball believe the viewing public will rush to their TVs to see wildcard playoffs?

Baseball has the Giants, who should be in Tampa. Baseball has no commissioner. Baseball doesn't know how to market itself. Baseball is bad television. Baseball is slow and getting slower.

Almost everywhere but Cincinnati, baseball isn't our favorite game. Almost anywhere else, today's baseball game is the warmup act for Michigan vs. North Carolina in tonight's college basketball championship.

Baseball is out of step with our rhythms and our culture. Basketball is the game now. Basketball is fast and hip. It plays to the MTV audience. Baseball hasn't had a Michael Jordan since Willie Mays. Baseball has never had a Shaquille O'Neal.

Baseball's best player is not its best face. He is Barry Bonds, a frequently sullen, occasionally strident young man who has the world by the nose and acts like he's the most tortured soul in the universe.

Baseball also has Kirby Puckett, the brightest of lights. He'd make a great ambassador for the game. Where is Kirby Puckett? What use has baseball made of his goodwill?

Baseball has so many messes, and appears so incapable of cleaning them, that it may lose its antitrust exemption. This is the law that allows baseball to pretend it's a game. Now that most of the reasons for that belief have been stripped away—a guy from Little Caesar's pizza owns the Detroit Tigers, Mr. Blockbuster Video has proprietary rights over the Florida Marlins—baseball may soon be deemed a business. It is, sadly, a fate that baseball has earned.

Baseball asks to be deemed special and unique, yet is afflicted with every social problem currently in town. Steve Howe, the habitual drug offender, is not special. Marge Schott, the tinhorn Steinbrenner and raging insensitive, is neither special nor unique. Neither is the greedy and sneering Bonds.

In total, baseball needs a whole bunch of Opening Days.

You have one here. One Opening Day. In Cincinnati, it is enough.

You pull out the gloves and the Neatsfoot oil. They're right next to the memories. You let the game back in. Because for all its faults, there is still something about it you just can't shake. Love can be like that.

The Reds won't win it this year. They aren't as good right now as they were a year ago.

Their defense is shaky, their middle relief is suspect. They are one Rob Dibble injury from big bullpen trouble, the Atlanta Braves have won the West twice in a row without Greg Maddux. And who knows what about Kevin Mitchell? The Reds won't win it.

Or maybe they will.

They have the best eight regulars in the league. Reggie Sanders is an emerging star, Tim Pugh will win 10 or 12. The Braves' starting pitchers will get hit this year. They just have to, right? And how 'bout that Kevin Mitchell?

You'll be in on it. In on all of it. Starting today.

Opening Day. Here, where it still matters. Here, where it all began. Baseball. Welcome home.

Game Tonight

August 9, 1994

*I*t is a Top Six night. Top row, very top, behind the plate, up by the moon, close enough to see the game and meet the velvet evening. The starry side of glorious.

It is a Booth G night. Outdoors, club level, first base line, next to the city cops working security. The press box is inside and cool, noiseless and anonymous. A cocoon. Watching ballgames from the press box is like watching a big screen TV. We prefer Booth G.

It hangs there like an aerie, a place to see baseball and the moonrise and to feel the flutter of a good crowd. On the good nights, breezes shiver the pages of your notebook in Booth G and summer sends you flowers.

Braves-Reds. Monday night of a dwindling season close to being done in by...what, exactly? Greed? Fear? Fehr? Who's right, who's not. Who knows? After Thursday, the doors will lock, the gates will close, the signs will go up. No Game Today.

It is a perfect thing, just about, to sit in the Top Six or in Booth G on a night like this, eating ice cream and arguing who is better, Ken Griffey or Barry Bonds, and what the Reds should do with Kevin Mitchell after this year.

The ballpark can still offer escape, if you let it. Baseball can be so right. We forget that sometimes. Most of the time. Especially this time.

"It's that childhood feeling you had. Smelling the grass, throwing the ball around. If you can maintain that perspective, it remains fun." This isn't some pie-eyed you or me talking. It's Tim Fortugno, the Reds pitcher who is, at age 32, about to see his best big-league season go up in strike.

In 1989, Fortugno was making $500 a month, to play ball in Reno, Nevada. He worked that off-season, and in the six off-seasons before that. "That carried me," he says. "My first six years in the minor leagues, I didn't save a thing. I spent money to play baseball. I always played because I loved to play. It's a game, right? Just a game."

My friend Cook tells me I'm full of it. (I have been known to be full of it.) Cook says people go to ballgames to be entertained. Winning is nice. Winning it all is thrilling. But not necessary.

"That could explain Chicago Cubs fans," I say.

Cook thinks baseball this week will be no different. Players will play and fans will yell. Baseball is still baseball, he says.

"I wouldn't go," I say.

If I'm a fan, I am skeptical there will be games after Thursday. If there are no games, there is no pennant race. If there is no pennant race, what is the point? The Reds are a good team on the road to nowhere. Next stop: Limbo.

There is no need to invest further emotion. Why care about a season that could be ending? I wouldn't go.

Cook sighs the sigh of a man who senses he is talking to a brick with a head. (I have been suspected of this as well.) You cannot talk sense to a brick.

"Most of the people who go to baseball games are not hard-core fans," Cook says. "They may root for a team, but it's mostly a night out."

Cook is right, of course. There may be an anger in fans this time. There may be an uncommon streak of to-hell-with-'em-all. But the resentment has not kept them from coming. Four games with the Braves attracted 179,223 paid admissions. Attendance Monday night was 35,041 paid.

They came for the evening, dreamy and blue. Not for the ballgame, exactly, but for the notion that the ballgame was a good place to be. Maybe, too, they sense the show was about to close for the summer.

"It brings back the childhood every time you come out here. This is how I dreamed it when I was a kid," says Brian Dorsett, the Reds catcher. "I think players realize that subconsciously, most of them. Maybe that's why baseball is so much fun."

The night arrives, soft and lovely. From the top row, downtown glows. Time, still, to grab some baseball. It's a game, right? Just a game. On a night like this, there is no game so good.

Little Big Man

*B*ret Boone claims he weighs 178 pounds. You could believe that. I believe if Boone tops 165, he's packing boulders in his Levi's.

If you are 5 foot 9, you look him in the eye. Bret Boone is one tough bud. He also resembles the kid who bags your groceries.

"That ain't no 6 foot 5, 250-pound boy over there," noted Reds reliever Jeff Brantley. "He's just a little guy."

Boone is not supposed to hit a baseball 421 feet to dead center field, as he did in the sixth inning Sunday against the Chicago Cubs. He is not your top pick to hit a game-winning, three-run homer to the opposite field, with two outs and two strikes in the bottom of the 10th, against the best relief pitcher in the National League.

But as we are finding out, this is not a season to be hung up on logic. Not around here, where it is a good time to be in Cincinnati and be a Red.

"I don't know if it's fate or destiny or what," said Barry Larkin, the shortstop, giving the best explanation he could find.

There are moments that define a baseball season. There are instants that, one way or another, produce the tone of a summer. One came Sunday afternoon in the 10th inning, when Bret Boone smacked a Randy Myers fastball off the outside corner and into the blue seats in right field.

The Cubs had led 3–0. They took a 5–3 edge in the top of the 10th, on a dramatic home run by Mark Grace. The Reds had tied things, 3–3, then won them, 7–5, because a skinny second baseman did something he had no intention of doing.

With his two homers Sunday, Boone now has 11 for the year, all of them accidents.

"I go up there every time, and the last thing on my mind, believe it or not, is hitting a home run. I promise you, if I ever think I'm going to hit one out and I do, you'll be the first to know," Boone said.

If you are Ron Gant, with arms like pistons, you muscle up to the plate intending to give the baseball a good, long ride. The 1995 Big Ron Machine is not without swagger. If you are Bret Boone, you whack it and hope it finds the outfield turf.

"Especially with two strikes," Boone said.

He was protecting the plate. Two outs, runners at first and third. Three balls, two strikes. "I knew what was coming," Boone said.

Myers throws very hard, but he rarely puts one across the plate. He nibbles. "He says, 'I'm going to throw a fastball away (from the middle of the plate), and you're not going to hit it,'" said Boone. Boone guessed he'd had one hit in his entire life against Randy Myers, in a spring game when Boone was playing for the Seattle Mariners.

This time, he took the fastball away and lifted it into a season that threatens to become magical. "You may be right," manager Davey Johnson said of that notion. "It's a hero every day. We've got a lot of heroes on this ballclub. I don't usually get excited. That had me like Rocky. Throwing my fist in the air."

In 1990, we knew the Reds were destined for special-ness when Norm Charlton ran over Dodgers catcher Mike Scioscia at home plate. In '93, we knew they were destined for the tank, when 10 showed up for Johnson's "mandatory" workout following the All-Star break.

In '95, we know about Boone's home run.

Baseball people do not trust success. They do not believe in fate. They believe in three-run homers. But this is one of those years in this town when fate happens. Fate has a place. If you didn't think that way before Sunday, maybe you do now.

"Against Myers," Johnson said. "That was large."

The grocery boy, winning a game with a home run, off one of the best pitchers in the business. What a thing.

Not more than 15 minutes after the home run, it started raining. A good, hard rain. The sort of rain that, had it occurred 15 minutes sooner, would have washed out the bottom of the 10th.

Fate? It was still raining at 8 Sunday night. No way they ever play the bottom of the 10th in those conditions.

The Recruiter

October, 1992

$\mathcal{S}$ teve Moeller once lost a basketball recruit because the kid's father needed new teeth.

True story. In 1978, in a poverty-pocket hamlet in western Kentucky, Moeller walked into town with a letter of intent for a blue-chip, 18-year-old basketball jones to sign, and walked out empty-handed. The last thing Moeller saw was daddy's new dentures, flashing pearly from the back seat of a limousine.

"The kid's father had three teeth in his mouth," Moeller is saying. "Suddenly, he looks like a toothpaste commercial."

It happens. In college basketball, it happens every day. They're starting practice now, gearing up for five months of Billy and Al and Dickie Vitale bay-bee! and what they all want most is to be cutting down nets in March.

They want it so badly they do the damnedest things. We're talking flesh-peddling, influence-brokering, chicanery, debauchery, greed, excess, and new teeth. And we're not talking about Congress.

Once, when Steve Moeller coached at the University of Texas, a sophomore basketball player from another school approached him about transferring.

Moeller was interested. The kid was a player. There were only a few minor details to be worked out.

"I need a new Camero and $20,000 in a safe-deposit box," the player told Moeller. "That's what I get every year at School X. I've had four other schools offer me the same thing, but I want to come to Texas."

The kid went elsewhere.

The damnedest things.

Steve Moeller has seen them and done them for twenty-eight years, as a high school coach and college assistant, from Colerain High to the University of Texas to the neat little office he currently occupies in Shoemaker Center at the University of Cincinnati.

Officially, he's an assistant to head coach Bob Huggins. He's also what's known in the business as a "recruiting coordinator," a scarlet title if ever there was one.

You see this 6 foot 9 kid who barely shaves, this pituitary case running the floor like a gazelle on safari, and you wonder: How'd he get here?

Literally.

Did someone buy that young man a car? Or was it just plane tickets for his mom, to all the home games?

Maybe he's simply using a car, a loaner from the local car dealer who's a "friend of the program."

Probably, it's neither. Surprisingly, considering the fan and alumni pressure to win, the monetary reward for winning and the back-biting competitiveness among coaches to beat each other, the majority of college basketball programs are clean.

Some aren't.

One thing up front: Steve Moeller doesn't cheat. Or if he does, he's never been caught. As far as we know, he's squeaky. But he has had a front-row view of the sleaze. Which, as you can guess, is impressive.

So come along with us, down the dark, dirty alleys of good-ol' amateur athletics, where nothing is as it seems and sometimes, you're only as good as your wallet.

It was the late '70s when Withrow High star LaSalle Thompson was going to sign with Texas. Moeller had been courting Thompson

68

the way Romeo courted Juliet, and he was rewarded with a verbal agreement from the best basketball player in Cincinnati.

Then thirty-six hours before Thompson was to sign with Texas, Thompson's mother called Moeller to say her son had changed his mind, and would be attending Purdue.

"I walked outside and threw up in the yard," Moeller says. Then he caught the first plane to Cincinnati, arriving four hours before Thompson would announce his decision to go to Purdue.

Moeller only had one question: "What happened?"

Thompson told Moeller that the Purdue coaches had shown him a letter written by his third-grade brother, Will. Will had written that he wanted his big brother to go to college close to home, so Will could come to his games and visit on weekends.

It was touching stuff.

Maybe too touching.

"LaSalle," Moeller asked, "you ever seen Will write a letter?"

"No, coach," Thompson said.

"You ever seen Will write a postcard or a thank-you note?" said Moeller. "You ever seen Will write?"

"No, coach."

Thompson went to Texas.

The damnedest things.

What else?

"What else?" Moeller says. He has to think about it. But only for a second or two. Twenty-eight years is a long time in the company of thieves.

How 'bout this? How 'bout the time the boys at the University of Houston kidnapped a guard named Rob Williams? Moeller says they spirited him away and stashed him in a hotel the night before national signing day, so even if he wanted to go somewhere other than Houston, he couldn't.

Williams went to Houston. Brilliant choice.

How 'bout the time the prize recruit jumped across the press table at a summer camp, chasing a loose ball, and the "recruiting coordinator" seated there managed to break the kid's fall, while slapping a business card in his palm?

How 'bout the time the coach from the not-so-prestigious Eastern school begged a recruit simply to mention the school's name every time someone asked the kid which schools were recruiting him?

And finally, how 'bout the player on his campus visit who played the radio over the phone to his girlfriend from midnight to 7 in the morning. Talk about your long-distance dedications.

"He was lonely," Moeller says. "The phone bill was $128. He signed with somebody else."

Moeller recruited ten of the twelve players on UC's Final Four team last year. Huggins got the Bearcats to the Final Four; Moeller got them to Cincinnati.

How? What is it about Moeller, or any recruiting coordinator, that would make a kid from L.A. (or in UC's case, three kids from L.A.) spend ten months in Cincinnati?

"He can tell you anything, and you believe it," Bearcats forward Terry Nelson said last March. "Recruiting is all bullshit, and Mo is the best in the business. Mo is a master."

Nelson says Moeller is "a sincere manipulator."

"He never promised us anything," Nelson said. "That's the thing that got us here."

"I'm honest with them," Moeller says.

He also works to ridiculous extremes.

Moeller has a ten-page, typed, single-spaced list of summer camps where players the Bearcats are interested in are playing. He has a stack of 200 player profiles.

At some point during the week, he will call or visit or watch play thirty-five or forty of those kids. Moeller will jet halfway across the country, just to watch a prospect play in a summer-league game, knowing it's against NCAA rules even to speak to him.

Moeller knows without looking that he can catch a 6:30 a.m. plane from Los Angeles that gets him back here in the middle of the afternoon.

He knows he can leave here at 9:05 and be in Houston at 10:45. He has a stack of frequent flyer miles from here to Bali.

"My whole deal is, I've got to out-work people. I've got to be on the phone more, sleep less, talk to more kids," Moeller says. "I want to know all there is to know about a guy. I want to know his girlfriend's name. I want to know his dog's name."

Along the miles somewhere, when he's looking at clouds out the airplane window and dreaming of signing the next Michael Jordon, Steve Moeller often wonders what the hell he's doing.

At the highest level, college coaching is a flesh trek, an never-ending odyssey to see who can get the best talent. You're running around, logging the miles, eating bad food, sleeping in lumpy beds across the wall from a guy who snores, all for an 18-year-old kid who can flip you off any time he likes.

What a life, to have your continued success, employment and fiscal well-being tied to the whims of post-adolescents with girlfriend problems.

Says Coach Mo, "I've been doing this for twenty-eight years. To chase what? To chase the Final Four. Okay, we got to the Final Four.

"Now, we could have a helluva year this year, but if we don't go to the Final Four, people will say we're not as good. It's a monster. You feed the monster. That's what we're doing here. Feeding the monsters."

To convince Nelson and his L.A. buddies Corie Blount and Erik Martin that UC was heaven in hightops, Moeller was up every night for three months until 3 in the morning.

He called each of them every night. Since they couldn't make it in before 10 or 11 West Coast time, Moeller worked the night beat. You couldn't expect the players to be considerate of him. They were the supply: Moeller had the demand.

The damnedest things.

"Recruiting is a vicious, dirty part of college athletics," Moeller says.

He says this while inspecting the bio of a seven-footer from Hong Kong.

71

Hong Kong?

"Sung Fong. I tried to call him," Moeller says. When he isn't a member of that world-renowned Hong Kong National Team, the immortal Fong plays at a junior college in California. Mo has him all scooped out.

"He's a great shooter, he gets up and down the floor, he'll have an AA degree...."

Mo went on vacation the next day, to St. Thomas with his wife. Maybe they were going to sit in the sand, sip rum drinks and ponder their toes. Or maybe there was a 6 foot 9 Virgin Islander with a vertical leap as big as a coconut palm that Moeller just had to see.

UC would have a shot at him, too. As long as his father didn't need teeth.

How Willie Invented the Sports Bar

October, 1995

Willie DeLuca collected "memorabilia" when memorabilia was "junk." His family ran a sports bar and called it a restaurant because, hell, no one ever heard of a sports bar back in 1956. Sorrento's became Cincinnati's first sports bar when Willie DeLuca noticed his house resembled a full-time swap meet.

That's the whole of it. There was no place else to put all the stuff. And Willie was not one to throw things out.

Today's sports bars are created by accountants. Open a place. Call it "Champions" or Tickets" or, should someone be missing the point, "America's Original Sports Bar." Hang some pennants and some big TVs. Offer drink specials during *Monday Night Football*. You are a sports bar. Willie DeLuca did none of this. Willie just had a lot of junk. Instead of putting it in boxes or between bicycle spokes, he hung it on Sorrento's walls. A simple concept, in the old days.

Now, Sorrento's Restaurant and Sports Bar is an archive of sports memorabilia. Thirty years ago, Willie DeLuca was a guy who'd frame the lint in his pocket. Now, he's widely thought to have one of the largest and most varied collections of memorabilia anywhere. Willie was, completely coincidentally, a man before his time.

Don't believe it? Fine. Go, then, and seek another collector with signatures from Pete Rose *and* Yasser Arafat. Johnny Bench *and* Adolph Hitler. When you find him, ask him if he also has the last check written by one Arthur Schlichter, noted football player, gambling addict and all-American check-kiter.

The check, payable to Willie, was for $1,000. It was colder than a dead man.

"I have all of (Johnny) Bench's stuff," Willie is saying. "Shin guards, chest protector, his jacket in '68 when he was a rookie. I have all of Pete's (Rose) bats. I have Ken Griffey, Jr.'s Moeller High School jersey."

Willie opens a manila envelope. "Got a letter right here. Signed by George Patton." Sure enough. (Signed) G.S. Patton, Jr. Lieutenant General U.S. Army, Commanding. "He's one of my heroes," says Willie.

Willie knows a guy in northern Kentucky, an 82-year-old veteran of the Big War, who helps him with the Sno-Softball Tournament he runs every winter. "He paints the balls orange," Willie explains. The old guy got him the Patton letter and the signature of Hitler. Recently, Willie acquired an autographed photo of the fighter John L. Sullivan and, at an estate sale, a ticket to the 1892 championship bout between Sullivan and James T. "Gentleman Jim" Corbett. These are not pennants on the wall.

How did this all begin?

"Jerry Lucas," he says. It began with Jerry Lucas. Willie was working at the Cincinnati Gardens in 1965, a high school kid on the maintenance crew, when he asked Lucas for a jersey. The Cincinnati Royals star obliged. I wonder if Lucas has ever seen what he hath wrought.

But the great thing is, all of this just happened: One day, you're a pack-rat, the next you're a collector. Willie didn't intend to get famous or rich. He never considered any of his acquisitions to be investments. Still doesn't. He just liked sports stuff.

Willie does spend money to acquire things ($300 for the Sullivan ticket). He once traded a middleweight championship boxing belt for a flannel jersey worn by Frank Robinson. He brokered the deal between Rose and a Cincinnati collector for the bat Pete used to break Ty Cobb's all-time hits record. But Willie does not engage in the smarmy horse-trading and money-grubbing rampant among collectors today.

"I hate it. Everybody's trying to cash in," he says. "Webster's dictionary says an autograph is a form of friendship." (Actually, it doesn't. But you get the point.) "This stuff is just on loan to me while I'm on this planet."

His family didn't intend to run a sports bar. They ran a restaurant that evolved into a sports bar. Truthfully, the metamorphosis isn't complete and probably never will be. Just because Sorrento's has a bar doesn't mean it is one. It's a mom and pop place. Literally. Enrico and Santina DeLuca arrived in New York by boat from Italy in 1956. They took a train to Cincinnati and wound up in Norwood, then a thriving suburb just north of town. Enrico had worked with prominent chefs in Italy. He knew his business.

They opened the restaurant, calling it Sorrento's after a famous Italian town not far from Naples. Today, "Come Back to Sorrento" is on the restaurant's juke box, sung by Pavarotti.

Thirty-nine years later, Enrico still comes to work. Santina makes all the sauces and the sausages and the pizza dough. Willie, now 45, takes to-go orders, works the register, and collects stuff.

In 1956, "the only items we had was a few pitchers of It-ly," says Willie, meaning photographs of his native land. Also, a TV. "My mom and dad couldn't hardly speak English. But they always had a TV behind the bar," Willie says.

The first standing-room-only TV event at Sorrento's was the 1968 basketball game between UCLA and the University of Houston. Lew Alcindor and Elvin Hayes. *Monday Night Football* progressed from program to phenomenon; Sorrento's bought the area's first big screen TV in 1974. Cable came to the area in about 1978. Sorrento's was in the local vanguard, packing its seats during the NCAA basketball tournament, the bulk of which could be seen only on ESPN.

Willie bought his first satellite dish 10 years ago. Sorrento's has two now, with a third planned. His parents watch Italian news programs bounced off the satellite.

The original restaurant had five or six tables; Sorrento's seats 300 now. Famous people sometimes come in. "Bench, Rose, Larry Bird, Danny Manning, Oscar Robertson, Jose Rijo, The Ramones," Willie says.

The Ramones?

"Johnny Ramone is a big sports (memorabilia) collector," says Willie. "He just sold all his baseball cards for over $40,000."

Sorrento's is what it is: a neighborhood restaurant. It's a dark place that could use some dart holes in its paneled walls. It is blessedly free of pretense. A joint. Unlike some other sports bars we know, Sorrento's would never encourage patrons to toss peanut shells on the floor.

Willie deliberately turns down the juke in his joint, "so people can hear the games." Sorrento's has ambience. And, of course, junk. The Willie Collection.

"This is stuff I been hangin' on walls for 39 years. I'm real choosy. It's all game-worn, authentic stuff." Not to mention a recently signed "pitch-er" from O.J. Simpson, received last spring, and Arafat's greeting: "To Mr. Willie DeLuca. best wishes, Yassar Arafat." Willie has this, yes he does. Don't ask why.

Willie also balances things on his large nose. Did I mention this? He has auditioned twice for *Late Night with David Letterman*, most recently in February. Willie does Stupid Human Tricks.

75

"For Letterman, I did a 10-speed bicycle. Fifty pounds, straight up on my nose," he says.

Alas, Willie did not make the final cut. He was beaten out by a man who could chatter his dentures rapidly, a girl who blew gum out of her mouth and sucked it back in (Willie claims the young lady attached the gum to a strand of hair) and, of course, two gentlemen who jiggled their pectorals to the tune of "Dueling Banjos." There are 4,000 sports bars in the country now; the first Champions opened in 1983, a mere 27 years after Sorrento's. Everyone thought it was a new concept. Everyone has not been to Sorrento's.

"What would you like me to do? A chair?" Willie is entertaining guests by balancing a chair on his nose. "I'll do a couple more for you. How 'bout Buddy Bell's bat with a hockey puck and a drink?" Well, okay. Iced tea glass on hockey puck on baseball bat. On nose. Done. Then comes the sword, its tip poking Willie's proboscis dead center, like a toothpick in a cocktail weenie. A female patron is impressed. "Doesn't this make your mother nervous?" she says.

"You ever heard of Art Schlichter? This is his Big 10 MVP trophy," says Willie. It must weigh 30 pounds. Willie hefts it upon his nose, balances it just right. The woman is aghast in wonder.

"We'll be back," she says.

Tough Guys

"This is war, fat boy."
—*Nose tackle Tim Krumrie, Bengal tenth round pick, to center Dave Rimington, first round pick*

The Toughest Bengal

November, 1993

$\mathcal{T}$he toughest Bengal there ever was has a foot long metal rod in his left leg and a canyon where the bridge of his nose used to be. Tim Krumrie always said the only way he'd ever leave a football game was if someone carried him off. When that finally happened, when his left leg was a flopping, shattered broken-in-four-places puree, the first words his wife said to him were, "Okay smarty, they carried you off the field. Now what are you gonna do?"

The doctors at Super Bowl XXIII had the idea that a man with a twice-broken tibia, a broken fibula and a broken ankle might want some medication to ease his pain. It wasn't what Tim Krumrie had in mind.

"How are we going to tape this sucker?" said Krumrie.

"Your leg is Jell-O," said the doctors. "We need to give you some pain-killing drugs."

"What will the drugs do to me?"

"They'll make you drowsy."

"Will I remember everything?"

"No."

"I don't want anything."

"You're going to pass out. You'll go into shock."

"Just give me a can of beer."

What Tim Krumrie did then was get his leg propped up on a table on the Bengals dressing room and sit there for three quarters, drinking a can of beer and watching Cincinnati play the San Francisco 49ers on TV. They convinced him to leave only by telling him the traffic would be hell after the game.

"I almost convinced them to take me out to the field in a wheelchair," Krumrie says. "But if I'd gone into shock, they'd have had a tough time getting me out of the stadium. I didn't want to make a scene."

The game is full of tough guys. Pain is in the contract, and if anything, football is more painful now than ever. The players are bigger, faster and stronger. The collisions become progressively more violent.

To stand on the sidelines of a professional football game is to bear witness to terrifying, mesmerizing violence. If it were a TV drama series, people would push to have it banned.

"Pain never bothered me," Krumrie is saying. He announces this matter-of-factly, as if pain were something to be flicked away like a fly at the family picnic. Pain is not his concern.

When Krumrie was about 9, he smashed his big toe on a rock as he was riding a dirt bike. The thing blew up like a balloon. The blood beneath the nail spread until his whole foot was fairly purple.

"Cry? Nope," Krumrie is saying. "I've never cried for pain. I stuck a pin in it, and watched the blood spurt everywhere. I was fine."

He has been a Cincinnati Bengal for eleven years, and he has never missed a game. He has played on Sunday after pulling a hamstring on Thursday afternoon. He has played with twisted knees and hyperextended knees and busted fingers and with a rod in his leg and with internal bleeding that swelled the back of his leg to the size of a grapefruit.

Krumrie plays nose tackle, and if ever a man were put on this earth to do one thing, it is Tim Krumrie, six feet one-inch tall and 273 pounds, a refrigerator with a head, plugging the middle of the defensive line like a dump truck in an alley. *You* try to get this guy.

He is a throw way-back. You could see Krumrie in one of those horizontal-striped rugby shirts, his leather helmet jammed in the seat pocket of his workin' pants, punching out of real life at 5 and heading for his part-time job with the Chicago Staleys or the Canton Bulldogs.

He'd be playing center and middle linebacker for $10 a game, and telling everybody about the time he lost some teeth making a diving tackle on a particularly fleet halfback.

"Picked 'em up, stuck 'em in my pocket," he'd say. "Don't eat so good now, but I made the damn tackle."

The notoriety to which Krumrie aspires has nothing to do with dollars, and only some to do with personal glory. He remains, at 33, an innocent, a dirty shirt in the land of players-with-briefcases. On durability alone, Krumrie could have, over the years, pushed the Bengals for a better contract. But he was also an All-Pro in 1988, and has led the team in tackles five times, mostly while being double-teamed.

Krumrie has never held out, never spoken ill of the organization, never decided he was above the general team welfare. All he wants to do is play. A high school coach he admires told him once that the worst thing any athlete can do is look back on a career and see regret. Says Krumrie, "That won't happen with me. I look and I don't regret one damn day. I busted my ass every single day."

Back to the Super Bowl. San Francisco 49ers halfback Roger Craig had taken the pitchout and swept to Krumrie's left. It was San Francisco's second offensive series of the Bowl, and Krumrie had yet to make a tackle. This, naturally, "pissed me off."

He vowed he would make a tackle on this series, regardless.

He went after Craig. His left foot caught in the soggy turf of Miami's Joe Robbie Stadium. Nobody hit him.

"I just had so much adrenaline going, with the hype of the Super Bowl. The torque caused the leg to break. The leg broke and then I took another step. I was so focused on making the tackle I didn't feel the break. My brain didn't register the pain.

"I actually took another step on it when it was broken. It broke a couple more times. That's where you get all the gruesome pictures.

"I did make the damn tackle, which was important."

He grew up in a farming town in Wisconsin called Mondovi, population 2,500. In the fields, he drove a water truck, but there was plenty of time for pleasure. "So I ran," Krumrie says.

Krumrie would run ahead of the trucks that sprayed pesticides into the corn fields. When he got too tired to stay a safe distance ahead of the trucks—"They'd have run me over. They thought I was a pain in the ass"—he'd return to his own truck, where he'd stashed a couple cinderblocks.

"I'd curl them," Krumrie recalls. "I'd curl them and lift with them, pretend I was playing football." What the good folks of Mondovi said about young Tim Krumrie was, "That boy is out of his mind."

And tough. The toughest there ever was.

"What about the time the referees had to escort you off the field because you wouldn't leave?" says Cheryl Krumrie. She is an athletic trainer, who revels in Tim's stories as much as he does. They met at age 15, and haven't been apart since. "I played fullback as a senior in high school and in our last game I was having just a hell of a first quarter."

"Seventy-four yards," Cheryl remembers.

"Right. Then on this one play, I got hit right above my knee. Hyperextended it. Hairline fracture of my femur."

"You have to leave," a referee decided.

"Bull," Krumrie said.

They dragged him off the field.

A week later, he was done with football and back on the wrestling team, as a heavyweight. "I was ranked number one in the state. I was so proud of that. I'd do anything to keep it," Krumrie says.

"I took a week off. We taped the leg. I couldn't get in a wrestler's stance. I couldn't bend the leg. I was undefeated."

Bad knee. Broken leg. Undefeated.

Tough. Toughest there ever was.

"I thrive on exhaustion and self-inflicted pain. I take myself over the edge," Krumrie maintains. "If someone says run a mile, I'll run two miles. I got cauliflower ear from wrestling. I cut my ear putting my helmet on every day. Even now, I call that my mindset for the day. It hurts like hell. That's how I know I'm ready to play."

As a senior at the University of Wisconsin, Krumrie played all year with a bad knee. It hurt him in the eyes of the pro scouts, but that didn't matter so much as the goal he had set for himself never to miss a game in college.

81

The Bengals drafted him in the 10th round, even though he was an All-American.

It was in college that Krumrie began cultivating the ditch at the bridge of his nose. It's from his helmet, acting like a backhoe, right between the eyes. As Krumrie explains, "I led with my head a lot back then."

It never quite heals. After every game, Krumrie bleeds like a boxer stuck with a jab.

"I had plastic surgery on it, after my senior year in college. It (the bridge) used to be lower, until they scraped it off and flattened it out. The whole surgery deal. To fix it, they'll have to draft some skin. Not 'til I'm done playing."

It has been a weekly ritual, this stitching of his face. Every week, for twelve years.

"Hundreds" of stitches, Krumrie says, gleefully. "Ten a crack."

This is the way you will remember him. The ultimate warrior, after the game, his uniform zippered with the black-green mash of blood and grass and mayhem, the white athletic tape frayed and unraveling from his hands. The nobility of a football player is forged in dirt and cast in blood.

Tim Krumrie will stand there after a game, just this way. The picture of a Sunday afternoon.

Occasionally, he'll wipe some blood from the bridge of his nose.

Kozerski's War

*I*f the Bengals really needed him, Bruce Kozerski could play on Sunday. Five days ago, he was playing center and someone sat on him during a pileup. These things happen in football.

He fractured a transverse process, a two-inch long piece of bone attached to either side of the lower vertebrae. Kozerski likens the transverse process bone to a "rib that didn't grow all the way around." He says, "I'd call what I have a broken rib."

You and I would call it a slightly broken back. That is, if we believe a back could be slightly broken.

He could play on Sunday. "In an emergency," Kozerski says.

This is the NFL. In the NFL, a linebacker named Jack Reynolds once played a playoff game with a broken leg. Bengals special-teamer deluxe Ed Brady hits people so hard on kick returns, his arms go numb.

Five days ago, Bruce Kozerski broke his back on the seventh play of the game. He played 23 more downs, until they wheeled him in for X-rays.

"The only reason I didn't play the rest of the game is they wanted to get it X-rayed. Once I did that, then laid on the table for 15 minutes, I couldn't get off the table. It locked up. I couldn't hardly move."

Five days ago, Bruce Kozerski broke his back. He could play on Sunday. "Only when I make certain specific movements am I in pain," he says.

Pain? Pain isn't the point. Playing with pain is the point.

At its most basic, the National Football League is a cult of pain. Pain is part of the basic agreement between a player and his body. Pain is in the contract.

For 16 weeks, what they do in the NFL is commit legal violence. Pain is expected, pain is tolerated. Pain is welcomed.

83

Says Boomer Esiason, "Monday morning? When I'm in pain? It feels good. On a Monday you don't feel like you're hurt you're thinking, 'Man, I must not have done anything out there yesterday.'"

Pain is the tie that binds players to the game, because no one who plays, plays without it. There is no more highly respected virtue in the NFL than playing in pain.

Sucking it up. Everyone sucks it up. Ten years from now, when it's raining and cold and their bodies are so stiff that they cry just getting out of bed, maybe they'll question that version of courage. Not now.

"That's just the way in the NFL," says Kozerski. "You don't make it anywhere in football without playing with pain.

"People play through pain every day, whether it's busted ankles, sore elbows, sore knees, sore shoulders. This isn't a sport for weak hearts. We're physically killing ourselves in this occupation."

Pain is what separates football from the rest of sport. Pain is what makes football our most popular and least rational game. In the body of every football player beats the heart of a homicidal maniac with suicidal tendencies.

I'm gonna kill that guy, even if it kills me.

It's more than a little ironic that a profession so dependent on health is run like a demolition derby. But that's football.

Esiason: "It's crazy. It's like getting into a head-on collision every week, then getting up the next day, giving yourself some treatment, practicing, then getting back into the car and hitting a pole."

There is pressure to play with pain. Subtle pressure from teammates ("When you comin' back, man?"), from coaches ("We could really use you this week"), from ownership ("We're not paying you to sit in the trainer's room, son.") Mostly, the pressure is within.

Football's super-heated macho environment isn't kind to those expressing a low pain threshold. Forever, the code of the NFL road has been, if you have a pulse, you have a chance to play.

You get muscle stimulation. You get wrapped, taped, iced, heated, shot up. You wear braces, flak jackets and foam rubber pads. You pop

84

anti-inflammatories as if they were jelly beans. You suck it up.

After the game, you may not be able to walk from the dressing room to your car without dragging a leg or slumping a shoulder. Your head is an explosion, your knees have been stomped by elephants, and your ribs, well, you won't even discuss your ribs.

But for 60 minutes, you played. You played.

"I don't think this injury is something that's going to cripple me," Bruce Kozerski says. It's a verbal shrug, a gentle so-what to a visitor who doesn't understand why someone, anyone, would try to play football with a broken back.

"Guys go to work sick every day," Kozerski says. "This is our way of being sick."

Think about that the next time you break a nail.

Through the pain, Kozerski finds one small consolation.

"I sleep like a baby," he says.

Officer Dibble

July 15, 1989

*T*his year, Rob Dibble has thrown a chair and five bats into a lake, a fastball behind Willie Randolph's head, a bat into the screen behind home plate and a pitch at Tim Teufel's spine.

As you might imagine, his baseball rap sheet is impressive. He has been fined three times, ejected three times and suspended twice. National League hitters might respect him. They also think he's certifiable.

When Dibble leaves the 15-day disabled list, he will serve a three-game suspension for giving Teufel lower back pain in New York last Saturday.

85

Then he will return as the best set-up man in the league, for as long as his arm and temper permit. Think of it as parole.

Says Dibble: "People think I'm crazy enough to hurt somebody. If I wanted to, believe me, I could. That's not beyond me."

You might think he spends his off days on the corner, pounding school kids for their lunch money.

You might picture Dibble walking, no, *riding,* in from the bullpen on a Harley, wearing leathers and some tattoos. He wouldn't strike out the side, just throw them all through the nearest plate glass window.

You might think that.

The fact is, Rob Dibble married his high school sweetheart. He drives a late-model Japanese sedan (very respectable), he'll be a father in a month, and he has a big dog whose picture he keeps in his locker. He listens to opera. Really.

Away from baseball, Rob Dibble is a very sensitive guy. Out of uniform, he's often mistaken for Phil Donahue. "I'm totally normal," he says. "I mean, I'm from *Connecticut.*"

Connecticut leads the nation in persons named Muffy. Everyone in Connecticut lives in a mansion. In Connecticut, you're underprivileged if you don't have a butler.

It isn't exactly a killer environment.

Rob Dibble? A maniac? From Connecticut? A guy could get the wrong impression.

"I don't need people to care if I'm crazy or not. Sometimes, people think you're putting on an act. When I get out there, I'm not even a part of myself anymore. I'm just out there throwing as hard as I can, trying to get people out," Dibble says.

Dibble plays hardball. Got it?

He isn't going to stand out there and let some banjo-hitting sometimes-infielder play slap shot with his fastball. No way.

You bat against Officer Dibble, you come to the plate thinking 100 mile-an-hour malevolence. You don't dig in, you don't lean your neck out over the plate like you just bought it. The Officer just might chop it off.

It's the way he plays. OK?

He doesn't apologize for New York, which cost him $400 and three days. (Teufel charged the mound and lost $200 and no days. "That's crap," says Dibble).

"I'd do it again. I'd do it in a heartbeat. I'll keep doing it until I run out of money or they get me out of the game."

When he was a kid, The Officer played hockey. Defenseman. He lost four teeth, he broke his nose four times. He'd think nothing of using his stick to dent an opponent's shins. It was part of the game, just like dusting a batter off the plate.

Dibble says, "I'm just trying to play the game the way it's supposed to be played."

Trouble is, baseball is a kinder, gentler game than it once was. Now, if you don't offer a hitter a hanging curve at least once every at-bat, you're asking for a fight. If Don Drysdale pitched now, NL president Bill White might lock him up.

If that makes Dibble a brushback throwback, OK. He's from a town called Southington, which rich Connecticut people pronounce "SUTH-ington."

When he was 14, he worked in a gas station. At 18, he was running a convenience store at night, "working so hard trying to show people I didn't need my parents' money."

His two older brothers went to prep school.

Dibble declined.

He does have his moments. A bad outing in Florida last March did upset him. "But people don't realize what I really did.

"People think I threw a bunch of chairs. I threw one chair. And about five bats. And turned over a bunch of picnic tables. I did a lot more than people gave me credit for."

A guy could get the wrong impression.

Dibble says, "The rest of the year, I have to be a good boy." Is this possible?

"If I throw a pitch inside now and knock a guy down by accident and the guy charges the mound, you might see me out for 10 days."

In '87, when he was pitching in Nashville, Dibble once reacted to the way he felt he was being misused in the bullpen by throwing his first four warmup pitches purposely into the Sounds dugout. A fifth bounced off the press box window.

The owner's wife picked up the ball.

Then what?

"They asked me if I was ready to pitch," says Rob Dibble.

The Hill

September 15, 1989

We earn our respect in different ways. Bengals halfback James Brooks gets a large chunk of his on an ungodly hill of dirt in Houston.

It's no higher than the length of the Bengals locker room. It was grass once, but hundreds of cleated feet over the last decade have changed all that. Now, The Hill looks like Baja, only vertical. Like where you'd film a truck commercial.

Running The Hill is like sprinting up a wall. It's where several college and professional football players go in the off-season for a guts checkup. "It's agony, man," Brooks says.

It's a place where you die daily, and feel good about it. What The Hill does is tell you how badly you want to play the game.

It is where James Brooks goes for two months every year to prove himself. All over again. Because the thing about being 180 pounds in a 280-pounder's game is, someone's always there passing out the doubts. Just last week, Chicago Bears coach Mike Ditka looked at film of Brooks and decided that Brooks, at age 30, had lost a step.

You believe what you want. I, for one, believe Ditka is the only man in America still wearing an Eddie Munster haircut.

Brooks believed Ditka must have been looking at super slo-mo instant replay. "Ditka doesn't know me," he said.

Evidently not. Too Old James had 134 total yards against the Bears.

Fooled 'em again.

At various times in his nine-year career, Brooks has been too: small, light, fragile, moody, cocky, and old.

Each year brings a new slight, be it real or perceived. There is a big chip on James Brooks' shoulder. That happens naturally when your whole life, somebody's telling you that, for whatever reason, you're not quite good enough.

Whether it was former San Diego Chargers coach Don Coryell making Brooks a blocking back—a 180-pound blocking back?—or the Bengals giving their offense to fullback Ickey Woods, then taking a halfback with their first pick in the '89 draft, James Brooks always felt like second place.

"Lots of people didn't expect me to be around playing halfback in the NFL after nine years," he said Thursday. They didn't know him.

Former Bengals and Chargers wide receiver Charlie Joiner first took Brooks to The Hill six years ago. The Hill had helped Joiner to a 16-year NFL career; Earl Campbell had credited The Hill with building his thighs.

Brooks loved it immediately. He loved the pain, because he knew he could beat it. "It hurts," he says. "That's the whole idea."

In a routine morning, Brooks ascends The Hill 45 times. "Once forwards, once backwards, once sideways."

He runs The Hill five hours a day for two months, thinking only that he has to be a better player the next year than he was the last one. "I always go to (summer) camp thinking like a rookie," he says.

"Everything's hard running on that hill. Everything's fast, fast, fast. Hard running. You'd think it might be boring, but it's not, because you think about what it's doing for you."

Brooks says he'll never meet a practice or a game tougher than

The Hill. "I come here," he says, "and I cruise. I'm in better shape than anybody."

The Hill puts football on pretty simple terms. Either you want to play, or you don't. Nothing comes without a price. Not if you're 30 years old and 180 pounds.

"Each year it's harder," says Brooks. "That's why I enjoy it. You don't get something for nothing when you're doing The Hill. It's not a clean place to be. Nothing pretty about it."

He grew up in a small Georgia town, one of 10 children raised by their mother, who had a hill of her own to climb.

"She never asked for anything from anybody," Brooks says. "She always taught us, if you can get it, do it yourself."

In junior high, Brooks played football with a brother five years older and 50 pounds heavier than he. "He figured I'd get hurt."

Ever get hurt? "Not to my knowledge. They couldn't tackle me."

Sunday, Too Old Brooks taunted Bears All-Pro defensive end Richard Dent. Occasionally, Brooks' assignment was to block Dent. Dent wasn't receptive.

Brooks, to Dent: "Why don't you stop crying? If you're so big and tough, why don't you knock me down?"

Dent never did. Too Little Brooks got away with one.

Brooks is the Bengals' second all-time leading rusher. Before they switched to a ball-control offense in '88, he was the Bengals' best offensive player. He remains the hardest-nosed.

The Hill is his teacher, and when it asks James Brooks how badly he wants to play football, Brooks always has the right answer. It's the pain.

"I love the pain," he says. "Say what you want about me. You can't say I'm not tough enough."

The Bogeyman

August 11, 1995

*B*engals emperor Mike Brown is a substance guy in a style world. That is very bad when you are trying to pitch sneakers or hamburgers, or a new stadium to an angry town. Substance guys don't manage public relations well. They don't dwell on their own reflections. They know what they know.

Bob Knight is a substance guy. So is Bill Parcells.

Change them? You might as well move a boulder.

So it is on this sunny Thursday afternoon of his 60th birthday, Mike Brown says: "I am what I am. I am who I am. I don't have a magic wand to turn me into Prince Charming. I happen to be a narrowly focused guy. Nothing particularly distinguished. That's what most of us are."

As the anti-stadia forces mutate, replicate and spread like fungi all over Hamilton County, Brown's predicament becomes painfully obvious: In his four years as the Bengals top executive, Brown has won more games than friends.

At a time when he desperately needs a shot of good public relations, the mere notion of it makes him wheeze.

Brown's problem is not that he is a dour, greedy man. His problem is everyone thinks he is.

"Some of the public isn't persuaded I'm a bad guy," Brown says, finally.

Oh, really? Which public is that?

The public that loves to be taxed to pay for stadiums? The public that wouldn't know Big Daddy Wilkinson if he took their drive-thru order? Or the public that thinks 3–13 is a swell way to spend an autumn?

"If people perceive me as a warty-toad, so be it," Brown says.

91

"Some people think I'm a sleek frog. Maybe there aren't enough of those."

Here's a tip: Take the warty-toad. Give the points.

As we tour around Hamilton County, we see the anti-taxers reveling in a prolonged ecstasy of Brown-bashing. We hear them say they won't spend money to buy "Mike Brown's stadium." There is no mention of a Reds stadium, even though they'd get theirs, too.

This is because Marge Schott understands PR. Dollar hot dogs, low ticket prices, etc. Brown hasn't a clue: price increases on Christmas Eve, poor records, hostage crisis, etc.

On one hand, Brown concedes his image "will be part of this debate." On the other, he says, "I don't think I can change it. I'm the bogeyman. I'm rich, I'm greedy. I know a lot of people in Cincinnati with fatter wallets than mine. Whatever I've earned, I've invested in Cincinnati businesses. But if you're against what we're doing, I'm an easy target."

He doesn't have to be. For a warty-toad, Brown's a swell guy. He is witty, personable, loyal and decent. The problem is, most of the people who know that were at his birthday party Thursday night.

There is a part of Mike Brown that lives somewhere close to 1955. It is the part that wonders why he can't just send his scrappy little 11 on the field and watch them play in the mud.

Except now, there must be more. Call it charisma, or shtick. Call it what you like. Image may not be everything. But it pays a lot of bills.

This week, the emperor decreed that WLW talk-man Andy Furman not be allowed on the Bengals pregame show.

"We're not looking for a talk show," Brown says. "Talk shows are for the American male what the grocery tabloids are for the American female. Last year, (Furman) called on people to burn their Bengals tickets in a bonfire. Well, guess what? We're trying to sell Bengals tickets."

Andy Furman is not the point. If the contract with Jacor allows Brown to pick his announcers, that's what he should do. But what results is a furthering of the notion that Mike is Scrooge in wingtips.

I ask Mike Brown: If you could dispel one myth about you, what might it be?

"I guess I don't know the answer to that," he says.

How I Spent my Summer Vacation

April 23, 1999

*I*n the first five minutes, he had eliminated all the reasons to be comfortable. Football is not about comfort, not in July, so the first thing he did Wednesday was take the metal, queen-sized bedframe from beneath the mattress and stack it up next to the dormitory room door. He would sleep on the floor.

Then he dumped his existence for the next 22 days onto a desktop. For his 14th and last training camp, Reggie Williams had packed:

—One black nylon shoulder bag containing a week's worth of clothes. "You ever wash these clothes, Reggie?" A visitor wanted to know. "No," says Williams.

—One small cardboard box filled with books. "I read a lot up here."

—One small electric clock. What, no sundial? "Not when there is a $100 a minute fine for lateness."

—One aluminum briefcase, this being councilman Reggie Williams and all.

That completes the creature comforts list. This blanket? Don't need this blanket. Bedsheet? Gone. Bedframe? History.

Other guys walking down the hall, moving in, carrying air conditioners, fans, televisions, radios. Carrying boom boxes, headphones, stereos, tape decks, compact disc players. Carrying picture frames. Carrying clothes on honest-to-God hangers.

Turning their rooms into...rooms. You can attack football training camp any way you like. It all depends on your interpretation of comfort.

Former Washington Redskins quarterback and Hall of Famer Sonny Jurgensen, for one, survived summer camp by launching frequent and devastating pre-emptive strikes on local watering holes.

Reggie, His Ownself, chooses to live in Wilmington like a Buddist monk. "Life at its most basic," he calls it. It is what makes him comfortable.

As with most things he attempts, Reggie Williams is different (some might say pretentious) with his training camp regimen. Williams' Spartan (some might say ostentatious) lifestyle begs to be noticed, if only because nobody with money to spend chooses to sleep on the floor of a second-story dorm room in July without the much-preferred AC option. Do they?

"Football is not a game you get comfortable to play," says Reggie Williams.

His room is painted an institutional blue. Room 263 is from the early Alcatraz Period: cinderblock walls, two built-in desks, one little window. A floor that resembles kitchen linoleum. Room temperature close to 90 degrees.

The point here, is suffering. Suffering is the object. You get reacquainted with it in July, so by November, it's second nature.

"With football, you can't say you don't play well because it's too cold or too hot, or you've got a cramp," Williams says. "Training camp, it doesn't matter how hot you get, or whether you catch a cold, or whether you have your allergies. The point is to be ready to play."

Say what you like about Williams, but for 13 years, he has been ready to play. Now, two months from his 35th birthday, he'll try again. One more time, with no air conditioning. One more time, comfortably suffering.

It's not strange (well, not totally) that Williams should subject himself to such preparation. Football players from Dartmouth who

94

play in the NFL do a lot of looking over their shoulders.

"The nerdy Ivy League," Williams calls it. He graduated from Dartmouth in January of his senior year, anticipating a February NFL draft.

As it was, the draft was postponed until May. But Williams had other problems. He had played poorly in the Hula and Japan bowls, two games watched heavily by pro scouts.

In one, an assistant coach actually appointed him a team water boy. In the other, an East versus West affair, the head coach's pregame speech on the deficiencies of West Coast football sounded fine, until he realized he had Williams, a nerdy Ivy Leaguer, on his roster.

Williams' agent was so embarrassed by his client's play in the two games, he tore up the contract he had made to represent Williams.

Embarrassed, Williams never went home to Michigan. He took a job as a janitor in a White Plains, N.Y., YMCA until the Bengals picked him in the third round in May.

In his first training camp, he shaved his head, because the other outside linebackers had done it. In his second, he irritated his roommate by turning off his fan in the middle of the night. It was the last year anyone agreed to room with him.

Now, he's back again. The nerdy Ivy Leaguer, looking over his shoulder, doing what he can to keep an edge. Suffering. The room is hot. Very hot.

"I usually have music," says Williams.

No music this year?

"Oh no," he says. "No music."

Goodbye, Mrs. Whatchamadoodle

April 23, 1999

*T*hey opened the doors to the Cincinnati Reds offices Tuesday, and the last 14 years blew out like an ill wind. Marge Schott was out. At 100 Cinergy Field, you could practically touch the relief.

The public doesn't know the half of dealing with or working for Marge. The public never will. It's barely relevant now. Schott is gone. All that needs deciding is if she keeps her 21 blue seats, an office at the stadium, and her place in the Findlay Market parade.

Give her the seats and be done with it. Don't let her be the Reds' mascot. This isn't meanness. It's the desperate need for the Reds to move on.

It is time to bring the joy of the game back to its oldest professional city. It's time to resume the business of making Reds baseball important again.

There used to be no baseball place like this. In the late '80s, the Dodgers would come in for the weekend, and it was all anyone wanted to talk about. The Reds would draw 35,000 Friday, 40,000 Saturday and 45,000 Sunday afternoon.

Now, people working for companies with free tickets give those tickets away. If they can. It's time to move on.

Lots of events have conspired to put this franchise in an unacceptable hole. The strike. Exploding salaries. A devastated farm system, the inexplicable departures of Lou Piniella and Davey Johnson, the classless ouster of Tony Perez, the stadium debate.

You name it, this team has suffered it. But the one ongoing, spirit-sapping illness came from the big office at 100 Cinergy. Time to move on.

Baseball is not a diversion here. It's not some beer-drinking, beach ball-bopping party. Other places, people go to ballgames the way they go to a movie. If you've ever been to Dodger Stadium or Coors Field, you know what I'm talking about.

They don't take the game personally.

We take it personally.

Time for the healing to begin.

Schott can help. She can put a shine to a corner of her discredited legacy. She can apologize. That's right. She can say, "To everyone I've demeaned and mistreated, I am sorry."

Nothing is so redemptive as an apology. Look what it did for Clinton. Look what it could have done for Pete Rose.

She can apologize to Eric Davis for not sending him an airplane in Oakland, for calling him a million-dollar you-know-what and for having him wear those stuffed dog ears at a press conference. Especially for having him wear the stuffed dog ears.

To Dave Parker.

To Bill Reik, Billy Hatcher and Lou Piniella. After sweeping Oakland to win the '90 World Series, the Reds returned to their hotel hungry. There was no food, though, only an open bar. Schott had sent the hotel's kitchen staff home.

Reik, now a majority partner; Hatcher, who had seven straight hits in the Series, and Piniella made a trip to a local fast-food joint. They bought burgers for the team.

Win a world title, get some fries. Damnedest thing I ever heard.

Sorry to Bob Quinn, for making him pay his own way to the All-Star Game and for making him scoop Schottzie's poop in the Reds offices. Really.

To Cam Bonifay, Chuck LaMar and every other scout who "watched ball games."

To those same scouts who, when traveling for the club, had to wash their clothes at a laundromat and plop quarters into motel pay phones because Schott wouldn't pay for inroom local calls.

To every Reds coach who had to share one rental car with three or four other coaches at spring training.

To Johnson and Piniella, who wanted to stay.

Sorry.

To Jon Braude.

To whatchamadoodle.

To everyone who deserved better, which was just about everyone who ever worked for her.

Schott could apologize and leave us with a good memory. Probably she won't. More's the pity.

Goodbye, Mrs. Schott. Thank you. Please leave gracefully.

5

They Would Be Kings

"If you don't catch the ball, you catch the bus."
—*Rocky Bridges, former Reds infielder*

Ickey Steps Out

November 18, 1988

*I*t has gone on long enough. Somebody has to say something now, before it's too late. A reputation is at stake here. People are starting to talk. OK?

Mr. Ickey Woods, fullback, Cincinnati Bengals, is too good a football player to go on like this. If he were just your average Ickey, it wouldn't matter. If he didn't have nine touchdowns, nobody would care.

But he does. And if you're lucky, he'll get more. The man is a truck. He is a refrigerator with a head. As a second-round draft choice from that football hotbed, Nevada-Las Vegas, he is making some Bengals scout look very smart.

He has one major problem. The man can't dance. In the end zone, he looks like a California Raisin with a milk hangover. He looks bad, and that ain't good. We thought it was time he knew.

Fred Astaire could dance better on his nose than Ickey Woods does on his toes. Ickey Woods makes me look like Michael Jackson. If Ickey Woods tried to moonwalk, he'd fall into a black hole.

Ever have one of those electric football games where the players moved by vibration? Ever watch the players when you turned the vibration control too high? Ickey Woods looks like that.

He's in the end zone, he breaks from the pile. He faces the crowd and does—what? What, exactly, is he doing?

Ickey Woods is hopping from side to side. There must be something wrong with his feet.

Upstairs, Paul Brown is concerned. "What's wrong with Ickey's feet?"

On the sidelines, Sam Wyche sends the team doctor out, to rub the cramps out of Ickey's feet.

In the end zone, Ickey Woods is like art deco. He's like 1950s furniture and 3-D movies. Paul Anka, Barry Manilow, Pat Sajak. He's so bad he's good. We thought it was time he knew.

In the end zone, the man is a casualty. He needs Arthur Murray. He needs help.

Rr-r-r-r-ing!

Hello.

Eleanor Lachman answers. She owns the Arthur Murray dance studios here. Arthur Murray is "the proven way to learn the newest steps," the ad in the phone book says. This sounds encouraging.

"Do you want something like classical? Would classical work?"

Eleanor Lachman is concerned. She loves the Bengals, she sees the star potential in Ickey Woods, football player. She knows it could all die, just fade away, if the man can't dance.

"We teach ballroom dancing. We teach rhythm dancing."

In the NFL, it helps to have a shtick. You can sell smoke without fire in the NFL (see: Brian Bosworth) but it's best if you have a gimmick. Eleanor Lachman can give Ickey Woods a legitimate shtick.

Rhythm dancing?

"He should learn the jive, or the swing. Or I would say maybe he should samba, mambo or cha-cha. It wouldn't be bad for him because most athletes have good directional movement."

Ickey Woods isn't big on people trying to change his dance. He likes his directional movement the way it is. "I don't need no mambo lessons," he said.

Woods created his end-zone bop before the first Cleveland game, two months ago. His mother was in town. He wanted to do something memorable for her if he scored.

"I didn't want to do something everybody else does," Woods said. "You see anybody else with my style?"

It's definitely one of a kind.

"I just jump from one foot to the other. The last time, I just hop on one foot. I do it one at a time, to give everybody a peek at it.

"I don't have a name for it. You can call it whatever you want."

101

I don't call it. I call Judy Hatterman. She runs the Fred Astaire studio ("You'll be dancing after your first lesson"), in Norwood Plaza. She will know what to do.

"Maybe if he did a few more leaps," Judy Hatterman suggested. She watches all the games on TV. She has seen the Ickey Bop. She says it needs help. "Maybe if he got a little more hip action into it."

Judy Hatterman talks about the movie *Dirty Dancing*. She says it "started a mambo craze." Maybe the mambo would be good.

Ickey Woods isn't convinced. He doesn't know from the movie *Dirty Dancing*. If he wanted dance lessons, he would have bought some. He's a football player. He thinks maybe the Ickey Bop has a future.

"My dance is good enough," he said. Ickey Woods is a proud man. "If people don't like it, they don't have to look at it."

Eleanor Lachman and Judy Hatterman said they would be glad to offer free lessons if Ickey Woods changes his mind. They only want to help. Until they do, Ickey Woods will be the best rookie running back in football. Just don't ask him to mambo.

Bound for Glory

November 28, 1988

*B*ruce Smith was a sack of potatoes. He was a pile of leaves. He was a 300-pound cat, tossed out for the night. Bruce (Morris) Smith. He needed help.

He was backpedaling four yards beyond the scrimmage line on the first play of the game, and he had Anthony Munoz's forearms doing the sledgehammer rhumba on his pectorals.

Maybe, probably, he wasn't believing this.

Bengals fullback Ickey Woods was downfield, way downfield. He ran right past Bruce Smith, All-Pro right defensive end, Buffalo Bills. Smith never saw Woods, only Anthony Munoz. Smith was a rowdy drunk at last call. Munoz bounced him.

Offensive linemen have dreams like this. They have scarred bodies and wrenched backs and fingers that could never play the piano. Their shirts never fit, because Arrow doesn't build shirts with size-50 necks.

We don't talk to them because they aren't quarterbacks. We write about Douglas MacArthur, not his grunts.

Except today. Offensive linemen work all year, all their professional lives, really, for a game like Sunday's.

Bengals 35, Bills 21 was a grunt and a snort. It was the Bengals' offensive line, beating the 11–1 Bills at their own Brand-X game. Take the first play, run it back 77 times—the number of offensive plays Cincinnati shoved at Buffalo—and you'll see lots of blocks like the one Munoz made on Smith.

That's why the Bengals gained 232 yards on the ground against the AFC's best defense. That's why they led, 21–0, before Bruce Smith could feel the turf burns on his elbows.

That's why (guessing here) the always loquacious Boomer Esiason left the dressing room relatively quickly. He wanted the linemen to get the credit that they deserve.

In the first half, the Bengals had 287 yards, more than Buffalo's previous six opponents had amassed in the whole game. That's why the Bengals are back to even-money to be in Miami on January 22.

Before we get carried away, be reminded that the Bills were playing for nearly nothing. They still can clinch the home-field advantage throughout the playoffs by winning two of their last three games.

They played without linebackers Shane Conlan and Darryl Talley, and cornerback Derrick Burroughs. They lost nothing but pride here Sunday. But...

The Bengals' game plan was simple. It was hightops. Black hightops, in the mud. It was 1950. It could have been drawn in the dirt by Paul Brown. Maybe it was. Get ahead of the Bills early, run often, don't make Esiason do a Dan Marino act in the fourth quarter.

Buffalo does not have a big-play offense. It gets no speed from its wideouts. By design, its offense plays just well enough so it won't mess things up for its defense.

The Bills play like champions mainly when they are ahead. The Bengals had the top-rated running game in the NFL. They wanted to use it often, if only to keep Smith and his friends off the field.

They did better than that. This game was a throwback to the future for Cincinnati, which played a Super Bowl-caliber game against a team that has worn out the rest of the AFC.

They ran 52 times, held the ball for 41 minutes. Super Bowl-winning teams dominate the line like this. It's what separated the Redskins from Denver last year, the Giants from Denver two years ago, the Bears from New England the year before that.

The running game was so strong, the offensive line so overpowering, the efficient Esiason hardly was noticed—or needed. Count on Joe Walter's twisted fingers the number of times you've been able to say that in the last five years.

How good was the line? Twice on the Bengals' final, nine-minute, Bills-killing drive, Wyche called runs *up the middle* on third down and five.

James Brooks gained eight yards the first time, 11 the second.

How good? "Unbelievable sometimes," Woods said. "Before I get hit, I'm five yards down the field."

How good? The Brand-X offense was so good, the defense never was seriously tested.

Bills Q.B. Jim Kelly is Steve DeBerg with better teammates. But Kelly threw two horrible interceptions, and Tim Krumrie forced a critical fumble when Buffalo was driving early in the fourth quarter.

This should have been the game that the defense won for the Bengals. As it was, the defense was spotty. It allowed 353 yards, but forced four turnovers. It played well enough not to mess things up for the offensive line.

Cincinnati offensive line coach Jim McNally has wanted to see these Bengals forever. He's in his office at 5:30 every morning, creating scenes like Sunday's. Sometimes, like Sunday, they all work.

"He's always trying to talk me into running more," coach Sam Wyche said. "My hearing is getting better."

No Dancing for Stanley

January 2, 1989

*I*t was nearly 9 o'clock on New Year's Eve when Stanley Wilson stepped from the Bengals' dressing room, the last player out. He left behind a few clubhouse guys, a TV cameraman, and a security cop impatient to turn out the lights.

Wilson was in no hurry. He'd spent too many years living too fast to be rushed. He knew, once, what it was like to be young and swift and immortal. Now, on this New Year's Eve, he knew none of it was ever quite true. He took his time.

"We got movement, I smelled 18 grand (in playoff money) and I decided to run over the cornerback and get into the end zone."

It was only two years ago that Stanley Wilson sat in the living room of Sam Wyche's house, eating ice cream. He was going to be tested for drugs the next morning. The coach took Wilson home and fed him ice cream to keep him from the streets, and from himself. Wilson failed the test.

He was a cocaine addict then. He remains one now. An addict can arrest his addiction. He can't control it. There's no such thing as an occasional addict.

The difference is, Stanley Wilson knows that now. Two years ago, no one worried about Wilson's football future. They feared for his life.

105

Now, on New Year's Eve 1988, they crowd his locker, waves of cameras and microphones and ballpoints. They ask about the two touchdowns he scored in Cincinnati's 21–13 victory over Seattle. He tells them much more.

"I feel reborn," he says. Addicts "feel like they're committing slow suicide. That's how I felt. This is almost like a second life."

You had wondered if, in this season of giddy success, Stanley Wilson's unique and singular triumph would be overlooked.

He had lost his starting fullback job early in the year, to injury and, ultimately, to rookie Ickey Woods. Wilson has spent the last three months blocking and taking play-action fakes from Boomer Esiason.

You wondered what this had done to his spirit. Usually, you wondered this while talking to Woods, whose stadium locker is adjacent to Wilson's. After most home games, so many reporters have crowded around the rookie/cult figure that Wilson couldn't reach his own locker.

How was he handling this? Says Esiason, "Stanley has had to sit and watch Ickey for the last nine or 10 weeks. He's had to watch his (Woods') Oldsmobile commercial. He's had to be quiet about it." You wondered if Wilson was lost in the Ickey shuffle.

He was not. He was the last player out. He stood wrapped only in a towel. For an hour, answering questions. His is a story worth telling and retelling. It's maybe the best story the 1988 Bengals have, even now.

"I'm just trying to keep everything together," Wilson is saying. "It has been a lot of hard work, besides football. It (football) is a lot easier than anything else I've done in the past few years."

There is pain in his voice, and more than a little irony. Cocaine put him in the hospital four times in 11 months. Twice, he was suspended from the NFL for coke use.

Now, he urinates in a bottle three times a week. Someone representing SmithKline Biomedical Laboratories—a lab used by the NFL to test its drug offenders—collects the specimen, seals it and sends it to be tested. Wilson will go through this three times a week for the rest of his football-playing life.

"On the previous play, we saw their defensive linemen slant outside, so we countered and went back the other way. They ran themselves out of the play, and I scored."

It was only because Woods was sick with the flu that Wilson played as much as he did Saturday. Wyche cares about Wilson, but mostly because he thinks Wilson is a good football player. It's a business.

Sunday against Buffalo, Wilson likely will be doing what he has done since October: lead Woods through holes at the goal line and take play-fakes from Esiason.

That doesn't change what happened Saturday, when Stanley Wilson rediscovered himself as a player, and lots of others discovered him as a changed, better person.

"No, I don't have a dance," Wilson is telling the man from NBC.

It's late. The clubhouse guys wheel big, gray hampers around the empty room, picking up towels. It's New Year's Eve. The security guard wants to leave.

Stanley Wilson is in no hurry. "Today was really good," he says. "I haven't felt this good in a long time. I knew that somehow, somewhere that something good was going to come out of it for me."

He went home, to Fairfield, in the Jaguar he drives too fast. "I got stopped last night," he says. "The cop said, 'If you win, no ticket.'"

He spent this New Year's quietly, with a friend. "No wild celebrations," he says. "Now, football is as wild as I get."

Montana to Taylor

January 22, 1989

*M*iami—"We were 34 seconds away," Sam Wyche said. "Thirty-four..."

He let the thought hang. His eyes were red. His voice cracked. What was left of it. It was late. For 59 minutes and 26 seconds, he was the head coach of the best team in football. Now, he was tired and teary. What else could he say?

A San Francisco 49ers wide receiver named John Taylor, who makes all of 14 catches in the regular season, who sells cars in the off-season, catches a 10-yard touchdown pass from Joe Montana with 34 seconds to play. The 49ers win Super Bowl XXIII, 20–16.

You go through a 4–11 fire storm, you fight the skeptics and the ridicule. You fight yourself, your own doubts. Am I really that bad of a coach?

You get a second chance, you make it work. You show the skeptics what they can do with their opinions, you show yourself what you can do as a coach. You take a city on a six-month joy ride the likes of which it has never seen. You win 14 games, more than any team in the NFL.

You know that, but for 34 seconds in the Super Bowl, yours was the best football team on the planet.

John Taylor was running a post pattern. Ten yards up, to the goal line, six yards into the middle. He got single coverage from Bengals cornerback Ray Horton.

Jerry Rice had caught 11 passes for 215 yards. On this play, Rice was in motion, right to left. Drifting, drifting, past John Taylor. Horton was conscious of Rice. He moved slightly to the outside.

Taylor ran the post, 10 yards up, six yards in, too quickly for Ray Horton. "He shot down inside. I stayed too far outside when Jerry came across. That's all it took," Horton said.

Horton looked as if he just missed tipping the ball. Later, he said he wasn't close. Sam Wyche, though, knew how close. "Thirty-four seconds," he said.

If they hadn't been playing against Joe Montana, the Bengals might have stood and cheered him, along with the rest of us. Montana painted a greatness portrait Sunday night. There is no disgrace in finishing second to greatness.

On the last drive, Montana completed eight of nine passes, for 95 yards, overcoming a crucial 10-yard penalty. The word here is surgical.

Montana saw that the Bengals' secondary was cheating towards the outside, believing that with 92 yards to go, the Niners would work the sidelines to slow the clock.

Instead, Montana went over the middle. Eight yards to Roger Craig, seven to John Frank, seven to Rice. Montana was a bug in your ear, a faucet that drips, an itch you can't scratch. He drove the Bengals to the edge and with 34 seconds to play, he pushed them over.

Maybe no other quarterback anywhere produces this drive in this game. The Bengals' secondary didn't play poorly, it just played Montana, who answered the post-game "pressure" questions with a shrug. Greatness is making the difficult seem routine. "You do it so much, it has to be second nature. You don't think about the pressure, you just react."

Seventeen yards to Rice, 13 to Craig, 27 to Rice. "I don't know how (Rice) made that catch," Lewis Billups said. "You couldn't get any better coverage."

Rice's brilliance—"When he attacks the ball, you can't beat him," said Montana—kept the Bengals from doubling up on Craig, who caught eight passes for 101 yards. He was the primary receiver on the TD play. "We just have too many weapons," Craig said. "Don't fault Cincinnati."

You work a whole season, a whole 12 months, really, and what you get is a loser's praise. The worst thing about losing in the Super

Bowl is that nobody but you remembers or cares how well you played to get there.

The Bengals *were* the second-best team on the field Sunday. The last drive confirmed that. Even with Tim Krumrie, who missed 53 minutes with two broken bones in his left leg, they would not have stopped Montana in the final 3:10.

They were courageous, but courage can't cover Rice man-to-man. They looked uncomfortable on offense, unsure whether to resurrect the passing game. Boomer Esiason's finger and ankle hurt more than he admits, but it was the Niner's secondary that really pained the Bengals.

Esiason threw for just 144 yards. But the Bengals still had enough to take a 16–13 lead on Jim Breech's 40-yard field goal with 3:20 left. That only made Montana's effort more of a masterpiece.

"We came from so far to get here," Wyche said. "That's why this hurts so much."

It was late. Maybe someday, the Bengals will come closer than 34 seconds to winning a Super Bowl. Maybe not. NFL success is a fragile, burdensome thing.

The Bengals played well in the best Super Bowl ever played. For 59:26, that was good enough. For 34 seconds, it was not. They lost to greatness. They ought to be able to live with that.

Braggs Snatches Reds a Pennant

October 13, 1990

*T*hey stood on the field afterward, all of them, for 15 minutes, a half hour, an hour, maybe. A long time.

One by one, the Reds marched from their cider-sodden clubhouse back onto the field, where 10,000 or so fans were going appropriately nuts. The Reds had earned what winners own. Through 168 games, they all took part in the deed. Now, after a 2–1 win over the Pittsburgh Pirates in Game 6 of the NLCS, they all took part in the joy.

The Reds won the National League pennant Friday night, because lately their outfielders and their relief pitchers have arms on loan from heaven. They won it because their everyday players did what was needed, and their bench jockeys did the rest.

They won it because Lou Piniella—driven by his own need to prove himself as a manager—coaxed the best from players that, until this year, never knew what their best was. And were never especially eager to find out.

But mainly, they won it because Glenn Braggs is 6 feet 4 inches tall.

"Exactly," he said. "Exactly 6 feet 4 inches."

How fitting. Ron Oester, banished to the bench all year in favor of Mariano Duncan, scores the winning run. Luis Quinones, in love with the bench for his entire five-year major league career, drives him home with a line single to right in the bottom of the eighth.

Quinones had fewer at-bats this season—145—than any player on the roster all season. His biggest job was to sit and watch. As a role player, Quinones was Macbeth.

Quinones lives for moments such as this. "I don't think in that situation," he said. "I just hit."

When we first met Piniella last November, he vowed his bench players would not rust. Everyone would contribute, he said. Eleven months later, everyone did.

Every Red played in the NLCS but first baseman Terry Lee and pitcher Jack Armstrong. At the very least, every Red did something useful. At best, they were heroic.

In the last week, you've seen things you've never seen before and, unless you're very lucky or very young or both, you may never see again.

"Eric Davis," general manager Bob Quinn is saying. "That throw. If you were to rank the finest defensive plays in the last 10 or 20 years, that's got to be in the top five."

There was O'Neill's throw in the second game that caught Andy Van Slyke at third, Billy Hatcher's throw in the third game to nail Sid Bream at home, and Davis', also in the fourth game, that nailed Bobby Bonilla at third and broke the Pirates' back. You watch baseball across 10 seasons, maybe you never see another throw like that.

But it was Braggs—another foot soldier in the Reds lately limitless supply of bench heroes—that clinched it all.

As Hatcher said, "Thank God he's 6 feet 4."

With one out in the ninth inning of a season for which you've waited 14 years, Pittsburgh's Carmelo Martinez hit a rising line drive toward Braggs.

Barry Bonds was on first, having worked a walk from Nasty Boy Randy Myers. Martinez sent Myers' 3-2 pitch on a line toward the 375-foot mark.

It's an eight-foot outfield wall that rims Riverfront Stadium from foul pole to foul pole. We've seen Paul O'Neill climb that wall a few times in recent years, to steal home runs, but never Glenn Braggs.

Glenn Braggs, they got for offense. The Reds got him from Milwaukee on June 9, for some right-handed pop, and because they were sick of pitcher Ron Robinson popping off.

They didn't expect this.

"I knew he hit well," said Braggs. "I saw it rising. All I could think of was, 'Get to the wall.'"

Ever hear a city hold its breath? As Braggs' glove touched the top of the wall, you could hear a heart beat at Riverfront.

Braggs stuck his glove over the wall and snatched the pennant back into the Reds hands. Just like that.

"This is a dream right here," said Barry Larkin, and it was.

Anyone who lives here and loves the Reds knows how fragile these things are. How close were these games with the Pirates? Pull a hair from your head, if you have any left, and measure its breadth. That close.

If you think this team wasn't touched by destiny or fate or karma or something, you weren't watching them for the past week.

Mainly, it was touched by Braggs, whose best move Friday night was being tall. And Quinones, who, through a cider bath, said this: "I could live a very long time and never feel like this again."

Davis Slugs Goliath

October 17, 1990

*E*ric Davis suffers in silence, exults in private and keeps his joy to himself. That's always been his problem here. You want Showtime, Davis gives you Garbo.

He has always had a Liz and Dick thing with Cincinnati. Judging the town's current relationship with its superstar is no harder than going to Riverfront Stadium and watching him hit once. The romance wavers from game to game, play to play, pitch to pitch.

It's torrid right now. All Davis did Tuesday was win the game. The first World Series Game in Cincinnati in 14 years was decided on a first-inning, first pitch two-run homer by a player whose left shoulder hurts so much he can barely lace up his spikes.

113

Did it hurt your shoulder to swing tonight, someone asked.

"It hurts my shoulder just standing here," Davis said.

The Oakland Immortals went down quietly after Davis' shot, stunned by its suddenness and the lack of respect it showed Dave Stewart, their best pitcher. Game 1 went smoothly and easily to the Reds, 7–0.

We may have to re-think this immortality business.

It was Davis' game, which may come as a surprise to the legion of Eric bashers, currently living in their closets. And to Davis' own shoulder, the inside of which is now the consistency of pudding.

On September 27, he ran into the leftfield wall to catch a flyball. Since, he has been unable to get much left-arm extension in his swing. That's important only if you think Davis should be hitting homeruns. With a bad left shoulder, a right-handed hitter loses the ability to drive the ball.

"The homerun shoulder," Herm Winningham called it.

Davis had looked so harmless batting fourth against the Pirates, manager Lou Piniella thought he might be more valuable batting first.

Davis said no, because he has a homerun hitter's bat and ego, and would rather not be seen on national TV striving for the ultimate single.

You said Davis was being selfish. You said Piniella should have told Davis where to hit, not asked his permission. Piniella's flavor-of-the-day lineups kept everyone else in limbo this year. Should Davis be special?

You said that until two out in the first, when Davis smoked Stewart's first pitch 429 feet to centerfield.

That popped the A's invincibility balloon right there. "Sort of put a dent in the steel," said Reds outfielder Glenn Braggs. Davis' homer gave Cincinnati a 2–0 lead and told the A's (and the Reds) we might have a Series here, not a coronation.

The homer also sent a small message to Piniella from Davis that went something like, "Let's forget this leadoff talk right now, shall we?"

114

Said Reds shortstop Barry Larkin, "Guys started saying, Here we go. Let's keep it rolling."

After the homer, it was like a spring game. This was March and Piniella was saying, "Just get your hacks in, fellas. Work on your timing and don't hurt yourself."

The Reds won in a walk—actually six walks, four in the first three innings—scoring at will and shutting down Oakland's vaunted power. Suddenly, the A's were. . . what?

Beatable. Mortal. Average.

"Everybody's human in here," A's catcher Terry Steinbach said afterward, but we were beginning to wonder.

"People expect us to win every time we throw our gloves out there," said Mike Gallego. "We know we're not invincible. So does (Stewart)."

That the A's clubhouse was alive with the strange sounds of humility was due to Davis, who now has made the two biggest plays of the Reds' believe-it-or-not postseason. The other was the throw in the third game against Pittsburgh. If you don't recall it, check out the highlight reels for the next decade.

Through all this, Davis has been Davis. He could pose for mugshots in his spare time. Davis is the same, win or lose, homerun or strikeout, standing ovations or boos. Healthy or injured.

In the A's third, Davis made a diving try for Rickey Henderson's sinking liner and came up with a jammed pinky. When he came off the field, Braggs said to him, "Man, I bet you can't wait for this thing to be over. If we go another month, you might not have any legs."

Braggs said Davis stuck his head in his hands. "You're not going to hear him groan," Braggs said.

Or boast. Davis has been the heart of the Reds for three years. Now he's assuming the dual role of heart and soul. You won't hear that from Davis, whose horn stays silent.

Improbable Dream

October 20, 1990

Oakland, California—The inevitability is so thick, you could walk on it. It hangs there like the sliver of moon above the outfield at the Oakland Coliseum. It is starlight time for the Cincinnati Reds.

They beat the Oakland A's for the third straight time Friday night, 8–3. Did we say beat? They laid the A's bare.

In one terrifyingly wondrous inning, the Reds put everything they've done all month into one, tidy package. We've talked about Cincinnati's eerie, hero-a-day competence during this postseason.

Billy Hatcher, the essential artificial turf player, playing slapball, using every field, smoking pinball shots to the gaps, playing eight-ball off the outfield walls. *Whap, whap, whap.*

Jack Armstrong, nothing but a roster spot since the All-Star Game, shutting the A's off for three crucial innings Wednesday.

Eric Davis, the Nasty Boys, Chris Sabo and Billy Bates. Beyond eerie and competent, how do you explain Billy Bates?

But there was nothing eerie or competent about the third inning Friday.

The third was murder. The third was a fist to the jaw. The Reds took the A's into the alley, rolled up their sleeves and beat them senseless.

After the third, the A's immortality lay in pieces on the ground. Greatness switched dugouts and, all in all, it was a very bad inning for invincibility.

The Reds played longball, they played slapball. They stole a base, they took a base. They did whatever they pleased.

"Everything we hit, fell in." said first baseman Todd Benzinger. "That was why it was incredible. They couldn't get us out.

"You know, once or twice a month you may get an inning like

116

that. You don't expect them. Especially not against the Oakland A's in the World Series."

Eleven batters, seven runs, seven hits. A Chris Sabo home run, the second of two. A triple, a double, four slaps through the infield.

Tradition dictates the show must go on, but tradition was asleep in the third.

A man's play-by-play:

"Hatcher singles to left. O'Neill double-play grounder to first, McGwire muffs. Davis RBI single to center. Morris RBI grounder. Sabo two-run homer to left, 2–0 count. Benzinger single, Oliver RBI double left field line, Duncan RBI single center, Larkin RBI triple left-center."

With that, the Reds swept the A's in three games.

"Score more. Score more." That was the mantra in the Reds dugout in the third. Sabo homers? Score more. Mariano Duncan doubles off a right-hander? Score more. Barry Larkin triples?

Bring him home. What's enough? Nothing is enough. Score more.

Oakland had to win Friday night. Win Friday, come back with Dave Stewart tonight and take your chances in a three-game series.

On Wednesday, A's left fielder Rickey Henderson had said Game 3 would "tell what kind of team you have." If that's the case, woe to the A's, who are indeed finding out what kind of team is theirs.

What it is, is a frontrunning team that responds to a test not at all. Oakland didn't lose to the Reds; it was clearly beaten. Part of the reason for that was the A's uncanny ability to sink to any and every challenge.

Friday night, they started Mike Moore, he of the 13–15 record and 4.65 ERA. How Moore—or anyone else—could lose 15 games on this team is a mystery.

Moore gave up three hits in the first inning; Sabo's first homer in the second and all hope in the third.

Improbable? Snow in August is improbable. There is nothing, absolutely nothing, improbable about what the Reds are doing to the A's.

The A's remain lost, quite possibly for the winter. They no longer need a tourniquet. After the third inning Friday night, they needed a priest.

Comparisons have been made to the A's five-game flop against the Dodgers in '88. But that's not it. The '88 A's were young and in love with themselves. What they did best was talk. And flex.

They were boys, and it showed. The '90 A's are men. Playing like boys.

The Reds may win it tonight, they may win it Sunday. They may light up the night at Riverfront Tuesday. No team has ever rallied from 0–3 to win the World Series. This A's team won't either. So eager to make history a week ago, the A's are running from it now.

And the Reds? They're standing in the middle of a dream. The view is good.

Who's the Boss Now?

*O*akland, California—The work is done. The points have been made, the mouths have been shut. Let the monkey light on somebody else's back.

Last November, Lou Piniella took a pay cut to come manage the Reds, a big goal being to stick it in George Steinbrenner's ear. Desperation is the best motivator, but pride is a close second. Steinbrenner twice fired Piniella as manager of the New York Yankees, for no other reason than he felt like it.

Now, on a sweet Saturday night he will remember always, Piniella stood in the tiny coaches dressing room at the Oakland Coliseum, a cigar in one hand, a beer in the other, remembering November.

"I said to myself, 'I have something to offer. Let me get something done.' I can manage in the major leagues. I know I can."

All Piniella did was take a team and teach it to win. You take everything he did in 1990—the hitting instruction, the fundamentals, the temper flares, the flavor-of-the-day lineups, the absolute intolerance for mental mistakes—put it all together and nothing mattered so much as Piniella's need to succeed.

"A refusal to be a happy loser," said Stan Williams, Piniella's pitching coach, roommate and soulmate. "That's what he brought. He harped on it, beat on it, insisted upon it."

Piniella didn't work at his job, so much as attack it. "We put in more hours than anybody I've ever seen," Williams said. "It was an exhausting year. I don't know why he's not completely mentally exhausted.

"His mind has been in it every minute, every inning, every pitch. He was working mentally all the time."

Piniella threw fits and bases. He was loud and brash and impulsive. He never let go of the whip until, down the stretch, his team no longer needed it.

If ever a team reflected the temperament of its manager, this one did. By October, the Reds were as dissatisfied with defeat as Piniella was. They were real unhappy losers. Anyone who had been around this team since it last won in 1979 could see the wonder in that.

The sweet October alchemy that made heroes of Billy Bates and Billy Hatcher began last November, when at his first press conference, Piniella said simply, "I didn't come here just to manage. I came here to win."

Piniella's need to prove to Steinbrenner (and to himself) what a mistake The Boss had made brought baseball back to Cincinnati.

We'd lost it last year. It was buried beneath the Dowd Report. Last year, Cincinnati was under the nation's boot heel. The Rose thing bumped us from one black eye to the next. Innocence died forever, and we thought baseball was a game played in courthouses, by men in robes and suits.

119

When we believed it could get no worse, they sent Pete Rose to federal prison.

Piniella brought baseball back. He offered the ultimate catharsis for a punch-drunk town and its sad baseball team. He wouldn't take losing for an answer.

The Reds were 9–0, they were 33–12. In October, they played two of the loveliest weeks of baseball you will ever see.

The Reds never were anything less than the best. All year.

All heaven broke loose in the clubhouse Saturday. To see 25 men in a winning World Series dressing room is to know that winning, not money, is the ultimate reward. The '90 Reds earned what winners own, and no amount of cash could buy that.

In 1990, everybody had something to prove. Everybody had a boulder on his shoulder. In his own fashion, every Red had a Steinbrenner to dump.

They all got sick of losing at the same time. If you think Piniella had nothing to do with that, you're missing the party.

"They just had to get the feeling they could win," Piniella said. "That was it. Once you taste that winning feeling, that confidence really exudes."

Once merely a winning team, a group dangerously adept at finishing second, the Reds are now a team of winners. The difference between the two is a 21-diamond ring.

The '91 Reds could fall off a cliff, but it won't be because they don't have character or a working knowledge of what it means to be a champion.

Sports dynasties come with a one-year warranty these days. And there isn't enough Marge Schott money to keep this team totally together in 1991.

These Reds may never pass this way again, but oh, what a ride it's been.

It started, all of it, with a fire in the manager's belly. If you ever want to thank George Steinbrenner for anything, thank him for that.

The night Lou Piniella won the World Series, George Steinbrenner hosted *Saturday Night Live*. You didn't know if people were laughing with him or at him. With Lou Piniella, the laughter was on the house. What a way to go.

Huggins on Fire

February 25, 1992

$\mathcal{I}$t's natural to think the referees gave Bob Huggins a pain in his chest Thursday night. It's natural because at least 27 times a year, he gives them one. Huggins will spend the better part of 40 minutes in a state of agitation most of us only have bad dreams about.

Truth: Have you ever yelled at anyone the way a basketball coach yells at a referee? If you did it in public, you might be arrested. There are times during Cincinnati basketball games when the only thing higher than Huggins' blood pressure is his decibel count.

Huggins isn't Denny Crum or Dean Smith, both subtle masters at leaving refs bleeding. He's not even Bob Knight. Huggins is louder. He is ZZ Top on the stereo, way up high, bass knob turned all the way to the right. For Huggins, the point is the officials will work as hard as he does, you better believe it. If they don't he'll make their ears hum for days.

Huggins has paid his dues. At West Virginia, he was the best player on the team and twice an academic all-American. He graduated magna cum laude. This is not a collegial trifecta one earns hanging out with mediocrity.

Huggins earned his masters a year after he graduated, and still had time to be an assistant coach. He made no quick flight to the top. It took him 11 years to get to UC. He worked and screamed all the way.

121

So maybe we can understand why this coach who gets the most from what he has tends to obsess on refs he feels aren't doing their jobs.

"The officials need to be made aware they aren't making the correct calls," Huggins said. "A lot of times they don't, contrary to popular belief."

You can't say his sideline act is getting old, because it's not an act. "I don't do it to intimidate officials," said Huggins. It's just Huggins doing Huggins. It's his Type A self, spilling all over the court.

You've got to think ulcers won't be a problem here.

Maybe Huggins' constant verbal barrage set his chest aflame Thursday night, maybe it didn't. Huggins himself doesn't know. Further, he doesn't care.

If the same Huggins temperament that lifted UC basketball from the outhouse is now giving him chest pains, he'll take the trade. "An occupational hazard," he called it.

You could ask Huggins to cool it, to limit his wars to those he can win, but that would be pointless. A personality can't be changed like a shirt.

"I never said I was going to be anybody other than me," Huggins said. "I don't want to be anybody other than me."

Huggins went nose-to-bald-spot with official Phil Bova Thursday night, in a scene that will be remembered for its ugliness. It wasn't the first such show and it won't be the last, causing a man to wonder:

Did the doctors tell you to calm down?

"Absolutely not," Huggins said.

What if they had?

"I probably wouldn't."

Huggins is 38. His father Charlie was a high school coach who had his first heart attack at age 36. Charlie Huggins underwent quadruple bypass surgery a couple months ago, at age 60. Huggins also had an uncle who died of heart failure. So the coach chooses to blame his pain on heredity, maybe because the alternative—toning his game-night self down to a dull roar—is not acceptable.

"I'm going to do my job the way I feel I have to do it. If that becomes unbearable, I'll do something else," Huggins said.

You wonder if Huggins' quest for perfection isn't wearing on his players. There's a suspicion his temper makes his players tight. It's a theory that looks good whenever UC blows a big lead in a big game. Maybe the only key Bearcat who has the coach's rages figured is Anthony Buford. But going 1-on-5 at crunch time is no way to win big games.

At South Alabama Saturday, Huggins used his pre-game time for an atypical soft sell. Instead of driving his players the way he drives officials (and himself) Huggins told them how much he appreciated their efforts. It was like a massage. The players responded by ripping the Jaguars with ease. Maybe there's a message here. Maybe not.

"You're talking to the wrong guy," Huggins said. "I haven't changed. I'm not going to change."

Before Saturday's game, Huggins told his assistant coaches he would try to sit on the bench. It's something he has never done.

The record stands. "They said I sat until the ball went up," Huggins said. Somewhere between screaming and sitting lies the perfect in-between. Not that Huggins is looking or anything.

Cutting Nets

March 30, 1992

Kansas City, Missouri—Terry Nelson was one of the first up the ladder, and what he did up there was slice just enough net to wrap around the third finger of his left hand.

"It's to keep my finger warm," he explained, "for the ring it's going to get."

OK. Sure. Why not? We never thought it could happen this fast. Truth: We never thought it could happen at all. The new University of Cincinnati basketball coach Bob Huggins stood up at his first press conference three years ago and said his goal was to get to the Final Four.

We said, "Uh-huh."

What did we know? UC beats Memphis State Sunday in the Midwest Regional final, just lays them out, and suddenly, the immediate future is filled with anything-can-happens.

Believe it. UC wins by 31 in a game that is supposed to be evenly matched. You don't walk four games on the post-season highwire to get a breather in the regional final, but here we were, watching a day the Bearcats pulled all the way from 1962.

This is the time of the year when dreams come dressed as pieces of net. If you're good enough and charmed enough, March Madness pays you a personal visit, atop a ladder. It equips you with a pair of scissors and a moment in time.

Said Bearcats forward Erik Martin: "It's everybody's dream, but when you actually get here, it's better than that."

Maybe the Madness works best at UC, where lots of the players are so new to the bright lights. The center, Corie Blount, didn't plan on going from Kmart stockboy to Final Four participant. It just worked out that way. If you want a working definition of the Madness, that will do.

What we have here, around this ladder, is a fearless team. It wasn't always that way, but it is now. The Bearcats started Sunday in the tradition of all really nervous teams, by singing rap on the team bus.

"They're in the bus on the way over here, banging the seats and making mouth noises," said assistant coach Steve Moeller.

Then what?

"We barked," Blount said.

Ah.

"Terry (Nelson) gets us into it. He says we're the only 'Cats that bark," said Blount. "Then we bark."

Does Huggins...bark?

"He's not in here too much when we do that," Blount said.

Anthony Buford, the senior guard, was wearing his piece of net on his ear, of course he was. "I will frame this," he said, "in a big glass frame."

The Bearcats ought to frame Sunday's game and stick it somewhere important. UC took the lead for good with 7:20 left in the first half. Point guard Nick Van Exel drove the right baseline, had no shot, but also nothing else to do but put up a playground jumper that swished. He followed it with a three-pointer from the other side.

UC led, 30–26.

We honestly don't know what the Tigers were doing after that. Maybe looking for Elvis.

After the first 20 minutes, Memphis was basically inert. It only took UC three minutes of the second half to push its lead to 15. From there, it was target practice.

What Memphis did best was hide its best player. It's hard to be inconspicuous when you're 6 feet 7, even on a basketball floor, but this is what we saw Sunday.

The Tigers didn't run any plays for Anfernee Hardaway. They didn't work to get him open. He didn't even take a shot for the first 10 minutes. It took him 30 minutes before he took a shot inside the three-point circle.

Truth was, Hardaway wanted nothing to do with the Bearcats, most notably forward Herb Jones. Jones is street-smart, tough and hungry. Hardaway is a first-year sophomore, who on Saturday had treated a UC rematch with all the optimism of a condemned man.

"You can't get a good shot off on them," Hardaway had said. "If I take (Jones), here comes another. If I get past *him*, here comes another."

Without Hardaway, Memphis wasn't much.

Up the ladder, the dreams were busting out all over.

Last March, Blount, Martin and Nelson played in the California state junior college championship, before a whopping 6,000 fans.

When they play Michigan Saturday, they'll greet some 35,000.

Snip, snip. They cheered loud Sunday when the game got out of hand and Huggins inserted Mike (Rock) Reicheneker, the 7-foot backup center. Reicheneker averages four minutes a game. He plays when the games are won. Rock is UC's victory cigar. His spirit is appreciated by everyone.

And here he was, up the ladder, cutting some net.

Thirty years ago, when Bob Huggins was 8 years old and screaming at his little grade school buddies to play some defense, the Universtiy of Cincinnati won a national basketball championship.

That picture is in focus again. Huggins has stressed this winter that every player is important, that champions leave their egos at the door. It is why UC still has a game or two to play.

The coach was up the ladder, snipping the last piece off the second net. Bob Huggins, on his way to Minneapolis, stopped for the smallest of moments. He handed the net, the whole thing, to Mike Reicheneker.

UC's Sweat Ethic

March 29, 1993

*E*ast Rutherford, New Jersey—It's an acre of soulless concrete in the tunnel beneath the stands at Byrne Arena. The trip from the basketball court to the locker room is a long, slow walk when you lose, so Erik Martin took his time.

From somewhere, a fan shouted to him. "Thanks for the two years," she said. "Thanks for the memories."

He did all he could. They all did. The Bearcats' sweat ethic raged Sunday. UC lost to North Carolina, anyway. There comes a time when effort matters not so much as a couple of 7-foot centers and a bench full of former high school All-Americans tossing three-point field goals into your hard work.

For about 10 minutes in the second half Sunday, 6-5 Erik Martin had to play center against North Carolina's 7-0 Eric Montross. Because Montross is an All-American who is also the size of New Jersey, this was a mismatch bordering on cruel and unusual.

Martin did all he could. With a minute to go in regulation time, he stood in the lane with Montross, slamdancing chest-to-cheek, and slapped the ball from the big center's hands. Martin scooped the loose ball and fired it to Tarrance Gibson, who took it at halfcourt and swooped in for a layup that tied the East regional final at 66.

The Bearcats had led by as much as 15 in the first half, before falling behind by four with 1:44 to play, and now they had come back to square it, by doing what they do best. Which is to fight you for everything you've got.

"I'm drained, man," Martin was saying. "I'm just drained."

The plan had been to win this game and give Coach Huggins a haircut. A haircut? Take the scissors and make Huggins as bald as UC-lover Dick Vitale. Instead, Martin was using the scissors to cut tape from his ankles. One last time.

"You have a tendency to run into his elbows," Martin said of Montross. "It wasn't like he was flinging them. They were just always there."

With 7:08 left in the first half, Nick Van Exel squared up from the top of the circle and drained a three-pointer, giving the Bearcats a 29–14 edge and feeling that anything was possible. They weren't considered an elite team. They weren't Duke or Carolina or Michigan or Indiana or Kansas. They were just here, and Van Exel was raining threes on the Tar Heel parade. He had 17 of UC's first 29 points. "I thought we had them on the ropes," he said.

Then center Corie Blount got his fourth foul with 13:26 left in regulation. Forward Curtis Bostic fouled out three minutes later, and it was Erik Martin in the little Bearcat middle, guarding Montross

127

and taking elbows like body shots to his ribs.

When Montross left for a breather, Martin got a real break. Carolina came in with Kevin Salvadori, a 7-footer weighing a mere 224. "They have, I don't know, eight 7-footers?" Martin said. "They just shuttle 'em on in."

Still, UC did what UC does. Salvadori scored on a follow-up to put UNC ahead by four, then the Bearcats responded with Keith Gregor's layup and Gibson's three-pointer, to take a 62–61 lead.

You wondered how this could be. Van Exel had 21 in the first half, two in the second. Blount was out of the game. Bostic was out of the game. North Carolina was running fresh troops in and out at every break. The Tar Heels have better players to begin with. UC led by one at half, but the consensus among the media geniuses was that the Bearcat ship was sinking.

It wasn't. The sweat ethic was working overtime. "It's what we have to do," noted forward Terry Nelson. "We don't have the talent to do anything else." UC survived the longest eight-tenths of a second in the history of the world to make it to overtime. Brian Reese's blown dunk at the buzzer kept the game tied at 66, and the Bearcats weren't the only ones sweating.

They scored the first two in the extra session, Blount floating a 10-foot turn-around jumper over Montross. "I thought it was our game," Martin said.

Then George Lynch scored for North Carolina, Van Exel turned the ball over and Carolina's Donald Williams dropped a three-pointer from the left wing. This is the difference between UC and UNC: North Carolina recruits Williams, a coveted high school All-American, to score. Period.

Until the last month, Williams was a bench player, brought in to juice up the offense. He scored the last nine points in the Tar Heels' Friday win over Arkansas. Sunday, he finished with 20, including two threes in the overtime.

UC does not have anyone to come off the bench and make three-pointers in overtime. Or any other time. Huggins does not yet have a stable of former prep legends cooling their shoes on the bench. The Bearcats don't win because they have great players. You wonder what would happen if they did.

As Nelson observed, "I can think of a lot of teams, if they played as hard as we do, they'd be undefeated."

As it was, Williams' second three-pointer in overtime put Carolina ahead 74–68, and the rest was Bearcats futility. They did all they could. Three wins from having it all, they would settle for memories instead.

Would Huggins really have let them shave his head? Someone wondered.

"Oh, absolutely," Huggins said. "Absolutely."

Eggs-avier's Biggest Win

March 19, 1990

Indianapolis—They talked with Bill Raftery—CBS!—and fought their way through the crowd. They were high-fiving, yelling, jumping, floating in the joy of the day, impossibly happy.

For a long time, the 6 feet 10 senior center Derek Strong stood on the court with his arms high over his head, preening, exulting, squeezing pride from the moment. Knowing what champions know.

It had been so long.

For four years, they had been Eggs-avier of Ohio, the nation's Nice Little Team. They won a lot of games, but they didn't play anybody. They were a top 20 or 25 team, but they played in a bargain basement league. They were Ann-Margret at the all-night laundry. They'd be middle of the road in the Big Ten or the ACC. We knew this.

Prospective, top 25-type opponents wouldn't schedule them home and home because Eggs-avier was not yet a "respectable" loss. They were on a treadmill. Too many mountains, not enough stairs.

That was yesterday. Today, they are packing for Dallas. There will be no more questioning the schedule, the league, the players, or their guts. The Little Team That Could, did, and now we run with the unbearably sweet notion that the Road to Denver must pass through Avondale.

Xavier 74, Georgetown 71.

Believe this: For every reason you can think of (and some you can't) this was the biggest win in Xavier's 70-year basketball history.

As guard Michael Davenport said, "This was a must win. Everyone was (saying), 'Well, Xavier, you're pretty good, but you're only *this* good.' We're saying maybe you're wrong."

The scoreboard says Xavier beat Georgetown on Sunday, but the Muskies started winning this one in 1987, when they lost their nerve and a second-round tournament game to Duke.

They won it the following year in the gym at the University of Nebraska, where they saw Danny Manning's 6-10 shadow and went into hibernation for the summer, losers in the first round.

Again and again, they've won this game. Against Louisville two Novembers ago, an 85–83 win at the Coliseum. Against Michigan in the first round last year. Loyola Marymount, Dayton, Evansville, UC. Games that tried their skills, but no more, maybe, than their souls.

After years of getting to Broadway just in time to trip over the footlights, Xavier has earned what winners own: The knowledge that sometimes, winning is no more important than believing you can.

Who thought they could do this? The national notion was that Georgetown would beat the MCC back into the Muskies. But here they were, 12 minutes into the game of their lives, leading the Hoyas, 28–15.

Tyrone Hill had just slipped in behind 6-10 Alonzo Mourning for a backdoor layup. Seconds earlier, Strong pounded a breakaway jam, despite being clotheslined from behind by Mourning.

The Muskies took no garbage from the Hoyas, who dish it with the best of them. They went elbow shot-to-forearm shiver with the Hoyas, who bring intimidation in their travel bags, along with the shoes and the socks and the basketballs.

By halftime, the Muskies had a 16-point lead and a look in their eyes. "I told the guys at halftime, it's no fluke we're up 16. It's no fluke we're here," Davenport said.

What were you thinking when you're up 16 at half? Someone asked coach Pete Gillen. "I wanted to be up 18," he said.

"He kept preaching courage," Maurice Brantley said. "He said we could win if we didn't back down."

All year, Gillen has held class in The Art of Winning. More so this year than ever, because Gillen knew he had the players to stay with the best, if only he could convince them that's where they belonged.

"I wanted us to stay aggressive, because when you're doing that, you're not thinking, 'Oh my God we're playing Georgetown on national TV.' You just react."

They led 65–57 with 6:15 left when Hill fouled out. They led 72–71 with 23 seconds to go and Jamal Walker at the free throw line. Walker embodies what Gillen preaches. He has the guts to win. More important, he has the guts to lose. He made both. The dream met reality at a sweet spot in time.

Down And Out

"In real life, you work thirty years for the company, or twenty
or fifteen, they give you a party and a gold watch. In the NFL,
they ask for your playbook. It's the only instance where a
working man has a better deal than a pro athlete."
—*Paul Daugherty*

Farewell, Straight Arrow

March, 1995

*H*e was always on the phone. Art Schlichter had one of those pocket cellular telephones that flipped neatly in the middle, like a wallet. His "business phone," he called it. He was using it most of the time.

We did a radio show together. Two afternoons a week, Monday and Friday on the old all-sports WSAI-AM in Cincinnati. Schlichter was good at it. He was candid, engaging and knowledgeable. He could tell you the starting five for the Lakers, and how each of them had done the previous night. Gamblers always know.

Every so often during the show, Schlichter would ask his producer to take an unscheduled break. The producer complied, filling the time with house ads while Schlichter slipped out of the room and pulled the phone from his pocket. It didn't take a genius to realize what he was doing.

Some people destroy themselves with a weapon. Art used the phone. He shot himself down, and out. Not with a gun. With his checkbook.

His reputation was no secret. Twice banned from the NFL for gambling. A declaration of bankruptcy. Debts from years before, which he claimed to be paying off.

He claimed to attend meetings of Gamblers Anonymous. He claimed to be a regular parishioner at College Hill Presbyterian Church. He claimed to take medicine for what he claimed was Attention Deficit Disorder.

In the tradition of all lost-soul gamblers, Schlichter once confessed to me, "You keep thinking the next win will pull you out. It's a sick way of thinking. I always thought I could pick 'em. I couldn't. Who can? I've never known anyone who could."

That didn't stop him from trying. It only stopped him from stopping. The more he lost, the more he bet. "Look," Schlichter said to me in the fall of 1992. "You go to the track. You start out with a couple hundred, and pretty soon you're betting a couple thousand. It could be in a day, in a week. I don't know. It just gradually happens."

Gradually, you slip into the abyss where Art is now. Last November, he asked a U.S. District Court Judge in Las Vegas for permission to spend the holidays with his family. He had entered a guilty plea to charges of bank fraud, for bouncing $175,000 worth of checks.

The judge called Schlichter an "economic danger" to the community.

Hands up! Nobody move! I've got a bad check!

The judge ordered Art into custody, where there are no cellular phones.

At press time, the former Ohio State quarterback remained in a Las Vegas jail cell, awaiting sentencing. After he is sentenced there, he will face additional charges in Ohio. Depending on the sentencing judge's discretion, Schlichter will be incarcerated for several months up to several years.

You could see it coming. So could he. It didn't stop him, not at all. Schlichter once called me at work and said, "Doc, I need you to loan me $10,000."

He would call a lot, all the time, always the same request. He needed money. He would pay me back Friday. Promise. C'mon. Art Schlichter is 34 now, was 32 then. He sounded like a 5-year-old.

It started to disrupt the show. The breaks were too frequent, the little phone trips taking too much time. "Let's do some business," Schlichter would say. And he'd be off.

After one such interruption, I said to Schlichter, "If you spent half as much time working on your radio show as you do scamming people and betting sports, you'd be the best talk-show host in America."

"Doc," he said, "you don't know the half of it."

Willie DeLuca knows. "Down through the years? Oh, boy." I ask him how much money he lent Schlichter. "I probably cashed over

$100,000 worth of his checks. Somehow, some way, he's always paid me back."

Schlichter sold most of his football memorabilia to DeLuca, who owns Sorrento's restaurant in Norwood. DeLuca has possibly the finest collection of sports memorabilia in the state. He says Schlichter sold him "all his trophies. His Big 10 MVP trophy. His rings, his watches, his jerseys, his game balls. I got it all."

Last spring, Schlichter called DeLuca from Las Vegas, where Art worked as a radio sports-talk host. "He told me there was an Ohio State alum who was a big collector and wanted his stuff," DeLuca recalls. "Art told me to sell all the stuff to this guy, and give him (Schlichter) half."

"He was desperate," says DeLuca, who also remembers a time more than a year ago when Schlichter walked into Sorrento's with a large, bound notebook. "It was his scrapbook," DeLuca says.

Said Schlichter, "Willie, this is all I have left. This is it. I need money, Willie."

DeLuca refused the scrapbook. "Save it for your kids," he said.

Schlichter is addicted to gambling. It is a hard concept for some of us, how a person could be chained to something you don't eat, snort, drink, inject or otherwise ingest. But for him, it's as real as a prison cell.

It has tyrannized his life for 20 years or more. As an All-American at Ohio State, Schlichter was a regular at Scioto Downs, along with his coach, Earle Bruce. Had he stayed away from gambling and stayed on sports-talk, he'd have been fine. Schlichter even got feelers from talk giant WLW while he was at WSAI. But the gambling stole his life and owned his soul.

It cost him an NFL career.

"A lot of people thought he was a top prospect," says New York Giants assistant general manager Ernie Accorsi. Accorsi was the assistant player personnel director for the Baltimore Colts in 1983, the year the Colts drafted Schlichter in the first round.

"But a lot of people didn't feel that way," says Accorsi. "Arthur wasn't like a John Elway or a Dan Marino. Those guys were either going to be good or very good. The spectrum was more diverse with Arthur."

As it was, another rookie, a third-round pick named Mike Pagel, got the starting job. "Pagel clearly won the job in training camp. He was just flat-out better," Accorsi says.

Says Cincinnati Bengals President and General Manager Mike Brown: "He was athletic, quick footed, nimble. But he was not a great passer by NFL standards. He didn't have the arm strength."

Yet after Schlichter's undistinguished three years with the Colts, Brown says the Bengals worked him out, and "probably" would have signed Schlichter as a backup to Boomer Esiason "if it hadn't been for his gambling problems."

Schlichter was passing cold checks as recently as two days before his arrest last November. He is the subject of a separate probe, for supposedly bouncing $200,000 in checks at Vegas casinos. Last October, he wrote a bad check at a Kroger in Upper Arlington, outside Columbus, for $1,150. A Cincinnati grand jury indicted him last March on charges of stealing more than $50,000 from a bank. The accusations keep coming.

"I want to do this radio show right," Schlichter told me two years ago. "I've already screwed up 10 years of my life." Now, he's in jail for an expected 18 to 24 months, with other charges pending. Suddenly, 10 years seems like a weekend.

"I don't know why I lent him the money," Willie DeLuca is saying. DeLuca also claims to have one other Schlichter memento: his last bad check. "He could have been a great actor, a great salesman, or both. But he just lies. He'd shoot his wife, then bet which way she'd fall."

Schlichter called him four nights before he went to jail. DeLuca was not pleasant. Art owed him $3,000. "If I'm not in jail, I'll wire you the money," is what Schlichter said to him. Only, Schlichter figured he would be in jail. Nothing stops a con man, not even imminent incarceration.

The conversation was brief. "I know I'm going to jail," Schlichter told DeLuca. "I'm glad it's over. I'll do what I have to do, and after that's over, I'll try to lead a normal life."

"I've never seen nobody with the disease as bad as he had it," says DeLuca. He still has all of Schlichter's memories. The good ones, anyway. They're up on the restaurant wall. DeLuca had one last word for Schlichter: "If you get your act straight," he said, "I'll sell all the stuff back to you."

The Curious Marriage of Mike and Sam

December 25, 1991

*I*t was one last surprise. One final walk on the wire connecting bizarre and outrageous. After eight years, Sam Wyche had pretty much worn that wire out.

On Christmas Eve, he quit as head coach of the Cincinnati Bengals. Or maybe he was fired. We never thought anything like this would happen. Then again, we could say that about a lot of things that happened to Samuel David Wyche.

Bright guy. Interesting, witty, charming guy. "Too decent a man to be a football coach," Boomer Esiason once said. Maybe.

But for eight years, ever since Paul Brown introduced him as "a very special individual," Sam Wyche made a habit of fighting battles he couldn't win. This one was no exception.

Wyche wanted to coach the world, and generally, he considered himself up to the task. But he could no more tell officials how to officiate than he could tell Mike Brown how to run his football team.

Wyche met with the Bengals general manager Tuesday. Each arrived with his own agenda. Brown wanted Wyche to clean up his tired act, to limit his wars to the game.

Wyche wanted Brown to allow him more say in who plays. He wanted the team to bolster its scouting staff and to begin running what he considered a first-class operation.

After 3–13, Brown was in no mood to hear the arrogant demands of his rhetorically windy head coach. Brown likely said something to trip Wyche's hot button (not a terribly difficult thing to do) and off they went, in different directions, for good.

Fired or resigned? Jumped or pushed? Maybe it's one for the lawyers. Whatever there was Tuesday, it didn't involve compromise. Wyche the crusader butted heads with another authority figure. This time, it cost him his job.

You knew that, at some point, Wyche would go out like this. Mike Brown wanted quiet, sober discussion. Wyche is as quiet as a cannon shot. Wyche once told me that my biggest problem was I couldn't keep my mouth shut. At least we had one thing in common.

In most places, Wyche wouldn't have had the chance to quit. A coach who loses 13 games, embarrasses his organization and then hints at a power play, has one move to make, and that's for his coat.

In any other NFL town, the Tuesday meeting would have been about Mike Brown asking Sam Wyche for his playbook. Yet here, the Wyche question dragged on longer than a touchdown drive against the Bengals defense.

What Wyche did best this fall was cover his own behind. There was blame for everyone but, of course, himself. When the defensive coordinator, Dick LeBeau, twisted beneath the critics' knives, Wyche kept his support for LeBeau to himself.

When the Bengals lost, it wasn't because they didn't play well or—dare we say it?—weren't well-prepared. The Bengals lost 13 times this fall because of bad breaks, bad calls and the lack of a big play or two. Most of the losses were satisfactory, of course, because the players tried hard.

This is baloney. All of it. But we bought it. Mike Brown bought it, to the extent that Wyche would have returned in '92 if he'd agreed to play by Mike's rules.

Ultimately, Wyche could not. You can't be a rebel and work for the Cincinnati Bengals. On Tuesday, we all found out who was running this team. It's not Sam Wyche.

We tried to find him Tuesday. We checked his house, his office, his haunts in Over-the-Rhine. We half-figured to see him in a kitchen in the West End, pouring soup.

And yes, we'll miss him. Whatever Sam Wyche was, he was his own man. He was aggressively different from other NFL coaches. He prided himself on that. Wyche didn't merely march to a different drummer. He conducted the whole band. We won't see his like here again.

But after awhile, we wished he'd knock it off and just coach. The one year he did, Wyche worked in the Super Bowl.

The oddest thing is that the Brown family ever hooked up with Sam Wyche. It was a curious marriage from the start. The wonder is that it lasted this long.

Wyche loved the attention. Wyche was a grandstander who could never resist shoving himself into the national bright lights. The Browns wanted him to draw Xs and Os and blend into the woodwork.

This year, Mike Brown had given up trying to rein in his coach. After the Monday night loss in Buffalo, when Wyche got crazy on national TV, Brown said this to me: "You could almost say he's a guy looking to sign his own death warrant. Most of it is a lack of emotional control. I can't stop him. I've told him and told him."

Wyche was never one to be told much of anything. It is why, ultimately, the Bengals told him goodbye. Sam Wyche the amateur magician could pull a quarter from behind your ear. He could never limit his wars to those he could win.

Ickeyville

*N*ow it can be told: Paul Brown was a closet Shuffler. By the time he performed the Ickey Shuffle to a rapt, standing-room-only crowd of media heavies at the Super Bowl ("Destined to be a classic! An enthusiastic two thumbs up!" raved the critics) PB had been rehearsing for weeks. In all things, The Great Man was always prepared.

During the fall of 1988, in front of family and friends, the Bengals founder would break into his own interpretation of the Shuffle, which, as son and current general manager Mike Brown notes, "would never make anyone forget Nijinsky."

The late PB was not by nature a Shuffler. He wasn't a Shuffling kind of guy. Anyone who knew him (or thought they did) could never imagine Paul Brown herky-jerking from side to side. They probably thought something was wrong with his feet.

Any other year, we'd have had him arrested and held overnight for observation; 1988 was no ordinary year.

It's just about over now. As a defining moment in time, it ended Saturday. The Bengals put Ickey Woods on their Plan B list of unprotected players. He won't play here again. Turn up the house lights, and have a safe ride home. The dance is done.

It was the singular nature of one Elbert Woods that he could make Paul Brown dance. Woods debuted the Shuffle on September 25, 1988, in Cincinnati's 24–17 win over Cleveland. His mother was in town and had wondered aloud what her son might do when he scored his first professional touchdown.

That got son to thinking, but thankfully not too hard, because the beauty of the Ickey Shuffle was in its silly simplicity. I mean, Michael Jackson is great, but try doing what he does at your next cocktail party.

That whole season, the Ickey Shuffle was the spontaneous symbol of a team flying high, but also by the seat of its pants. Every team would like to go from 4–11 to 12–4, as the Bengals did. No one can claim drawing it up that way. The Shuffle wasn't choreographed; it just happened.

It quickly assumed a life of its own. The Shuffle worked because the Bengals were winning, but also because it wasn't taunting or threatening or remotely athletic. No Butch Johnson "California Quake" here. Just a little celebration that even corporate America could do.

So we did. Men in suits Shuffled in December on Fountain Square. Companies sold towels and posters with the steps printed in them. There were Shuffle contests, judged by Ickey himself.

There were local dance instructors, offering tips: "I would say maybe he should samba, mambo or cha-cha." A dance studio owner named Eleanor Lachman told me that, in November 1988. To which Ickey replied: "I don't need no mambo lessons."

A Boston sports columnist in town for the AFC title game datelined his piece, "Ickeyville."

By Super Bowl Week, Ickeyville had gone national. Woods and his mom did a car ad on TV. No one could have imagined then that Woods would become nothing grander than a marketing phenomenon. The sporting version of the hula hoop.

Now, Woods is more of a concept than a player. "I'd like to stay here," he is saying. "But I'll probably be moving on."

He has two bad knees and a weight problem. For three years, ever since he stood during a team meeting and said "(Expletive) you, homeboy," to then-coach Sam Wyche, he has been in the doghouse.

If anyone ever represented the fragile nature of success, it is Ickey Woods. "I grew up in a place where I didn't have any notoriety," Woods says. "Notoriety comes and goes with the weather. One minute, you're a star; next minute, you're a bum and they're booing you. I've seen it all."

"My dad appreciated showmanship," Mike Brown says. "Ickey's

act caught his eye. Even when he voted to curtail (on-field demonstrations), my dad felt that Ickey's little dance was always a plus, not something to be penalized."

The Bengals stuck with Woods through three years and two knee operations, hoping for a little happy nostalgia. It never happened. "I think Ickey could have been great," Mike Brown says, sad words rippling the air.

Ickey will be going now. Business is business, and, on that score, nobody cares about 1988. Except, maybe, those of us who remember the dancing.

Maybe Ickey will make it, maybe he won't. There isn't a real thriving market out there for a running back with two bad knees.

The rest of us, we're in his debt. Sports at its best is a glad thing. Ickey, in his way, certainly was that.

Mostly, fame has the shelf life of warm milk. Memories are easier to keep, and we'll remember Ickey's happy dance. So too, we suspect, will Paul Brown.

The Coach and the N Word

August, 1993

*H*e won't say the word now. It has vanished from his lexicon. In the confused and confusing '90s, the word is stuffed at once with hatred and admiration. It is a venal descriptive and a term of endearment, and woe be to those who don't know the difference. The protocol depends on who says it to whom. It depends on how it is said. Denny Holthaus may never stop wondering why he got fired for using the word "nigger" when addressing his high school football team. He only knows that it is a word he will never use again.

So when in the summer of 1993, four years after the Cincinnati school board fired him, he says his former players at Aiken High School referred to him as "their favorite N-word," it sounds so stilted, you almost have to laugh.

He is seal-coating driveways now. That is his business, along with another small company he runs that sells sweatshirts to area high schools. These are concerns he runs himself. There is no one to fire him, no one to question his motives. How do you pass judgment on a man who seals driveways and sells sweatshirts?

Holthaus collects disability from the school system, for the ulcer he got from the firing and all the publicity it received. .

He'll probably never be a head football coach again.

We live in a time when what you say is held more closely to the light than what you do or who you are. Denny Holthaus discovered that too late. He could work in the Cincinnati schools for eighteen years as a teacher and coach. He could win some championships at Aiken. He could be coach of the year twice.

He could find his players summer jobs and drive them to the airport when they were being recruited for college scholarships. He could, as most coaches could, be a father and a shrink and a confidant and a friend. He could be all that, and none of it would matter so much as a single word.

"Whoever says it now is going to get fired," Holthaus is saying. He is 43 years old. His hairline travels north. He has seen a dream come and go, and there is a bitterness to that he wears on his face. What are the rules, and who has to live by them? What is important, and what is not? What is real and what is cosmetic? Does anyone stop to think about any of this? This is what Holthaus wants to know.

"I wish I had punched some kid in the face or sold drugs. I could handle that in my mind, that I should have gotten fired.

"It's amazing. I work to try to help these kids, and people of their race stereotype me as being a racist. To the black guy on the street, I'm probably a racist," Holthaus says.

This is what happened, in September of 1989. These are Holthaus' words, but they have been substantiated by others, including former Aiken players.

"We had team meetings before two-a-days (summer practices). We talked about rules, what kind of kid we expected. We talked about drugs and ACT tests, a lot of different things.

"We also talked about hearing the N word. The players talked about it. They said they were tired of being called a bunch of you-know-whats. We (coaches) talked to them about it. We said everybody in Cincinnati respects Aiken football. I said people would say that word because they're jealous.

"You go beat a school that has a band and a booster club and lots of fans, they can't handle that. You're stereotyped as being not as intelligent as them, which is not true. You're stereotyped as low IQs, no dads and coming from low-income families, which is not true.

"I said there are people who are prejudiced out there. If you hear them say the N word, bring it to me, don't react to it on the field. Handle yourselves with class. If we keep playing good football and act like decent people, we won't hear it."

There was a time when the Aiken players returned to their bus following a game to see "KKK" scrawled on the windows. There was a time when they needed a police escort to get in and out of Portsmouth, Ohio. There was a time when the door to the visitors' dressing room was locked and Holthaus asked for the key.

"Why don't your boys just break in?" came the answer.

All of it built up within the team. Players went to Holthaus for solutions.

"About two weeks later, we were having a bad practice," Holthaus says. "Everybody was loafing. I blew the whistle. I said, 'You guys told me you don't want to be called, you know, this word. If we practice like this and play like this, you're going to hear it in the stands. You guys are a bunch of you-know-whats.

"I didn't think anything of it. I was saying it to try to protect them from being called that word."

145

A parent of a player called the high school anonymously, recounting Holthaus' use of the word. The Aiken principal passed it on to the school board. Word was given to the papers and the TV. A week later, Holthaus was fired.

"School board members thought I was a lowlife," Holthaus says. "I made a mistake. A verbal error. If in Teaching 101, they said if you teach in an all-black school, you could never say that word no matter what, then okay, fine. That was not the case."

About half of Holthaus's players, most of them upperclassmen, reacted to the decision by boycotting Aiken's next game. "As a team, we love the coach," one player said. "We didn't like the statement, but it's no more than what a black coach would have said."

"I wish that someone had taken the time to find out who I am, where I was coming from, and the context in which it was said. Once it got in the papers, there was no context," Holthaus says.

He went to court to get his job back. A judge agreed with him, but the school board appealed the decision and won. Holthaus has applied for head coaching jobs at four schools since—Lakota, Roger Bacon, Sycamore and Withrow—and gotten just one interview, at Bacon.

Now he's a volunteer line coach for the freshmen at LaSalle, where his son plays. Holthaus feels aggrieved. Depending on which side of the hazy, wavy and ever-changing line of political correctness you tread, you agree or you don't.

More likely, you stay out of things altogether. It's safest that way, if not particularly courageous.

"We had rules," Holthaus is saying, "We had discipline. Like, if you missed one practice, you couldn't start. If you missed two, you couldn't play. We made them say 'Yes, sir' and 'Yes, ma'am.' My wife would get on the phone and tell the kids to go to class. We helped them pay for team pictures.

"If you talk to these kids, they're street smart. If you try to lie to them, they'll see through it. They'll lose respect for you."

He brings with him to our meeting a briefcase full of positive job appraisals, letters of recommendation, newspaper clips, and judges' rulings. Holthaus talks about playing football at UC, about rooming with two black players, about coaching and teaching for eighteen years in a system of predominantly minority students. "Why would I want to turn forty kids against me?" he says.

"I lost my identity, I lost my self-confidence. I'd always been extroverted and enthusiastic. I lost all that. I was paranoid, or whatever. What I was trying to do and what I stood for was totally out the window. It hurt the kids, it hurt the school system, it hurt me. Nobody won."

Except the sweatshirt business. The sweatshirt business is booming. He hands me a business card. "Holt's Sportswear," it says. "Quality Embroidered and Imprinted Garments."

Denny Holthaus, "Your Complete Sports Apparel Representative."

He looks up from his salad, and you think you see him wince. "It's a living," Holthaus says. "I guess."

The Fall of The Hawk

May 15, 1990

*B*oxing is a sport so terrible you can't take your eyes off it. A boxing ring is the most elegantly brutal place on earth, but it's no place to save a soul or a life.

As of this moment, Aaron Pryor will step into a ring in Madison, Wisconsin, on Wednesday night. Unless someone connected with this event comes to his or her senses—never a safe bet in the world of boxing—Pryor will fight one Daryl Jones for the princely sum of $5,000.

If boxing were sensitive or rational or fair—if boxing were anything but the golden cesspool it is—someone would not let this happen.

Someone would wrap Aaron Pryor in their arms and never let go. Hold him. Tell him that saving his sad and weeping life involves more than a $5,000 payday against a bad club fighter in a small-time arena.

There's more to the rest of Aaron Pryor's 34-year-old life than this. There has to be.

It's a thin line in boxing between courage and foolishness. Thinner still between foolishness and desperation, and that is the line Aaron Pryor will walk Wednesday night.

Pryor is off to another war. He's less a soldier than a migrant this time, less a warrior than a servant, more an indigent than anything.

If there's an emptier dream than his, it doesn't come to mind.

He can't see. From his left eye, vision dances like fog. His left eye sees pastels, a soft, gauzy haze of fuzzy shapes that stay out of focus forever, no matter how close they are. Depending on the doctor doing the testing, its power ranges from 20/300 to 20/700. It is legally blind.

What is it like to see the world through a 20/300 eye?

"You can't recognize the face of somebody sitting across the table from you," says Cincinnati ophthalmologist Dr. Jerrold Levin.

With his left eye, Pryor cannot see to read a book or drive a car. He cannot see clearly his own outstretched hand.

That Wisconsin's Department of Regulation and Licensing can see to approve Pryor's request to fight is a tragedy of the worst sort.

Pryor is classified as "handicapped" in Wisconsin. What Wisconsin is saying is that to prevent Pryor from fighting after he has been medically approved to do so would be discrimination. What Aaron Pryor is saying is that, for $5,000, he's willing to gamble that this fight won't cost him his sight or his mind.

The most recent ophthalmologist to peer into the deadness of Pryor's left eye was one Dr. Rodney Sturm of Madison, who somehow concluded that Pryor "is fit to continue boxing."

Meanwhile, Dr. David Smith, the consulting ophthalmologist

for the New Jersey state boxing commission, examined Pryor in February. He has this to say: "Aaron Pryor can't even see the big 'E' on an eye chart. He has a problem like no other boxer I've ever seen, and I've examined more than 300 boxers."

To this, Marlene Cummings says, So what?

Cummings is the head of Wisconsin's Department of Regulation and Licensing. She is a civil libertarian. She upholds laws. She says Aaron Pryor has a right to pursue his trade. Even if common sense (and decency) says otherwise.

Marlene Cummings says, "What you're looking at is basic human rights," which, basically, means that if a man wants to blind himself, well, that's his business. "This is a free country," says Marlene Cummings. Let freedom ring.

At the moment, Aaron Pryor is subsisting in a $42.88-a-night Super 8 Motel in Madison, doing whatever it is that condemned men do.

They called him The Hawk once, when his performances were praised for their savageness. In November 1982, The Hawk successfully defended his junior welterweight title, stopping Alexis Arguello in the Orange Bowl in a fight that sports columnist John Schulian called "the greatest fight since Muhammad Ali and Joe Frazier dueled in Manilla" nearly a decade earlier.

That was a long time ago. Now, The Hawk is on the phone, a soft, distended voice, a monotone from a sparrow.

"The doctor tells me if I get hit in my right eye and it's bad, I can still drive with my left eye. I got glasses," he says. "Lots of folks got glasses."

Someone once said that in the kingdom of the blind, the one-eyed man is king, but this does not apply to one-eyed Aaron Pryor, who whispers into the phone.

"I was the greatest fighter in my division once," he says. "With the vision I have in my right eye, I can beat most of these guys out here now. All I want is to leave the fight game with a better name than I left it before."

Cry for Aaron Pryor tonight, if you care. Grace his memory with your tears and hope beyond hope that tomorrow night in Madison, Aaron Pryor will exit the boxing ring in the same condition in which he arrived.

Slim Pickens

August 31, 1997

*C*arl Pickens could stand to be left alone. That goes for the heathen media and opposing defensive backs. Why all these questions?

Why do you want to talk to me? I play football, man. That's what I do. I don't need the spotlight. I don't want the attention, and if I do, it's going to be my call, not yours.

Pickens begins his sixth season as a Bengals wide receiver today. He's arguably the best they've ever had at the position. He's probably the best in the AFC right now. If Jerry Rice ever allows age to creep into his personal game plan, Pickens could be the best in the entire league.

About the rest of him, who knows?

Pickens is funny. (He does impressions). He is multitalented. (He plays several instruments). He wants to make rhythm and blues records. He's taking bass lessons.

He is country. (He still spends the offseason at home in little Murphy, N.C., high in the Smoky Mountains). He is family. (He lives, yes, in the basement of the home he bought for his parents.) He rides horses, he camps, he washes his father's truck. But these are all things you really don't need to know. Do you?

Pickens is mercurial. He could write the book on mercurial.

"Eloquent, quick-witted, clever, shrewd, thievish," is how Webster's defines it. "Volatile, changeable, fickle."

Yes and yes.

"Why do you want to talk to me?" he asks.

I am standing in the parking lot at Spinney Field. Pickens is walking to a bus that will take the team to the Meet The Bengals Luncheon on Friday. That he has even acknowledged my existence is a great leap in the history of our relationship.

I made the same request an hour earlier, as the Bengals were coming off the field after a morning workout. Pickens looked right through me, said nothing, and ran right past.

"Because you're here six years," I say, "and we've never really talked. And you may be the best receiver playing now."

"Are you saying that because you mean it, or because you want to talk to me?" he says.

Strictly speaking, all Carl Pickens owes anyone is a good performance on Sundays. And really, knowing Pickens the athlete is as easy as watching him play. Watching him on one particular play, actually.

It's called Stroke X Dancer. It's the fade route Pickens works with quarterback Jeff Blake. They work it so well, the ball could be attached from Blake's right hand to Pickens' long arms by a string.

By now, every team in the world knows what the Bengals are likely to do inside their opponent's 15-yard line. "Guys are over in the corner waiting on it now," Pickens says.

What makes it work is partly Blake's touch, but mostly Pickens' will to catch the ball. Once Blake lets the ball go, more a jump ball than a pass, the play becomes a free-for-all in the endzone. Whoever wants the ball more will probably get it. Pickens wants the ball.

A teammate and fellow wide-out David Dunn says, "He feels like every ball in the air is his."

Putting it another way, Bengals emperor Mike Brown says, "We've never had anybody here who was more of a competitor."

The ultimate competitor can be prickly. Most competitors are.

151

"I'm just now learning to play at a controlled pace," Pickens says. "I'm still learning how to concentrate and relax in games."

When I suggest his work ethic seems borrowed from Rice, Pickens says, "I take everything from Jerry. He's the best. But I don't want to be like Jerry. I want to be better than Jerry."

We will not hear about Pickens in trouble. We will not see his name on a court docket or a police report. Football "is the easiest job in the world," he says, "if you keep your head clean and your nose clean. Look at (lineman) Joe Walter and (punter) Lee Johnson. They know how to work. They're disciplined.

"But you have some guys that would rather go to a club, get in a fight, bring girls to hotel rooms. We get a big ol' book on July 17. It says from July 17 to December 22 you need to be here or there at this certain time. Some guys can't follow that."

He does not endorse products. He doesn't sign autographs for pay. "Cheap money," Pickens calls it. When the season is over, he goes home.

He is a millionaire who lives in the basement of his parent's house. He takes out the trash. "My parents have been married 29 years. I know what commitment is about. They've kept me level-headed. I know to this day that if I screw up, my dad would be right in my face."

Pickens stays in Murphy, because it is where he trusts people and things. "People there are real," he says. "You can get caught up in this lifestyle. Fancy suits, fast cars, big houses. There's nothing like that in Murphy."

He goes camping for days at a time. He plays music with his father Carl, a blues guitarist. The stuff Pickens used to complain about when his mother Mary dialed it up on the radio—old Motown, Bobby Womack, the O'Jays—is what he wants to play now.

During a practice break at training camp last summer, Pickens led a group of players through several R&B standards, including the Bill Withers' tune "Lean on Me." He played piano.

And on any given day, he could look right through you when you ask for a minute or say hello. Mercurial.

152

"I'm a very moody person," Pickens says. "I trust the people I have to trust. I have close friends, but not a lot. And I don't need for you to know me."

Personally, I could talk to Pickens all day. Personally, Pickens would probably rather take a flaming stick to his eye.

In the end, all we really need to know about Pickens we can find in that one play. Stroke X Dancer. You get the impression that's how he prefers it.

Just as Barry Larkin is an impossible play behind second base lunging, twisting and throwing out a baserunner all in one sweet, poetic motion...just as Boomer Esiason is a play-action TD bomb to Eddie Brown in the righteous autumn of 1988...just as Pete Rose slides headfirst into forever...so is Carl Pickens, already in that select company, over there in the back corner of the end zone, fighting for a popup thrown by Jeff Blake.

It's the surest thing in Cincinnati since Procter & Gamble and the Republican Party. George Foster didn't hit bad curveballs any better that Blake hits Pickens with that pass.

Stroke X Dancer.

"You are being completely gracious to me now," I say to Pickens. "But why do I get the feeling that if I were to say hello to you next week, you'd act as if I weren't there?"

"Because," Pickens says, "that's how it is."

The Man Who Had it All

January 31, 1999

*M*iami—Ten years ago this week, Stanley Wilson ruined his life.

It was just before 8 p.m. the night before Cincinnati was to play the San Francisco 49ers in Super Bowl XXIII, when the Bengals fullback walked down a hall in the team's hotel and made a U-turn back to his personal hell.

"I forgot my playbook," Wilson told several teammates. "I'll meet you guys downstairs."

As the Bengals gathered for their last meeting before the game, head coach Sam Wyche took a head count. Players were responsible for their roommate. Wilson's was wide receiver Eddie Brown.

"Stanley went back for his playbook," Brown said. "He'll be right down."

"We'll wait," Wyche said.

Upstairs in his room, Wilson saw the white powder. The devil takes many forms. One of them looks like white powder in a plastic bag. Wilson was already a two-time loser under the NFL's drug policy. The league suspended him the entire 1987 season. Once more and he would be banned for life.

Cocaine had once put Wilson in the hospital four times in 11 months. He knew its lure. He also knew it could kill him. "Cocaine is seductive, man," he said that September. "Mentally, you're not convinced it's hurting you. (But) I don't think about the end of my football career if I use again. I think about dying."

He had stayed clean the entire '88 season. He passed three drug tests a week. Wilson scored two touchdowns in a divisional playoff win against Seattle. He was a tough, tough football player.

"Our resident street bully," in the words of Cris Collinsworth.

"Stanley brought an edge to our offense."

Solomon Wilcots, a safety, and his defensive teammates called Wilson "Taz" because his playing style reminded them of the hyper cartoon character the Tasmanian Devil.

"He had this bravado," Wilcots said last week. "You know, 'You don't hit me.' He would tell rookies, 'You aren't going to make the team off me."

The Bengals waited for Stanley Wilson.

Ten minutes.

Fifteen.

Wyche left the meeting room. He returned a few minutes later. His eyes were red and brimming wet. "Stanley has had a relapse," he said.

Boomer Esiason remembers thinking, "Is this another of Sam's motivational stunts? With Sam, you couldn't be sure. He was always doing that stuff."

Not this time. "Sam broke up crying so hard, he had to leave the room," Esiason recalls.

"Come back in 10 minutes, when I can compose myself," Wyche said.

Stanley Wilson used cocaine that night. He snorted it. He smoked it. He couldn't stop. Some 20 minutes after the meeting was to begin, running backs coach Jim Anderson found Wilson in the bathroom of his room at the Holiday Inn in Plantation, Fla., a few miles north of Pro Player Stadium. The player was sweating and shivering. White powder flecked his nose and upper lip. The devil was back, for good.

"Oh, Stanley," Anderson said to his fullback. "Why?"

Nobody knows that. Wilson once compared a cocaine high to an athletic high. He said the feelings of elation, confidence and well-being were similar. Maybe so. You can talk to 10 addicts—drug users, alcohol abusers, gamblers—and each will say he doesn't know why he does what he does, or what makes it so hard to quit.

All know one thing, though. The only place it ends up is in trouble. Trouble could be in a crack house or a bankruptcy proceeding or a failed marriage. For Stanley Wilson, trouble currently is in a West Los Angeles courtroom, where on Friday he stood accused of first-degree residential burglary, Case No. SA031810.

If convicted, Wilson will go to jail for the rest of his life. Wilson had three strikes in the NFL; this is his third in the California legal system. The face of trouble for Wilson looks like an 8-by-10 cell from now until forever.

It's a sad and terrible gaze, which is ironic, because the face everyone remembers on Stanley Wilson was not that way at all.

"Stanley is a likeable guy," Jim Anderson said recently. "He's a good person."

Said Wilcots, now a reporter for ESPN, "Stanley had the biggest smile of anyone I ever knew. He also had a big man's laugh. You know how big guys can have a laugh that carries a room? That was Stanley."

Wilson was quiet and thoughtful, almost shy. He had trouble talking about his addiction, but once he started, he was candid and realistic. "I can arrest it. I can never control it," he said in '88. "(Football) is a lot easier than anything else I've done the past few years."

After the two-touchdown show in the playoffs against Seattle, Wilson said, "I feel reborn." Addicts "feel like they're committing a slow suicide. That's how I felt. This is almost like a second life."

His third life began that night at the Holiday Inn. January 21, 1988. It has taken him to where he was Friday, a 5-foot, 10-inch man, 225 pounds in his playing days, 270 pounds now, fearful, in front of a jury ruling on the merits of his life. Collinsworth, now an analyst for Fox Sports, interviewed Wilson early this month for a story that will air today on the Super Bowl pregame show. His was the only interview Wilson allowed.

Collinsworth said Wilson admitted in the piece that the numerous burglaries he committed were to feed his cocaine habit. Wilson has done time in prison and in rehabilitation centers. Late in 1990, Long Beach, Calif., police found him in a crack house and arrested him on burglary charges.

"He was at the bottom of the pit, in a place filled with trash and needles," police Sgt. Robert Gillissie said at the time. "it was almost like he was asking for help."

"He's desperate to get it figured out and pieced together," Collinsworth said.

You never know what people are looking for when they turn to drugs. Wilson knew what he was looking for the night before the Super Bowl, and all the next day: More drugs.

The Bengals secreted Wilson out of the Holiday Inn and back to the Omni Hotel downtown, where the team had stayed all week. While team business manager Bill Connelly talked on the phone, Wilson slipped out of the room, down a fire escape, and into the night.

According to Wilson's account in *Penthouse* magazine, he took a cab down Biscayne Boulevard, bought liquor and found street dealers to supply him with cocaine. He checked into a motel.

He surfaced on Monday, the day after the 49ers beat the Bengals 20–16 in the Super Bowl. "You have to let my family know I'm alive," he told lawyer James Kidney's secretary.

Kidney frequently represents local athletes. Wilson hired him after the player had been charged with indecent exposure, when Newport police arrested him for urinating in the parking lot of Rumors, a now-defunct bar, days before the AFC title game.

Kidney recalls Wilson a week after the Super Bowl, arriving at Kidney's Newport office in his Jaguar, and sobbing. "I (messed) up," Wilson told Kidney. "I let my team down. I let my son (Stanley Jr., then 6) down." Wilson gave Kidney his black game jersey as a token of his gratitude, and left.

"Stanley had a lot of things given to him," Kidney said this week. "Athletes think God gave them the ability to get away with everything. Even when he was down, Stanley had things given to him."

Everyone tried to help Stanley Wilson. Almost everyone tried to save Stanley from Stanley.

Boomer Esiason put him up at the Westin early in the '88 season. Until then, Wilson had been sleeping in the Jaguar he bought with money from his first contract. He was broke.

One night two years earlier, Sam Wyche took Wilson home with him and fed him ice cream all night. Wilson was to be tested for drugs the next day. Wyche was a compassionate coach, beyond the NFL norm. He didn't want Wilson on the street. Wilson failed the test anyway.

Jim Anderson treated Wilson like a son. After the '87 suspension, Anderson went to L.A. to see what the layoff had done to his fullback. He returned to Cincinnati recommending the team give Wilson another chance.

Anderson and Wilson were frequent visitors to Wyche's office in 1988. Wilson spent an unusual amount of time sleeping in the players lounge. His moods were erratic.

Was he OK? Always, the conversation was the same:

Wyche: "Are you having any problems we should know about?"

Wilson: "No."

After the Newport incident, Wyche suggested Wilson see a psychiatrist; Wilson declined.

He was having a very good year, riding the wave of the best season in Bengals history. Wilson was a devastating lead blocker. His execution of the play-action fake was textbook.

Nine years later, the resurgent Esiason would tell rookie running back Corey Dillon to "sell the play-fake like Stanley Wilson did."

"I'll never forget," Esiason said. "It was '86, up in New England. The first time we used it. Twenty-nine Boss, we called it. Bruce Coslet designed the play. Stanley ran like he had the ball. I mean he leaped into the line with everything he had."

Eddie Brown ran a post pattern. The safety bit on Wilson's fake. "Eddie was wide open. A play was born. A system was born," Esiason said.

The Bengals offense destroyed the league in the first part of '88. The play-action was a big reason why: so were James Brooks and Ickey Woods, following Stanley Wilson into the hole.

"Second (down) and one," Solomon Wilcots recalled. "Stanley would throw his body up in the air, and you just knew he had the ball. And he didn't just block. He tried to cave your chest in.

"He was hell-bent for leather. He didn't do anything halfway. On the football field, that was a good thing. In life, maybe not so good."

Wilson could not do just a little coke. He could not drink just a little booze. The first time he drank at Oklahoma—where he started as a freshman, in a backfield that included Billy Sims—Wilson imbibed until he blacked out.

He wasn't using in '88, but he was drinking. And his moods were erratic. One teammate recalled an incident at the end of training camp. Several players had rented limousines to take them to a Dayton nightclub. The evening ended early when Wilson, rebuffed by a woman he'd asked to dance, started "getting physical," the player said. Teammates had to escort Wilson from the club.

Then came the incident at Rumors. Kidney maintains that Wilson tried to use the club's restroom, but was interrupted when "two women came in there and wanted to take a picture with him."

The case was dismissed. Wilson's demons were not.

"My God, what have I done?" Wilson says to Collinsworth in the Fox story. That was Wilson's reaction to going AWOL in Miami, 10 years ago this week. Wilson claims to have gotten the coke from teammates, an allegation he made a decade ago in the *Penthouse* article.

Collinsworth doesn't know what the national impact from the story might be. Who outside Cincinnati remembers Wilson? Ten years later, who cares? Collinsworth said he did the story as much for himself as for the network.

"I really wanted to know what happened. It put the story to rest for me," he said.

"At the end of it, I ended up more upset with the people involved that gave him the drugs."

Could the Bengals have beaten the San Francisco 49ers with Stanley Wilson in their backfield? The field was a mess, muddy and chewed up. Wilson ran with short, sure steps.

The game plan featured the running of Woods and Brooks; that depended some on Wilson's presence. The night before the Super

Bowl is not the time to change a game plan to account for the loss of your lead blocker.

Then again, as Wilcots noted, "Had Stanley not gotten caught, how effective would he have been in the game anyway?"

No one will ever know. It's no more knowable than why Wilson, a smart kid from the middle-class L.A. suburb of Carson, where he grew up with both parents, decided to embrace a demon he has never been able to shake.

He hasn't left much of a wake. Collinsworth's producer at Fox spent six months tracking him down; Wilson blew off their first interview.

His last contact with the media came more than two years ago. Wilson was a volunteer coach at a small Christian school in south-central L.A., where Stanley Jr., then 13, was playing eight man football. The *Los Angeles Times* reporter who wrote the story, Bill Plaschke, went intending to do a feature on the program. He had no idea Wilson would be there.

When you call the Crenshaw Christian Center now, asking to speak to Stanley Wilson Jr., the woman on the other end of the line tells you he isn't there. When you begin to ask her if she knows where Wilson Jr. might be, she hangs up.

Former teammates, upset once with Wilson for hurting their Super Bowl chances and a second time for ratting them out for money in the *Penthouse* article, haven't kept in touch with him. Collinsworth said the friends Wilson has now aren't aware Wilson ever played football.

James Kidney still hears from his former client, though. Wilson even sent him a Christmas card this year. "Real religious," Kidney said.

"God is on my side," Wilson wrote. "God is in your spirit."

Several years ago, Wilson would call Kidney, who tried to get him work in the Canadian Football League and with the L.A. Raiders. Wilson never asked the lawyer for money, though Kidney suspects Wilson had none. His last NFL checks—from the playoff wins in '88—were used to pay debts, Kidney said.

Wilson is married. His wife is seven months pregnant. She cried throughout the Fox interview. Wilson worked construction until he found trouble again.

Said Collinsworth, "Stanley is the toughest guy I ever dealt with. If cocaine can own Stanley Wilson, it can own you."

Maybe that's the lesson. It's not about a football game lost or a football franchise that has lost its way in the decade since. The minute Stanley Wilson returned to his hotel room and put the powder to his nose, the Cincinnati Bengals began a free fall that continues to this day.

It's not about that. It's about a man on the verge of having it all, a strong man who was powerless against the demons. Stanley Wilson is on trial now, closer to hell than not, a victim of his own urges.

After they talked, Cris Collinsworth prayed with Stanley Wilson. Both teared up over their fond memories and Wilson's sad waste of them all. "This is a soul worth saving," Collinsworth said.

If only that could be.

A Rose By Any Other Name

"I'd be willing to bet you, if I was a betting man, that I have never bet on baseball."

—*Pete Rose, 1989, before his banishment from baseball for gambling*

Dowd 1, Legend 0

*H*e stepped into the late afternoon sunlight and adjusted his tie. John Dowd is a big man, maybe 6 foot 2, with a long and melancholy face that suggests he has seen too many unhappy endings. And that, quite soon, he would see another.

"Human life is very fragile," he said.

The suit that Pete Rose has brought against major league baseball looks like the desperate act of a beaten man. Its basis—that baseball commissioner Bart Giamatti already has decided that Rose bet on baseball—was flimsy to begin with. Thursday, in Room 516 of the Hamilton County Courthouse, it was all but buried.

John Dowd was why. Dowd is baseball's special counsel in the Rose investigation and the author of the damning 225-page report on Rose's supposed gambling activities. If Rose's career is shot down, Dowd will hold the smoking gun.

For 90 minutes Thursday afternoon, Dowd was brutally articulate. His testimony kicked Rose right in the credibility. It left anyone who heard it wondering how Rose could win acquittal in any forum, public or private.

Rose's lawyers were to cross-examine Dowd this morning, hopeful of stopping the hemorrhaging of Rose's reputation. But the damage already has been done. The question, from Major League Baseball's lead attorney Louis Hoynes Jr., had been about betting sheets.

Why are they called the Pete Rose betting sheets?

"Because witnesses have testified that they came from Mr. Rose's house," John Dowd said. "That they were in Mr. Rose's handwriting. And that a handwriting expert has stated that the handprinting on those sheets belonged to Mr. Rose."

He went on. Baseball has phone records that support the testimony

164

of Ron Peters, who claims Rose bet heavily on baseball and on the Reds. Baseball has canceled checks signed by Rose that it claims were used to finance wagers. Baseball has nine witnesses who have given investigators information about Rose betting on baseball or the Reds.

Baseball has what it calls the betting sheets.

"Three pieces of paper with handprinting on them," Dowd said. "Some have dates. There were basketball teams, baseball teams on there."

Dowd takes no pleasure in this. Rose's lawyers may have portrayed Dowd and Giamatti as vindictive and prejudicial, but there is no joy for John Dowd in taking down a legend.

"I grew up in Boston, loving Ted Williams," he said. "I used to sit out in the left-field bleachers and watch The Splendid Splinter play. Take the subway or the train in to Fenway Park."

Was Williams a hero to you? A man wondered.

"Yeah, he was. A magnificent guy. I just loved him."

You wonder what John Dowd must have been feeling during the three months he rummaged through the unmade rooms of Pete Rose's life. Ted Williams, hero, was a man of many faults. None were investigated by baseball.

Times were different. Standards were different, gentler. Williams left the game with his records and his dignity.

Deep down, John Dowd, who recognizes the need for heroes, isn't happy with the way things have worked out for Pete Rose. Deep down, nobody is. "Pete Rose is a human being, just like me or anyone else," Dowd is saying.

It's hot downtown. Dowd pulls a red kerchief from his breast pocket, dabs his forehead. He has a stiff, bow-legged walk. Thursday, he walks slowly, away from Room 516.

"You have feelings of sadness. It's very difficult," Dowd said. "He has to live with it. I have to live with it. He has done a lot, achieved a lot in his life. It's all very fragile."

Dowd said he interviewed Rose on April 20 and 21. Two of Rose's lawyers were present. "We exposed Mr. Rose to the evidence we had.

His testimony is woven throughout my report. His deposition is attached. Every subject that we covered in the report was covered with Mr. Rose. I showed Mr. Rose the betting sheets twice." A handwriting expert reported to Dowd that the handwriting was Rose's.

Dowd shot down the notion that baseball had made life difficult for Rose's lawyers. "There was more information in my report than you would receive in any criminal or civil case that I've ever seen.

"I don't know what else a lawyer can have than when the fellow on the other side completely exposes his case."

In 1974, Dowd was the chief of the federal organized crime strike force. Later, he led a federal probe of Pennsylvania congressman Daniel Flood. For the last decade, he has been in private business, conducting internal investigations for corporations.

He is a heavy hitter, with a heavy heart. He thinks what he has done in this case is right. He doesn't have to like it.

"There isn't a day," John Dowd said, "that I haven't felt enormous sadness on this matter."

Cincinnati in Black

August 25, 1989

*T*elevision lights bounced off Pete Rose's face, flinging garish shadows across the back wall of the room. On the day baseball fired its all-time hits leader, Rose wore a navy blue suit, a white shirt, a red tie, and a look of deadpan anguish. Cincinnati simply wore black.

Standing perfectly still, hands clasped in front of him, Rose looked like a mug shot. He was surrounded by lawyers and media. He looked very much alone.

The lawyers couldn't save him. The legal system couldn't save him. After he had taken his game through six months of needless sadness, baseball wasn't interested in the job.

He was the game's best and brightest once, a beacon for anyone's little-boy dreams. For so many years, in so many ways, he was the best baseball had to offer.

But save him? No, on Thursday baseball wanted only to wash him from its hands. "The matter of Mr. Rose is now closed," said commissioner Bart Giamatti.

What's left for Rose is to save himself. After Thursday, you wonder if he can. Rose barrelled through his 20-minute press gathering with typical bravado. The gravity and sadness of the occasion would have humbled other men. It barely scratched Rose's terminally cocky surface.

Rose puffed his chest. He drew back his shoulders. If he'd asked for mercy, he'd have gotten it. He didn't, and after a few minutes, the notion stuck that Pete Rose didn't believe he had done anything wrong.

"I don't think I have a gambling problem at all," Rose said. "Consequently, I won't seek any help of any kind." He needs it. Denial didn't help Rose the last six months; it won't help him now.

That was clear Thursday, when it was obvious Rose had no case against baseball. He had six months, four lawyers, two courts and one lawsuit to clear his name.

Assuming he was interested.

Which he was not.

What Rose did was spend an estimated $500,000 in legal fees to delay the inevitable and stonewall the opposition, which happened to be the game he loves.

Rose had no case. On Thursday, Giamatti said, "In the absence of any evidence to the contrary. . . I have concluded he bet on baseball."

Rose had no answer to that. He had no answer to the Dowd Report. He had no answer to Paul Janszen or Ron Peters. He had denials.

"Read the document," Rose said to me, as he made his way out. I did. What Rose bought for his six months and half-million was 29

167

words on Page 4, which read: "Nothing in this agreement shall be deemed either an admission or a denial by Peter Edward Rose of the allegation that he bet on any Major League Baseball game."

In other words, maybe Rose bet on baseball, and maybe he didn't. What a stinging rebuke of the charges. Baseball must be reeling.

Giamatti didn't formally find Rose guilty of baseball betting. He just charged him with it in a nationally televised news conference.

Rose had no case. If that wasn't plain before, it was Thursday morning. The only thing the commissioner left with Rose was the knowledge that baseball would embarrass him no further.

Rose called that a "compromise."

He has a problem. It may be a gambling addiction. More likely, it's his attitude. He said he had made "mistakes." When asked to elaborate, Rose later said he had chosen the wrong friends.

Others had gotten him banned from baseball. This was the implication. If that's really what Rose believes, his troubles run deeper than a penchant for betting illegally. Rose needs to look in the mirror and stop seeing a legend. He needs to confront himself. He needs to confront who he has become.

On a day he had every reason to be repentant, Rose was defiant. When he needed to lob humility, Rose threw arrogance. The day is done when Rose can suspend reality—or create his own—simply because he is Pete Rose. That was Thursday's message.

If Rose wants back in baseball, he needs to stop gambling. To do that, he needs to lose the attitude. He has spent six months denying, rationalizing and lying, all with a swagger that could belong only to him. Look where it got him.

In 1978, Rose sat in this same room discussing his 44-game hitting streak. Seven years later, he was in here talking about 4,192. Thursday, he sought redemption, the best way he knew. You only hope his effort is good enough. One last time.

"It's a very sad day," Pete Rose said. On this, everyone agreed.

Local Hero, Passing Through

August 2, 1993

$\mathcal{H}$e comes back rarely, on little cat's feet. Sometimes, Pete Rose will do his nationally syndicated radio show from a local studio. He will play golf here once, in a charity tournament in the fall. At the moment, he's talking to local food merchants about carrying his latest product. Hit King Ballpark Frozen Pizza, coming soon to your grocer's freezer.

He makes no lusty entrances. He is in, he is out. He is in Cincinnati, but no longer of it. It is his best and worst place, a place of such roiling and conflicted emotions it makes even Rose's legendary stoicism buckle at the knee.

The room at Riverfront Stadium where he celebrated with the media his 44-game hitting streak and the surpassing of Ty Cobb was also the room where he left his baseball life in pieces on the floor.

When Pete Rose was the universal idol, you could spot him just about anywhere, all over town. He liked the attention almost as much as the hits. It's different now.

The helicopter made one pass over the new Crosley Field in Blue Ash, then landed in the outfield grass just beyond second base. This was somebody else's idea. Rose had spent Saturday night at a Blue Ash hotel. He could have walked to the Reds Oldtimers game Saturday night.

Instead, he stepped lightly from the copter, and 6,000 people cheered his name.

"You belong in Cooperstown, Pete!" a woman yelled.

"Wouldn't be here then," Rose answered.

On the day Reggie Jackson became a Hall of Famer, Rose played baseball for the first time since 1986. He had been invited by Jim O'Toole to the game. After working out a few kinks that could only

169

be caused by the Hit King's nebulous stature in the game of baseball, Rose appeared in a white uniform with red and blue trim, a few pounds thicker than when he last chanced a jersey in public.

"They didn't have no door on that helicopter," Rose said. Usually, 3,000 fans gather for this game. Sunday night, there were twice that.

"We've missed you," longtime Reds TV announcer Ed Kennedy said over the PA. "I don't like snow," Rose said.

He lives in Florida. Boca Raton. Still sounds odd, even after four years. "My wife don't like snow."

Wittingly or not, Rose betrayed the trust of his hometown four years ago. He hasn't been here much since. Rose has been in Florida, making good on promises to be a good family man and businessman. Keeping clean the nose he still presses to the Cooperstown glass, waiting for someone to open the door.

"I'm doing the right things. I guess you could call it taking the high road," Rose said.

His son Tyler is 8, and he goes most places with Rose. He was there Sunday night. It is said Rose keeps with him a wallet-sized photo album, filled with pictures of Rose and his family. He'll show it to you if you ask.

He came to bat in the bottom of the first inning Sunday, just as the sun was sliding away from the terrace in left field and over the green painted wall. Rose hit left-handed. He was deep in the batter's box in that coiled, back-foot leaning scrunch. For an evening, Rose was Rose again, and it wouldn't have mattered if the old pitchers were throwing dinner up there.

It is not possible to erase the recent past with a stance, a swing and a line drive. But the distant, better memories are worth having, too. They came back last night, delivered by helicopter.

His first at-bat, Rose stroked a double to left-center field. It resembled closely Hit No. 4,192, made almost eight years ago, a liner that found the grass in the seam of the outfield between left and center. He batted twice more, Rose in the eternal Pete crouch, smacking line drives again.

"The wind's blowing in, and I haven't had batting practice in eight months. But I'll hit the ball," Rose had said. "I don't know where I'll hit it, but I'll hit the ball."

Rose had never wanted to play in an oldies game. One, because he was vain and aging pained him, and two, "I was always worried I'd hurt somebody. It don't matter where I play or how I bat, I hit the ball hard up the middle. I don't want to hit somebody in the nose with a line drive."

He went 2-for-3 in the five-inning game. It was his first game in seven years, and now you wonder when the next might be. Recently, someone asked Reggie Jackson about Rose and the Hall of Fame. "There's a piece of him that's not alive," Jackson said.

Rose returned to Florida Sunday night, exiting so quickly his appearance here seemed a mirage. The local hero took flight again. Cooperstown was miles in the opposite direction. So was Cincinnati.

Son of the Legend

May, 1997

He is close. This much he knows. Maybe this month, maybe next. Maybe September. "Pray somebody gets injured," is what his father tells him, only half-joking.

All this time. My goodness, so much time. Nine years, four organizations, 10 towns. Ten towns? He isn't sure. Let's see: Frederick, Erie, Sarasota, Columbus, Ga., and Kinston. Hickory, Birmingham and South Bend. Prince William, which isn't so much a town as an exurb of Washington, D.C., with, he recalls a great shopping mall. If he were a road, he'd be Route 66.

171

What is it they say? It's not the destination that matters, but the journey? Yes.

Nine years. Eighteen years old to 27. Boy to man, single to married, tears to cheers and back and forth. Bus to town to splintered dugout to bad-hop infield to Waffle House, the slumping batter's friend, where the food always comes with two or three hits, guaranteed.

His mother was there for him every step of the way, in person or on the phone, crying or laughing or yelling, there for him like no one else. His mother could star in an opera. His mother *is* an opera. "If I was down to my last hundred bucks and she needed it, I'd give it to her" is what he says.

To which she answers, "With him, I'm always first. It's a beautiful thing to be first in your son's life."

His father was there, too, mostly in thought and memory. It's a wonderful, painful thing, the father-son dynamic, never so deep and precarious as when he is the all-time hits leader and you are his son. You carry his name and his trademark tenacity, and his lovely gift of treasuring the game.

You look so much the way he did as a rookie, you'd swear the mirror had cracked and granted him 34 years of renewed youth.

He stays away, though. He hasn't seen you play this year.

But now, you are close. And you know, just know, that the day you walk onto the Cinergy Field turf, he will be there, in the stands. "No question," you say.

A life without pain and sadness isn't much of a life. Without it, you never appreciate the good. Pete Rose Jr., nine years into his baseball career, sweetly lugging his bittersweet heritage from here to there and back, hearing the hurtful bleats of ill-tempered drunks, wondering how many more gambling jokes he can take before the lid pops off his good nature, counting the days and the hits until somebody up here notices him down there, well, he appreciates the good.

Boy, does he ever.

"If I get called up, I'll never throw a piece of my uniform onto the floor," he says.

172

What?

"I'd never make Bernie Stowe pick up anything of mine." Stowe is the Reds equipment manager. "I'd never take a thing for granted up there. Ever."

There are people you wish to succeed in life, and people you don't. Most fall in between. If ever a person deserved to turn the copper of faith into the coin of reality, it is Peter Edward Rose Jr.

Says Bill Doran, a Reds roving instructor, "You pull for everybody. But boy, when you see a kid like that..."

And now, he is so close.

"I dream about it," Rose says.

"Well, sure," I say. "Everyone dreams about it."

"No, I mean I *dream* about it."

This is the dream: Pete Rose Jr. is taking batting practice at Cinergy Field. He's wearing white uniform pants and a red warm-up top with "ROSE 14" stitched on the back. Every ball he hits flies into the green-level seats.

Suddenly, he's in the dugout, and he can't read the lineup card. It's his first night here. Is he playing? "I can't tell," Rose says. Somebody tells him he needs to have his eyes checked.

Nine years in the minor leagues could do that to a man. I'm in the big leagues? Somebody read me the lineup. I don't believe my eyes.

But playing in the big leagues is all he ever wanted. "What would a shoemaker do if he couldn't make shoes?" Rose Jr. asks. "What would a Rose do if he couldn't play baseball?"

The nine-year wander was meant to do more than teach him the world is a good and suffering place. It had a purpose, to which he has devoted his entire life.

It's a lucky man who gets to do the only thing he ever wanted to do. Pete Rose Jr. is close.

He walked the halls of Oak Hills High wearing a Reds ballcap. He had a batting glove in each of his back pockets. He kept a bat in his car. That was when he went to school.

Some days, he didn't. He would ask his mother, the indomitable Karolyn Rose, if he could skip school and hit in the batting cage. In his front yard.

"Yes," Karolyn admits now. "I'm afraid I let him do that."

He'd hit all day. When it got dark, he wheeled his Chevy Blazer up, turned on its headlights, and hit some more.

Honest to Cupid: When Pete Rose Jr. asked his wife, Shannon, to go steady as a senior in high school, he was on the phone, gripping a lucky bat. "My dad's," he says. "An ATHL—All Time Hits Leader—Mizuno black bat. My dad used it in a game."

Rose still has the bat, but has not used it. He will break it out the day the Reds bring him up, for his first at-bat only. "After that, I'll never use it again," he says.

Sometimes, loving your dad feels more like an obligation than an emotion. For Pete Rose Jr., it amounts to both. After divorcing Karolyn, remarrying, being expelled from baseball, moving to Florida and starting a new family, Pete Sr. hasn't had much time for his son.

Says Karolyn, "My son's father was the greatest hitter ever. The greatest *ever*. And he doesn't take the time.

"I don't think (Pete Sr.) knows how to converse with him. How to say 'good game' or 'you're not swinging level.' It hurts me, because Big Pete should be paying more attention to his son."

The elder Rose did not answer repeated phone messages for this story.

Junior has talked recently with his dad. In a small slump, he received some advice over the phone. "Spread out," Senior advised. "Try to hit the ball the other way. Stay back. And keep your same approach."

Petey acknowledges the hurtful distance between his life and his father's. It is as wide as 4,256 hits. It may never be closed. But he honors his father. He endures his father's legacy, in doses large enough to still a lesser man.

Three times in his first two years as a pro, Petey had to go home, for breaks from heckling fans. Karolyn recalls a conversation she had

174

with one heckler, at Frederick, Md., in Petey's first season:

"He was waving dollar bills and hollering," she says. "I said, 'Hey, numbnuts. You got two things you can do. Hit the pavement, or take your best shot at me.'"

He still gets it. "You hear the same old things. *Hey Pete, there's a casino right down the road. Hey, Pete, I bet you can't do this or that.'* I used to come home and cry. Now, I block it out. Those people aren't worth it," Rose says.

You wonder what some sons might do, faced with a wrath they did not inspire. You guess at the twin conflicts of burden and inspiration that a famous father can bring to bear on his first-born son. You wonder how a kid can do this for nine seasons in the backwater and still come back for more, never with bitterness. Not with Rose Jr., though. You don't wonder. Because he is some kid. You know what he does. You can see it.

He is standing at his position, third base, for the first time of the night. He hops on the bag, and off. He kneels down behind the base, draws in the dirt with his right index finger: "4,256." He circles the number.

He does it every night. Every Southern League ballpark bears the tribute son offers father. "My dad can't be on the field," Junior says, "only with that, he is. He's on the field every time I am."

The great thing about it is, Big Pete doesn't even know his son does it. Says Karolyn, "He's proud of his father. But he wants to be Pete Rose. Why can't people give him that? My son is a self-made man."

Just like his father. He plays the game with passion. He has some wide-eyed kid in him. He runs out pop-ups like a 7-year-old chasing an ice cream truck. Just like his father.

"It's nice to see," says Rose's Chattanooga manager Mark Berry. "There's not a lot of guys like him left. Every flyball this kid hits, he's on a dead sprint to second base."

His father never got cheated. Not in baseball. Not one day, one at-bat, one pitch. So it is with son. It is the good, pure part of the legacy.

175

"I'll keep playing as long as I've got a uniform," Petey says.

Perseverance is what it is, whether you are chasing Ty Cobb or a bus to Huntsville. Maybe Pete Jr.'s pursuit, unadorned as it is by the rewards of major league glory, is the purer of the two. Nine years. Maybe it offers the larger lesson.

There is irony, too, if you're looking. Junior and Senior have arrived, over time, at the same place: Noses pressed against Major League Baseball's window, hoping someone will let them in. More irony: Junior is likely closer to admission now than Senior is.

"The way he's swinging now, he could play anywhere," Berry says. It's not a universal sentiment.

By June 5, Rose was hitting .319. Off-season workouts helped him add 20 pounds; he has 11 home runs and 39 RBI hitting cleanup for the Lookouts. But the Reds see Aaron Boone as a better third base prospect. They see Rose as a September call-up. Rose has a good feel for his own destiny.

"He hopes to become a utility guy," says Rose's agent, Brian Goldberg. "He feels there have been enough late bloomers that he still has a shot (but) he harbors no illusions."

Rose does wonder about the politics of the game, though. "Mike Kelly's up there. He's a good player. But he can play up there, I can play up there."

Chances are, he will. Karolyn Rose isn't sure what she'll do when that comes. She hasn't been to the stadium since September 11, 1985, the night the elder Rose broke Cobb's record.

"I don't know how I'll handle the emotions of it," she says. She struggles with the sentiment she feels for the good years, and the bitterness she has toward Pete Sr. for what she sees as his neglect of Pete Jr.

"I was a single parent my entire marriage," she says.

"If I was Pete Rose, I'd say to my son, 'Come down to Florida in the winter. We'll go to the batting cages.' I know he's not allowed on the field. But he could sit in the stands. Petey didn't get a divorce from his father. *I'm* the one who asked for the divorce."

176

He is so close. If Junior's rise to the big leagues after all this time brings together a tangle of jagged emotions, it's still better than not having the experience at all. A life without pain isn't much of a life.

It is remarkable, given Petey's heritage and own, middling success, that he still plays baseball because it's what he wants to do most. And he is close. This much he knows.

"Just to go into the locker room where my dad played," he says. "Hopefully, they'll give me his locker. I believe it's going to happen. I really do. I don't want it to be because of who I am. I want it because I can play."

If attitude made the big leagues, every player would be Pete Rose Jr., and we'd all love the game as much as we once did. When he says, "I'm proud to be who I am. I'm glad to be playing baseball," you want to build him a monument, stick it under every major leaguer's nose and say, "This. This is what it should be about."

Mostly, the honor is in the striving. The truth is in the time put in honestly, with little reward. From the nine-year crucible of expectations, comparisons, cat-calls and wandering, Pete Rose Jr. has emerged a truly honorable man. You'd be amazed at the character forged in towns like Frederick and Kinston and Chattanooga.

Inside the bill of his cap, Rose has written this: *I Can. I Will. I Am.* "I can play in the big leagues. I will play in the big leagues. I am going to stay in the big leagues," Rose says. This is what it means.

Someday, maybe soon, he will run to third base at Cinergy Field, touch the bag, kneel and draw with his index finger in the dirt: 4,256. And for a day, Pete Rose Sr. will be back in the big leagues. Right by his son.

And wouldn't that be something.

Karolyn's Sweet Ride

September 2, 1997

*T*he ride to a dream should be done this way: In a long, black limousine, 5-inch color TV by your right elbow, cellular telephone across the leather acreage of your luxury seat.

A man named Clarence is chauffeuring Karolyn Rose to the ballgame. This is right and good. Also safe, because Karolyn is in the limo, trying to paint her nails red and her lips pink with hands that are sweaty and shaking. Wouldn't want her to be behind the wheel, tooling down Fort Washington Way. Somebody could get hurt.

"It's starting to get to me now," she says. "I'm starting to get sick to my stomach."

Twenty years ago, when she was still Mrs. Hit King, Karolyn would drive to K mart in a Rolls Royce. "They'd see me coming," she says, "and they'd say, 'Quick, turn out the blue lights!' They knew I liked the specials."

On Monday, she arrived at Cinergy Field in the limo. It was her first game there in nearly 12 years. Her son Pete was starting at third base. You might have heard. "To be able to go down to my seat and have him look up at me," she says. "That's my moment."

Karolyn was emoting like only Karolyn can. "I remember when he was a little boy," she says. Seven years old, Karolyn guesses. At spring training.

"He'd help Bernie (Stowe, the Reds equipment manager) clean and stack the players' spikes." Petey was paid for the job, and he asked for his money in a white envelope, the way the players received theirs.

With his earnings, he spent $20 on a pair of Joe Morgan's cleats. "I can still see him with those things. He wore 'em to bed," Karolyn says.

The Reds chewed tobacco, so Junior chewed black licorice. Once,

Doug Flynn and Mike Lum gave him bubble gum with tobacco stuffed inside. Petey, believing he could be like a major leaguer without suffering some consequences, dived in.

"Come get me, mom," he said soon enough. "I'm sick."

The stories rolled on. The limo eased downtown, past Fountain Square and down to Pete Rose Way.

Some people get what they deserve, some people get what they don't, and some get both. This Rose family—mother, Hit King, son—has gotten it all, and then some.

What a strange, wonderful day. What an odd mix of triumph and sadness. The son with zero lifetime hits receives the standing ovation. The father with 4,256 is not allowed on the field.

Rose Junior holds a postgame news conference in the same room his father reacted to his ban from baseball; Rose Senior conducts his press conference outside the stadium, in the players parking lot.

Junior scrawls "4,256" in the third base dirt. Junior uses Senior's black Mizuno bat his first time up, the same model Senior used to set the hits record. Waiting on his first pitch, he crouches low in the batter's box, weight on his back foot. "The Hit King mode," he calls it.

The Hit King says he got stuck in traffic on the way to the game. This bizarre coming together of father and son, in the city that treasures each . . . it was more like a class reunion than a ballgame.

Junior on the field, and in the dressing room he used as a playground when a child. Junior a big leaguer. Senior, sitting in the stands, still on baseball's black list, outside the circle, nose pressed against the window.

"We're talking about it," is what Senior says about that. "The ball's rolling. Today don't hurt me."

Junior welcomed warmly. Labor Day, for a kid who knows what that means.

Senior, hoping for a reprieve.

Karolyn, somewhere in the middle, living the day of her life.

"Gimme the beer," she says, to no one and everyone. "Gimme the pretzels."

179

When they announce her son's first at-bat, she cries. Then she says, "We could go to Philadelphia. He's playing in Philadelphia next week. We could drive."

Honor the Player; Punish the Gambler

September 30, 1997

*I*t's interesting how baseball gets religion when the subject is Pete Rose.

Baseball's recent past is stained by jaywalkers and wife stalkers. It is weighted by the occasional Albert Belle. It is fat with men who demand millions in raises, then claim "it's not about the money." It is run by Bud Selig, who canceled the World Series.

Pete Rose has applied for reinstatement to the game. He wishes to be a party to all of this again. He must have his reasons. After eight years of pressing his nose to the glass, Rose has decided to knock politely on the window. He'd like to know what, exactly, the game still has against him after years of living the exile's life.

I'm not sure why Rose has waited until now to request reinstatement, or why baseball still views him as a leper. But neither Rose nor the game is going away, a trait they share with taxes and the common cold.

Has Rose really "reconfigured" his life, as Bart Giamatti advised him to do? Beats me. Who judges that? Selig? Come on.

Selig runs baseball's executive committee. These executives couldn't agree that two plus two equals four. Poor Pete, held hostage by a bunch of guys who have put a shine to the phrase "gross incompetence." To those of us not as smart as Bart Giamatti, "reconfigured" means "keep your nose clean." Has Rose done that?

He still goes to the track. He still signs his name to anything inanimate. He signs in Cooperstown the day before the Hall of Fame inductions. He often does his radio show in Las Vegas. He used his son's Major League debut to promote his own reinstatement. Shameless.

But as eye-rolling as this stuff is, none of it is very damning. It's just Pete, being who he is.

Rose is no more deleterious to baseball's "image"—such as it is—than Wil Cordero or Tony Phillips or the knaves who run the game and own the teams.

That said, Rose does not belong back in baseball. Not now. Not ever. But he does belong in the Hall of Fame.

Rose bet on baseball. Anyone who doubts it is delusional. You can't have someone like that involved with running a team.

Rules can't be selective. They can't apply to everyone but someone with 4,256 hits. The rules say if you bet on the game, you are no longer a part of it.

By insisting on his innocence, Rose has backed himself against a wall he may not escape. If he admits to betting on baseball, maybe he's never reinstated. If he cops a guilty plea, feel free to question his sincerity.

Rose is done inside the game. A man lives long enough, he wears the face he deserves. But he also gets his due, and no one is more due of a place in Cooperstown than Rose. It's easy to separate Rose the ballplayer from Rose the gambler, and that is what should be done.

Remove the lifetime ban that keeps him from the Hall. Eliminate the self-righteous baseball hypocrisy that says, "We're too good to admit a man like that into our most exclusive fraternity." Because you're not. Obviously.

Think of the fans. That'd be a switch. Just guessing, but when parents take their kids to Cooperstown, they probably don't say, "And over here's Babe Ruth's plaque, son. He was a fine citizen."

Put Rose's plaque up next to Ty Cobb's, if that makes you feel better. Two examples of baseball's eternal commitment to morality and altruism, side by side.

Declare that while Rose is no longer in baseball, he most assuredly is of it. None but the petty and the pompous believe Rose's achievements as a player are diminished by his actions as a person. Lots of bad guys are great players; few are punished to the extent Rose has been.

The definition of a hero, as we have seen, is flexible. Rose heroically played the game. That should be enough to get him in the Hall of Fame.

Admit him now, and be done with it. Baseball is bigger than Pete Rose. So are its problems.

8

Politically Indecent

"Son, if you're interested in business, politics, law, illegal pharmaceuticals, and semi-automatic weapons, you really ought to consider a career in sportswriting."
—*Paul Daugherty*

Big Kat Exposes Sham

September 6, 1998

*M*organtown, West Virginia—Andy Katzenmoyer is eligible. Everyone knew he would be. All it cost Ohio State's stud middle linebacker was a little ridicule and a lot of mindless public scrutiny.

Now we know that the Big Kat is proficient in Golf and Music. He is AIDS Aware. Here is what universities need to know:

There is a difference between students and athletes. Universities need to make the distinction clear. If they determine the millions of dollars and priceless publicity athletes produce for them are a good thing, they need to recognize athletes are as important to the general, ivy-covered welfare as honor students.

Then, they need to cut the jocks some slack.

Do we publicize the straight-A chemistry major that cannot throw a spiral? Do we recognize the English Lit major's deficiencies in running, jumping or throwing?

Do we test them for drugs? Do we allow the number of times they take entrance exams to become public knowledge?

This is not an apology for Andy Katzenmoyer. OSU coach John Cooper said Katzenmoyer became an academic what-if because he didn't go to enough classes last winter. After football season ended, the Big Kat checked out of any classroom that didn't have a film projector or a whirlpool.

And you can bet that once this season is ended, Katzenmoyer will be even less attentive to his books. Probably, he will decide to enter the NFL draft, in which case, why does he need Shakespeare or square roots?

But this notion of jocks as students needs to stop. It is the NCAA's core hypocrisy. It is the business of jamming square pegs into round holes. It embarrasses schools and athletes. It is unnecessary.

184

I have written this half a dozen times, almost as much as I've urged a football playoff. Here it is again:

An athlete should have the option of majoring in his sport.

If he is Andy Katzenmoyer, he should be allowed to declare a football major. He should get credit for games and practices and film study. He should take courses in subjects relevant to his major: Coaching, refereeing, physical education.

He should be given instruction in life skills such as finance and money management. So many star players leave college without even the most basic skills. That's why they lean on agents to do their bidding. Negotiating a contract is something they should learn while they're in school.

Here are some things athletes should not have to learn:

That they are expected to be students, similar to everyone else. They're not everyone else, not until everyone else practices 20 hours a week and rolls out of bed Sunday morning feeling like a boulder fell on their spleens.

They should not take courses simply to stay eligible for sports. What did Katzenmoyer get from AIDS Awareness that he didn't already know?

"He needed to take courses he could be successful in," Buckeyes athletic director Andy Geiger said.

Fine. But make them relevant to his career choices. How about a course in athletic training? Maybe then, the next time someone asks him to play in pain or take a shot, he'll know what he's getting into.

Jocks shouldn't be open for public ridicule because they are not students. They don't claim to be; the NCAA "member institutions" do it for them. They have a talent that is equal to—or in Katzenmoyer's case, superior to—the academic skills of the normal student.

Geiger told the *New York Times*, "A musician who plays tenor sax and wanted to be a jazz player had to learn in clubs and bars. Now they can go to a school of music and get a degree in jazz. We've never accepted sports the same way."

If colleges don't mind profiting from the Katzenmoyers of the

185

world, they should make allowance for their unique abilities. They should cut the sham of student-athleticism.

Let Katzenmoyer major in football. Perhaps he'll get an education.

Why Pay Dues?

May 18, 1997

*T*he question is really whether you want to be around people who don't want to be around you. That's what clubs are all about.

Ohio legislators, in a bit of can't-lose do-good-ism, want to make sure private clubs don't discriminate. In the case of country clubs, they'd like it if all of us were free to make a nine on the first hole of the annual member-guest event. Equal access for everyone, to the pond guarding the 18th green.

Great. But who wants to be in a place where he feels out of place?

I worked at Congressional Country Club, site of this year's United States Open, for eight summers. I was a waiter. Occasionally, when members wanted service, they'd snap their fingers at me.

I did not want to associate with these people. I wanted to dump ravioli in their laps.

I wouldn't belong to an exclusive club. I wouldn't belong to any club where a jacket is required to enter the grill room. I wouldn't belong to a club that had a grill room.

Those places require a measure of personal pretense that's beyond me. If their members are OK with that, good for them. Personally, I'll eat my *foie gras* with my own buds. If I want to go somewhere I'm not wanted, I'll go to the Reds clubhouse.

This is what has me puzzled by this need for governmental

interference. Or, in Deborah Kline's case, legal muscle.

Deborah Kline never saw herself as a pioneer or a trailblazer or an enemy of every heathen male who has ever played poker on an oak and velvet table in a country club men's grill. She just wanted to golf with her husband and son on weekends.

She couldn't do that at Terrace Park Country Club, where the only golfers allowed on weekends were men.

So Kline took it to court in 1993, and finally won last May. She is now a voting member at Terrace Park. She can golf whenever she likes. But who wants to golf with people who don't want to golf with them? Aren't clubs, by nature and definition, exclusive? You don't form a club intending to offer universal membership. If you did, what would be the point of the club?

Argues Al Gerhardstein, Kline's lawyer in the Terrace Park case: Country clubs "are really VFW halls for the rich."

Yup. And your point is?

The whole notion of a club is to keep people out that you don't want. Which, in lots of cases, works perfectly well. I never felt any urge to become a Daughter of the American Revolution. I was not a Brownie. Somehow, my life is fairly full.

If Congressional invited me to join now, I'd agree only if I could kick out everyone who currently belongs.

Despite Kline's victory, country clubs will always be exclusive, until the day they stop charging dues.

Equal access at Terrace Park or anywhere else comes to those with the cash to pay for it. Those with money are more equal than those without. Which we've pretty much figured all along.

Shoal Creek, the club in Alabama that played host to the PGA Championship several years ago, ran afoul of mainstream opinion because it had no minority members, nor much intention of seeking or accepting any.

Was that stupid? Yes. Illegal? Yes again. The club changed its policies, as did Augusta National, site of the Masters.

If I'd been excluded from Shoal Creek, so what? I wouldn't have wanted to belong there, anyway. I'd have seen them as silly bigots and dropped my $50,000 initiation fee elsewhere.

Deborah Kline says her effort at Terrace Park was worth the fight. "It is a lot better," she says. "They recognize all women as members."

Meanwhile at Hyde Park Country Club, women still aren't allowed tee times between 11:45 and 1:30 Tuesday through Fridays; they can't get on the course before noon on holidays.

These women shouldn't fight silly Hyde Park CC, though.

They should quit and apply for membership at Terrace Park.

Court of Peeves and Extended Snits

October 22, 1995

tlanta—Let's get something straight: The social significance of Atlanta Braves versus Cleveland Indians is limited to boxscores. We are not attempting something of lasting global effect here, and thank goodness for that. We are playing games.

The impact of the tomahawk chop on the lives of American Indians is absolutely none. Lord help a country that applies social significance to Albert Belle.

They are here again. The protestors. Well-intended Native Americans are seeking an end to the use of their people as mascots for sports teams. "Messages of racism," one man called them. His name was Cleto Montelongo. He claimed to be a Cherokee Indian. An elder in his clan.

At 5 p.m. Saturday, Montelongo stood on the plaza at Atlanta-Fulton County Stadium and let his anger run. "They are having a good time at the expense of our culture," he said. "As long as America

188

continues to show us as monkeys and clowns, we are nothing."

Behind him, a woman held aloft a poster on which team pennants had been drawn. The New York Jews. The San Antonio Latinos. The Chicago Blacks. "No other race of people is disrespected in this fashion," Montelongo said.

No argument there. If you choose to see Braves and Indians and tomahawk chopping as means of invoking malicious, deliberate disrespect against the first Americans.

I don't see it that way. I don't think most people do. Judging from the sparse turnout of Native Americans at the pre-game rally Saturday, neither do the supposedly offended people themselves.

I see it as 50,000 people expressing their loyalty to their favorite team in the currently popular manner. I don't think anybody has any ill feelings about Native Americans. But I can understand the outrage.

We have digressed to the point in this county where everyone is always angry, no one is able to laugh at himself and you cannot have frank discussion without being labeled a bigot. The level of discourse has descended to the symbolic.

At least one newspaper in this great land has eliminated all references to Braves and Indians from its pages. The *Star-Tribune* in Minneapolis now refers to the two clubs as "the team from Atlanta" and "the team from Cleveland."

That's workable, in a ponderous sort of way, but way too cumbersome. Why not the Atlanta Flaming Janes? Why not the Cleveland Frozen Tundra Soot-Breathers?

What about inventing one of those groovy symbols, like the one now used by the artist who used to call himself Prince? At least it would save space. Even if no one knew what the hell you were writing about.

Personally, I'm in an extended snit over the University of Notre Dame's insistence on calling its sports teams the Fighting Irish. Being 100 percent, dyed-in-the-Guinness Irish, I'm more than a little peeved.

Why not the Notre Dame Noble Pacifists? Why not the Notre Dame Nurturing Hibernians?

Oh, the insensitivity.

Also: Must they maintain that little green leprechaun twit as a mascot? That guy couldn't go three rounds with PeeWee Herman. As I am neither a fighter nor green, I object to this casual and demeaning stereotype of me and my ancestors.

As long as America continues to portray us Irish as short, green, fighting twits, we will never get the respect we deserve. I think it's degrading and disrespectful and, of course, racist. Isn't everything racist now? Set my people free, I say.

Meanwhile, I read of the tragedy of the Indian reservations. Poverty, crime, illiteracy, substance abuse, unemployment. I wonder how much an Indian man in South Dakota who can't find a job cares about people who buy foam rubber tomahawks in Georgia.

If he could choose, I wonder if the high school dropout with a needle in his arm would pick a new start in his life, or a new nickname for the Indians.

I wonder why Cleto Montelongo doesn't wonder more about that.

No Love for the Brickyard

May 27, 1989

I hate the Indianapolis 500. I hate the Brickyard. I'd rather poke myself in the eye with a dipstick than endure another checkered flag.

I hate wasting a day off to drive to Indianapolis to pick up my press pass. They won't mail it, because they need me to sign a piece of paper that says if I get close enough to a speeding race car to die in a thrilling, fiery explosion, it's not their fault.

190

I wouldn't get that close. I hate race cars.

I hate getting up at 5 in the morning on race day to get into the Brickyard, so I can wait around half a day for an event I hate.

It's because of the crowds. I hate the crowds. Every year, about 400,000 alleged people worm into the Indianapolis Motor Speedway. Some 75,000 cases of arrested development wriggle into the infield. I hate the infield.

Who sees the 500 in the infield? Who cares? The infield makes Woodstock look like a tropical vacation. To sit in the infield, you need $15 and proof you're a Homo sapien. Every year, lots of creatures with $15 are turned away.

"They'll put people in there as long as they can get 'em in," says track spokesman Bob Laycock. "They start gathering the night before. There's no place else to go, so they just line 'em up someplace outside the gates."

And what? Shoot 'em?

Gee, this sounds like terrific fun. Next time I get the urge, I'll gather 20,000 of my closest friends and sit in a submarine for a few hours.

If you are rejected for infield space—which is a lot like being deemed unfit for latrine duty—take heart.

You can approximate the Indy infield experience at home by hosing down your backyard, wearing your worst clothes, drinking cheap domestic beer, playing heavy metal or country tapes at a decibel level that would reverse the Amazon River and doing doughnuts through your wife's petunias in your 4-wheel drive. Vroom.

By the end of the day, you will be drunk, sick, deaf and unconscious. This is the essence of the Indy experience.

I hate the race. I hate sitting in the treehouse press box and craning my neck back and forth to catch the "action."

Anyone who finds it entertaining to watch a few dozen automobiles go around in circles for three hours must also appreciate TV test patterns, anthropology lectures and meetings of the city planning board.

191

I hate the track announcer. He talks constantly, usually to shill for this motor oil or that engine additive. That's if you can hear him. Usually, the "action" is so loud, you can't.

I hate the advertising. Breakfast by Marlboro, lunch by Pennzoil. Smoke these Winston cigarettes, drink this Valvoline orange juice, wear this Pontiac badge, drive this STP race car. The official sponsor of the Indianapolis 500 is hype.

I hate the whole scene. I hate the jargon. I hate it when some guy with enough 30-weight beneath his fingernails to fry 56 chickens tells me a car's out of the race because it's front wing adjuster failed.

Front what?

I hate Indianapolis. It is Detroit without the tuneup. I drive into Indianapolis on a road that has more liquor stores than people. I hate driving on all those freeways. Take 74 to 465 to 64 to...take a wrong turn, you're in Chicago.

You'd think a town famous for an oval race track wouldn't have pretzel freeways. I hate Indianapolis.

I hate the thrill of the Indianapolis 500 because thrill at Indy is a code word for death. People like this race and this sport partly because it flirts with disaster. "Pushing the outside of the envelope" Tom Wolfe called it.

In his book, *The Right Stuff*, Wolfe wrote about military test pilots pushing the outside of the envelope. Their objective was to fly faster. If that implied a certain increase in risk, so be it. Fear was inherent in pushing the outside of the envelope. So was death.

Some of Indy's appeal is wrapped up in the same morbid fascination. How fast is too fast? How fast before someone's car "gets upside down" as the stock drivers say? How fast before someone dies?

Rick Mears set a track record, qualifying for the pole position with an average speed of 223.885 miles an hour over four laps.

Isn't that great? Soon enough, someone will discover that his race car has too much technology, that the good ol' Brickyard oval wasn't meant to handle such speeds.

That lucky someone will wind up in a wreck that will make the usual Indy G-forces seem like a back rub. He'll be dead. Won't that be thrilling?

I hate it when people refer to Indy as sport. Come on. The guy with the best machine usually wins, right? A driver could pop a hamstring and win the 500, but he couldn't pop an engine rod. If this is a sport, so is a tractor pull.

I hate tractor pulls.

Costing out The Big Mike

I called Len the termite guy. A few years ago, termites were eating my house. Len killed them all dead. First, he came out and gave me an estimate on what all the murdering might cost. It was $1,400. I said OK. Make 'em disappear.

Len's bill came. It was $1,452.

"So, Len," I said Thursday. "What would happen if you made a habit of giving people $1,400 estimates to kill termites dead, then presented them with a bill for, oh, $3,000?"

"I wouldn't have a job," Len said.

I called Bob the tree guy. I needed someone to cut down some dead trees, and a giant hickory limb living over the back of my house. Bob estimated the job would cost $350. I said, OK, fine. Bob's bill was $328.

"Bob," I said. "If you estimated $350 and the actual bill was, oh, $800, how long would you be in business?"

Bob said, "Not very long."

"If the job is going to be a lot more than the estimate, I call back and say it's going to be a lot more," Bob said. "Then they tell me if they still want me to do it."

"So," I wondered, "you mean an estimate is a reasonable and educated guess as to how much a job is supposed to cost?"

Bob said, "Yes, sir. That's right."

"Interesting," I said.

My heating/cooling man is named Adam. Adam has fixed my air conditioning in the heat of the moment. No estimates. When it's 95 and feels like Guam in the bedroom, you don't mess with estimates.

Still, I asked Adam, "What happens if a job ends up costing you a whole lot more than what you estimated to the customer?"

"I have underbid jobs," Adam said. "The thing to do is get the work done and keep a smile on your face. You eat the job and act like it tastes good."

The bill for the Bengals stadium used to be $245 million, and now it is $400 million. And now I am waiting for Hamilton County to produce a knife and a fork. Because it doesn't matter what the commissioners say or how they say it, there is a difference between $245 million and $400 million that nobody bargained for.

We were had. We believed that the original cost was an estimate. In the real world, estimates usually end up being close to what we pay. This Bengals stadium, though. It's just a whole different deal.

John, my mechanic, was on the line. "John, if I came in for a clutch and you wrote me an estimate for $400, could you add a transmission to the bill without my approval?"

"Nope," John said. In fact, Ohio law prohibits auto repair shops from charging any more than 10 percent more than an estimate. Maybe we should extend that to apply to counties building stadiums with public money.

I feel stupid today. I feel like I've signed every blank check in my account and turned them all over to Bob Bedinghaus and Mike Brown. I feel like I've just walked into a showroom and paid $100,000 for a Maserati, then had the salesman say, "Oh, you wanted an engine with that?"

I don't care about inflation or land acquisition costs or prevailing wage laws. We agreed to build the Bengals a palace. We should have been offered the simple decency of knowing approximately what it was going to cost us.

All of it.

What we know now is the cost of Paul Brown Stadium—hereafter known in this space as the Mike Mahal, or simply, The Big Mike—is rising faster than the Dow. And we're stuck with the bill.

If it's $400 million today, what might it be tomorrow?

It's unconscionable. It's unreasonable. It's just incredibly, amazingly arrogant. And it's wrong.

The only guy who's smiling today is Tim Mara, the man who fought the sales tax and predicted the current calamity. To him, I say, "Can I wash your feet or something?"

Me, I feel taken.

Adam, the AC man said this: "I don't know. When I give somebody an estimate, I usually stick with it."

Good for you, Adam. Do you do stadiums?

The Allure of Killing Deer

November 10, 1988

*F*rom the trunk of the car, you could see all four of the big deer's legs. They were stiff and sticking straight up. If you plopped a slab of oak on top of them, you'd have a very nice table.

The 15-mile trip along Route 28 Friday morning, between Milford and Blanchester, yielded four more deer sightings. Three deer were in the backs of pickup trucks; a fourth was tied to the roof of a

Land Rover. All were quite dead.

In Ohio, the six days a year we can kill deer with guns ends today. The state division of wildlife is optimistic that hunters will have killed more deer than ever this year. With luck, the total will exceed 100,000. The more, the better. It seems there are just too many of the pesky critters roaming our state.

The deer are running wild. They are along the highways and in the backyards, eating the shrubs and the flowers and, who knows, helping themselves to the Bibb lettuce at Kroger.

This is the argument the hunters use. The deer are everywhere, a veritable plague. They must be stopped.

Living in the rugged, untamed wilds of metro Cincinnati, I somehow have never crossed paths with a single deer. I am in the minority. Give 'em a few years free of shotgun blasts, and they'd be taking over our neighborhoods. This is what I hear.

The hunters kill the deer as a public service.

No. That's not it. Hunters "harvest" deer, so as to make the act seem benign. Deer are a crop. You know how it goes: In the spring, farmers plant corn, wheat, beans, and deer.

Hunters harvest deer to "manage" the wildlife population. Otherwise, Bambi might be out there menacing our streets and ransoming our children for an extra ear of Silver Queen white. There are, in some places, "shooting preserves," though what shooting preserves hasn't struck me yet. In publications devoted to hunting, frequent mention is made of "serious" hunters. Help us if there is any other kind.

Hunters consider themselves "sportsmen." This is a curious conceit, seeing as how most deer don't pack guns. Give a buck a 12-gauge, then we'd have ourselves a sport. *Webster's New Universal Unabridged Dictionary* says a sportsman is someone "who treats his opponents with fairness, generosity and courtesy."

Forgive me, Rudolph, while I spray you with buckshot.

It would be sporting to report that every deer that is shot is actually killed, or that every killer dresses the deer and takes the meat home to the freezer. When the state reports 100,000 deer killed, it isn't counting those that leave the glorious harvest gutshot or missing a leg.

It would also be enlightening if I had ever actually witnessed an attack of the killer does, on a deadly rampage through the swingsets and tulip beds of suburbia. Then maybe I'd understand the need to manage the menace.

In a fabulous bit of twisted logic, hunters will suggest that they are actually conservationists, and that without hunters thinning the deer ranks, the poor creatures would starve to death.

Hunters kill deer, so deer can live.

Apply that logic all the way up and down the Darwinian line, and see where it takes you.

I met a guy Friday, at a place where hunters go to check their deer. He runs a sporting goods store in Milford. His name was Dave Spurlock, 57 years old, a lifelong hunter, and everything he told me about hunting made sense. Until he talked about pulling the trigger. Then he lost me.

He said deer have no natural predators now. No wolves and only a few coyotes. Coyotes know when a doe is ready to give birth, he said; they will pounce then. It is a natural way of controlling the herd, and which is better? A deer killed by a 12-gauge, or by a hungry coyote?

Without natural enemies, deer reproduce like, well, rabbits. State wildlife people claim there are as many deer in the state now as there have ever been. Spurlock said," When I was a kid, you couldn't find a deer in Ohio." Now, by state count, there are 400,000 or more. That's good wildlife management, Spurlock said.

He also knows a guy whose brand new Jeep Cherokee recently had an unpleasant encounter at 55 mph with a buck. More than $7,000 later, the guy still had a leaky radiator. I suppose if a buck front-ended my Cherokee, I'd want to hunt down his whole family.

And I have been convinced, over the years, that there are many more responsible hunters than not. Just like with anything else.

But here's the thing: If the greatest enjoyment in hunting comes from simply being in the country—and this is what most sane hunters will tell you—then why not pack a Nikon or a Minolta instead of a Winchester?

It makes you think people kill deer because they like killing. Who can defend that?

The Sad Lot of Scholarship Athletes

December 13, 1994

*I*t's chic to lament the sad lot of scholarship athletes. These poor, used kids. They make millions for their schools and get nothing in return. All those hurdlers, rifle teamers and golfers, making the university cash register sing, receiving zero.

It's an awful life. A real struggle. Why, we're taking advantage of them.

Well, no. We're not. Here's what we're doing:

—Giving a fair number of academically underqualified people a chance to go to college for free.

—Taking scholarships from people who really want to be there, and giving them to people who really don't.

—Creating a caste system where high-profile athletes are both exalted and scrutinized beyond the norm.

Lots of basketball players leave school after two, three or four years, with no degree, or much intention of ever getting one. Somebody is being chumped there, absolutely: The school.

Ah, but these kids make money for their universities. Well, no. Not unless they play football or men's basketball or, in a very few places, women's basketball. Athletic departments all over scramble to

198

break even while funding non-revenue sports. No school makes a killing fielding a volleyball team.

But athletes deserve to be paid. As it is, they're nothing more than slaves.

Sure they are. Go, slave, and toil for millions in the NFL or NBA. If you can't make that grade, go make some others, in the classrooms where someone is trying to help you with a more realistic future.

If you don't want to do that, don't blame the NCAA. Find a mirror.

If you really want to pay jocks, swell. Who gets paid? How much?

Base it on the revenues they bring to the school, you say? OK. Pay Danny Fortson, UC basketball star, several thousand dollars a month. Charge Mr. or Ms. Swimmer a fee to swim, because they are taking from the treasury, not supplementing it.

But does the swimmer work any less diligently than Fortson? Fewer hours, less sacrifice? Probably not.

So pay them. Go ahead. You figure out how. And be sure to make it fair.

Because as everyone knows, the current system just isn't fair.

The NCAA does silly things. Parents of athletes should not have to pay their way to an NCAA basketball tournament game. On Senior Day, mom and dad should be flown in and put up in a nice hotel. This isn't an "inducement." It's decency.

Athletes should have the same rights and responsibilities as the rest of the student body. They should be allowed to work. They shouldn't be drug tested. Their test-taking abilities should not be held so closely to the public light. They shouldn't be stereotyped as "dumb jocks."

Unless they are quoted saying "the kids aren't getting anything" as a local women's basketball player was this week. Someone needs to grab her by her insouciance, show her some classrooms, swing her by the bookstore, take her to her dorm room and the cafeteria and let her see all the nothing she's getting. My parents, who paid for me to go to school, would have been delighted with all that nothing.

199

I did a column once, comparing the non-payment of basketball players at UC and Xavier to what I made as a college senior, working in the cafeteria dishroom. I estimated the hours they spent practicing, playing and traveling. I divided it into the value of their full rides.

Guess what? Their nothing beat my hourly wage all to hell.

But that's not the worst of all this. What's awful about the persistent whine for money is, it's saying a college education is worthless. It's suggesting that the value of learning can only be measured by the almighty buck. We're not getting paid for it; therefore, it's not worth our time.

I'd love to find a Division I athlete who thinks playing sports is a good deal. This would be someone with the wisdom to realize what he or she gets from athletics doesn't have to be measured in coins.

Dedication, discipline, sacrifice, perseverance. Sports can teach those. They're nice little life lessons.

They make you a better person. At some point, they just might help you make more money as well.

If that's all you care about.

Which, hopefully, it's not.

Bury the Athlete-as-Role-Model

August 7, 1990

*T*he next time a player is pulled over for breaking the sound barrier in his Maserati or tossing an autograph-hound through a plate-glass window or attempting to snort a baseline, someone will decide athletes are no longer the Boy Scouts they evidently used to be. They are no longer fit to serve as role models for our youth.

200

Oh, the horror.

It is amazing that anyone can still equate strength and speed with grace and virtue. It's astounding we still expect jocks to perform like Superman and behave like Clark Kent. Old clichés never die. Some don't even fade away.

I suppose at some long-ago point, it made sense for kids to look up at athletes with the same glazed admiration reserved for mothers, fathers, teachers and clergymen. That time is done. It expired sometime after Joe Namath's first Brut commercial and before Jim Bouton wrote *Ball Four*.

Athletes are not role models. Athletes *need* role models.

Athletes act illegal, immorally and selfishly. They act like most of the rest of us. Yet we insist on holding them to a higher standard, as if high-average hand-eye coordination and 100 mph fastball somehow bestow righteousness.

The subject arises because Reds pitcher Tom Browning had a marijuana cigarette in his truck and New York Mets outfielder Vince Coleman injured a toddler with an M-100 explosive. The role model theorists would have you believe Browning and Coleman are corrupting our youth. A little dope in the ashtray, and there goes the neighborhood.

Fact is, jocks are less equipped than almost anyone to serve as gurus for proper behavior. There is no school for athletes than includes classes on being a good person. Role Model 101 never has been offered.

Because they are given special talents does not make them immune to tragedy, bad judgment or immaturity. Often, it makes them more susceptible.

Athletes aren't role models. They're heroes. There's a difference.

"When I was a kid, I used to run up and down the street in the snow, imagining I was O.J. Simpson gaining 2,000 yards. I envisioned me being Mercury Morris on that undefeated Miami Dolphins team. These guys were heroes to me.

"Mercury Morris was convicted for drugs. O.J. had problems with women. These are not people whose lives I would emulate. My

201

role model was my mother."

This was Mike Martin, on the phone Friday. The ex-Bengals wide receiver has been on both sides. What he thinks of the jock-as-role-model concept merits some attention.

"There's nothing wrong with looking up to an athlete for what he does in his sport," Martin said. "But don't make that person be the image of how you want to be as an individual. Athletes are human. They are not going to live up to expectations."

Admire them for what they do. Pick and choose what's admirable from the rest of their lives.

Mike Martin has an office in Winton Hills and a new, struggling program for kids called Commitment to Character. A few times a week, he will pull his car up to the office and wait for the kids to appear. Often, they want nothing more than to talk.

Some of these children, in this battered neighborhood, have no role models at home. They hitch their identities to Martin and his partner, ex-Bengals linebacker Ron Simpkins.

Martin and Simpkins accept the burden. They hold sports clinics, they take kids camping. They hold cookouts. They are around. Their presence makes a difference. They welcome the role-model responsibility. They can handle it. Most athletes cannot. Nor should they be expected to.

When Charles Barkley shills for a shoe company by saying, "I'm not a role model," he's honing a bad-man persona that has helped him sell lots of sneakers. He is also speaking the truth.

Parents who rely on athletes to shape their kids' perceptions of good and bad are not working hard enough as parents. People who see Tom Browning, Vince Coleman or any other strayed jock as corrupting the lives of youth need to give youth more credit for having good sense.

Kids don't expect athletes to lead them down the bright and shining path. The adults do that.

It way past time to bury the notion of athletes as role models. Athletes owe us nothing more than effort and solid citizenship. As

Martin said, "If you hold them in high regard only as athletes, they won't let you down." Otherwise, they just might.

The Autograph Biz

July 28, 1996

*H*ow do you remember Mickey Mantle? I remember him as The Mick. There were never any home runs like the home runs The Mick hit in Yankee Stadium. There are people and places that define for us a sport and a time. This is what Mantle did for me. He defined the game.

If you are on the short side of 30, you remember another Mantle. He is the man bent behind the banquet table in the cavernous convention hall, grimly signing autographs until his wrist cramps up.

Unless, of course, he is the sad and shriveled Mantle, holding a press conference to damn his own boozy lifestyle. A lifestyle fueled by his appearances at autograph sessions and card shows.

This autograph thing has gotten out of hand.

What used to be the purest form of appreciation between player and fan is now a business dominated by people with cash registers for hearts. An autograph used to be the closest bond a ballplayer could forge with a fan. Now, it is a reason for fan and player to dislike each other. We already have enough of those.

Who's worse: The ballplayer who signs 20 autographs, but not 21?

Or the fan who insults him when he walks away?

And what, exactly, is gained in the exchange?

A letter appeared the other week, from a reader complaining of a card show at the convention center downtown. The reader had paid $50 for the show, expecting to get signatures from several Reds, including Ron Gant and Reggie Sanders. Problem was, neither Gant nor Sanders showed up.

Was this before or after Duke Snider and Willie McCovey appeared in court for stiffing the IRS? The two former stars had not paid taxes on money paid them for a card show appearance. They are the newest members of baseball's Brown Paper Bag Club, reserved for those who take the cash and run.

Pete Rose was the charter member; Darryl Strawberry his first lieutenant.

Prosecutors and IRS agents promise the investigation will continue. While they're at it, they ought to check out the growing collection of desperates who have made collecting autographs so distasteful.

These are people who can't tell you how many home runs Frank Thomas has, but who know to the penny the market value of his rookie card. I'm not sure what the players mean to the kids now, other than signatures. Ken Griffey Jr. may be the best player of his time; he's nothing if the Griffey rookie card you won has a crease in it.

I recall Rose on the night of his banishment from baseball, appearing on a TV shopping channel, selling pieces of himself. How sad. How smarmy.

"I don't look at it as pieces of yourself," says Cal Levy, owner of Position Sports Marketing in Cincinnati. Levy's clients include Rose, Johnny Bench, Joe Morgan and Tony Perez. "It's just another product. A commodity. Does it make them bad guys because a business was started that pays them for their signature?"

It has gotten out of hand. It's not worth it when the players are so busy signing, they never look up from the table to acknowledge the fans.

It's not worth it when kids hound players everywhere in public. When the civility of please and thank you slumps to the brazenness of "Sign this" or, a personal favorite, "Are you anybody?"

It's not worth it when the gesture is wrapped in commerce. When it causes heroes to commit crimes. It has become a joyless enterprise. For everyone.

On the field at the All Star workout three Mondays ago, I saw a man conferring with two kids. At his feet were two boxes of fresh baseballs. The man was about 30. The kids were 12 or so. The man was telling the kids which players he wanted to sign the balls.

He knew the players would sign more readily for the kids.

He was not interested in saving the baseballs for his grandchildren.

No wonder today's players have a problem with autograph seekers.

"It's a business now," Cal Levy says. "For better or worse."

Uncommon Valor

"Each 24 hours, the world turns over on someone who is
sitting on top of it."
—*sign in Sparky Anderson's office*

Blind Determination

January 1, 1995

*H*e can still move. George "Sugar" Costner stands in the small light of a hall in his one-bedroom place in Walnut Hills, bobbing, ducking, weaving, jabbing and remembering who he was.

He is six feet tall and near 170 pounds. He's wearing a set of black satin handmade lounging pajamas that could pass for a fighter's robe. He's dancing the way boxers do, a little two-step, shoulder-shimmy up on the balls of his feet.

"Jab-jab-jab-HOOK!" he says, and forty-one years since his last fight, there is still a cadence to this for him, a fist rhythm. "Jab-jab-jab-HOOK!"

He's remembering things now. Sugar Costner's shadow bounces eerily off a living room wall, and the punches snap across fifty years.

"I didn't do much backin' up," he says. "Jab-jab. I was a target puncher. I'd go right up under the heart. Made the heart quiver. Take away a man's stamina.

"Then I'd get in underneath the rib cage. Jab-jab, man. To the gall bladder. You hit a man there, he's paralyzed."

The imaginary man across the shadows is hunched over now. Sugar Costner rips into him with a right hook. "That's when you drop him," he says, and he does a tribal ballet to who he was before his eyes died.

Costner is 67 years old, and blind. Boxing was his first love, his best wife and what it did was take him within a kiss of the top, then drop him into an eternal sunset.

There was a straight right hand from a hot young Cuban named Chico Varona that ripped across the night and into the left cheekbone of Sugar Costner. It was the sixth round of a welterweight non-title fight on May 9, 1949, in Philadelphia, the seventy-ninth fight of a

208

career that began in Cincinnati in 1940. A fight Costner would win.

"But that punch, man, it was like somebody just took a ball of fire and threw it into my face. It didn't drop me, it just made me dizzy."

"Things began to dim," Costner says. Ironically, it was the right eye that was immediately affected. "Things started getting dark."

He knocked out Varona in the tenth round. "I knocked him out of the ring the first time. The people pushed him back in, so then I knocked him out cold."

The doctors said it was broken blood vessels. They gave him shots to deliberately drive up his body temperature, thinking that would dry up the wayward blood they believed was clouding his right eye.

Costner went on fighting, because that's what fighters do.

No fighter is ever a coward, not when the only thing between his brains and the business end of a six-ounce glove is his chin. Boxing has coughed up its share of blood and deceit and death, but its nightmares occupy no more space than the courage and the skill and, ultimately, the hope that the game produces.

We'll tell you momentarily why this impossibly sad story has such a sweet ending. But since so much of the fight game's heroism is born of tragedy, grimness and plain bad luck, we'll start with the sadness.

Back before the world went fuzzy, then dim, then utterly dark, Sugar Costner had one fight to win to become the welterweight champion of the world. He chased his dream with a pure, hot eagerness not found in the fights today. Today, the fights are a hustle and a con, a street serenade sung by corner boys wearing diamonds as big as a brick on their pinky fingers.

Back in the 1940s when boxing was truly alive, George Costner fought ninety-two times, from Cincinnati to Oakland to Philadelphia to a little, one-holer of a town called Jenkins, Kentucky, where Costner can tell you today that he knocked out Tiger Kiggins in two rounds on the fourth of July in 1942.

Costner fought the great Sugar Ray Robinson twice. He fought Jake LaMotta when LaMotta was young and vital. He once had twenty-three knockouts in a row. He fought three times in four days, and won them all by knockouts.

Sugar Costner beat Kid Galivan and seventy-six others. On July 12, 1950, he was a 6-to-1 underdog when he defeated Ike Williams in ten rounds, to become the No.1 contender in the world.

They took Williams out of Shibe Park in Philadelphia in an ambulance, and the sports writers were calling 26-year-old Sugar Costner the best welterweight in the world. Sugar Ray Robinson was leaving the welterweights to fight middleweight. His title was vacant. It was Sugar Costner's for the taking. Just one more fight.

It had been a long run. Costner was born in Mt. Auburn in 1923. He wanted to be a baseball player until he realized blacks were not permitted in the majors.

He became a professional boxer at age 15. He won his first fight less than two years later, a second round KO of one "Red" Knox, for which he pocketed $1.50.

He kept fighting, and winning. "I was so fast. I was like lightning," Costner recalls. He trained each afternoon in a gym on Pleasant Street, after spending the morning driving a city sanitation truck.

Costner was a barnstormer. When he ran out of opponents in the Midwest, he went to California. From there, it was back to the Midwest and, finally to the East Coast. To Philly and New York, to big-time boxing's soul.

"Many boxing experts believe Costner is the best welterweight in the country today," said an article in the Camden (N.J.) *Evening Courier*. "He can do everything required of a good fighter, even to getting up off the floor and going on to win."

In 1945, Costner fought Robinson and LaMotta just six weeks apart. Robinson KO'd him in the first round, LaMotta in the sixth. But Costner was barely 21 years old. He had a big jab and a rock jaw, one that cleaved nothing but pure future.

A rematch with Robinson was set for March 22, 1950. "I'd had sixty-five fights since the first one with Robinson," Costner says. "I felt I was ready to take him."

Three days before the fight, ten months after Varona made him see rockets, Costner worked his last sparing session, against a tough welter named Joe Blackwood. Costner remembers all of it.

"We was bangin' pretty good. After I got through, I went down to the dressing room. My body cooled off, and I couldn't see nothing out of my right eye.

"I said, what the hell's going on here? I couldn't see. I was devastated, because fightin' Ray Robinson with one eye was suicide, man."

Costner already had signed to fight Gavilan and Williams after Robinson. Both would be big paydays. He knew he had no chance against Robinson. He also knew if he forfeited, his career might be over.

Costner took a dive. "It was the only thing I could do," he says. "I lay down in the first round. Sorriest day of my life."

The eye got no better. He saw nothing from it but black, a big black haze, as if a curtain had been drawn across the right side of his face.

He passed his physical for the Gavilan fight because "the doctor liked me quite a bit." This is how things sometimes work in boxing.

"I beat Gavilan with one eye. It went the whole ten rounds. If it had gone another round, I'd have knocked him out. He was bleeding pretty bad."

A month later, he beat a journeyman named Charley Cotton. A month after that, July 12, 1950, he fought Ike Williams, in Philadelphia.

The day of the fight, the Pennsylvania state athletic commissioner summoned Costner to his office. He had seen the doctor's report from the pre-fight physical.

As Costner recalls, the commissioner said, "I know you can't see through that right eye. My wife and I stayed up all night last night, pondering whether I should let you go through with this. We came to the conclusion that we felt you could win, so we'll let you go on with it."

211

That night, Costner decisioned Williams in ten rounds. "I liked to kill him. I felt sorry for him. He was so swollen, he looked like he had two faces. Ambulance took him to the hospital," Costner says.

He was summoned the next day, to meet again with the commissioner.

"He handed me the gloves I fought Ike Williams with. He said, 'That was a helluva fight. But that's the last fight you're going to have, George.' I broke down and cried.

"I was at the top. Right at the top. I had beaten everyone [ranked] in the top ten in the world, and now none of it mattered."

Costner had fought fourteen months with a detached retina in his right eye. In the next year, he underwent two unsuccessful operations to repair the damage.

He bounced around after that, working menial jobs and plotting an empty future. From his left eye he began to see what looked like streaks of lightning. The doctors said it was a cataract. They removed one the size of a shirt button.

Two days after the operation, a doctor came to Sugar Costner's room. "He put his hand in front of my face. I could see his hand so beautiful. I could see the wrinkles in it, the joints on the fingers."

Costner's eye was wrapped in thick gauze. The doctor returned the following day and unwrapped the gauze. Costner stifled a moan.

"I can't see doc. I can't see a thing." He was 27 years old.

The way Costner tells it, the cataract had obscured another retinal detachment. He assumes the punch from Chico Varona ruined both his eyes. But since he fought thirteen times after beating Varona, it could have happened any time. Not that it mattered.

Between 1951 and 1958, there were six operations, all unsuccessful. "I made up my mind then that I was going to be blind. Totally blind, and that was that," Costner says.

For the next decade, he didn't do much but take low-wage jobs and leave them. He subsisted on a military pension, social security and the notion that nobody has much use for a blind man.

"I wasted eight or nine years, man," Costner says.

Costner doesn't recall why he went back to school, really, only that some acquaintances suggested he try it. A man has his life, his love, snatched from him, just as it is in full bloom. Who's to say how anyone would react?

Nothing in the ring had wobbled him the way this had. And after a decade, he decided that nothing else would. After ten years, Sugar Costner found his legs again.

He moved to Cleveland. He went to Cuyahoga Community College and earned a two-year degree and a 3.7 grade point average.

He persisted. At age 52, he enrolled in Cleveland State University. He couldn't see anything but opportunity.

Costner missed two classes in four years. He lived alone in a little apartment on the east side, and it took him four bus rides to get to school and back every day. Sometimes, he would get so cold while waiting that he would deliberately take the wrong bus, just so he wouldn't freeze.

He taped all his lectures, he got all his books on tape from the Sight Center in Cleveland. He paid his tuition out of his savings and his pension.

Sugar Costner graduated from Cleveland State on August 30, 1979, with a 3.0 grade point, a degree in business administration and an education no one will ever take from him. He was 56.

A month later, Costner's name was heard on the floor of the U.S. House of Representatives. Ohio congressman Louis Stokes said, "George Costner pooled all his resources to surpass every conceivable odd to reach his goal [of] a college education."

"I had run a great race and I had won," Costner says. "It was a long run, man, between the time I went blind and when I got that diploma."

He is 67, and his face is smooth. It was never a fighter's gaze, not even after ninety-two bouts. He never got hit much.

No scar tissue bloats his eyes. His nose was never pugged or pancaked or shoved to one side or another. It's a civilian's face, a white-collar face.

213

Costner worked for the Civil Rights Commission in Dayton until 1985. Now, he is retired and he passes his days in the apartment off Gilbert Avenue, listening to scratchy jazz on the radio.

"What I really wanted was to fight Ray Robinson again," he is saying. Costner is a dignified man in black satin, reliving the best years of his life.

On a shelf in his living room is a bronzed glove from the Gavilan fight. From a drawer in his bedroom, he pulls a glove from the Williams bout. It's red leather, six ounces, soft as a dream. He pulls it on.

"The welterweight title was empty. It was mine. All I had to do was be rematched with Gavilan or Williams and *boom*, just another night. But what I really wanted was Robinson. One more time."

Sugar Costner pirouettes around the room, tossing straight punches at a long ago time. *Jab-jab-jab-hook*. Maybe somewhere, the great Sugar Ray Robinson is taking one in his gall bladder, right below the rib cage.

George Costner, nicknamed Sugar after his third pro fight by a knockabout heavyweight named Sammy Mack, says, "I'm just very satisfied with myself, man. What do they call that? Self-esteem?"

He says this while he's throwing punches into the glorified past, and what you think about that is, it sure is remarkable how a blind man can see things so clearly.

Boomer's Best Crowd

*W*e asked him how he felt. We always ask that. It's the best and worst question. And almost always unanswerable, because the deepest feelings can never properly be expressed.

How did Boomer Esiason feel?

How does a sunrise feel, making its way across an ocean? A crocus in April, a parent in the first few minutes after a child is born? There are no words.

Even for someone as talkative as Esiason. Boomer would be in the Sportswriters Hall of Fame, if there were such a thing. He's in the front row, a box seat, 40-yard line. He always has something to say.

But words can fail even him: "Very fulfilled," was what Boomer managed. "Very satisfied inside."

Here is what he did, on this glowing day of football, witnessed by 55,158 at Cinergy Field:

Threw for two touchdown passes and 211 yards.

Brought a composure and presence to the Bengals offense. "A sense of success" was how guard Scott Brumfield put it.

Created an excitement at Cinergy Field that had been lost, while helping the Bengals beat Jacksonville, 31–26.

Brought again to the public conscience the fight for a cure for cystic fibrosis.

Gunnar has that. CF. Gunnar is Esiason's son, born six Aprils ago. Boomer's very own crocus.

On Sunday, Gunnar watched the game from the enclosed box his dad bought for the season. Cold weather aggravates Gunnar's condition, but inside the box it's no problem.

He saw his dad turn the clock back a decade. Gunnar pronounced the effort "Really good. It was good to see my dad out there."

215

Yes, it was. A town searching for something, anything to cheer for from its mournful football team needed No. 7 to do what he did Sunday. He was a walking reason to believe.

The first time the Bengals had the ball, Esiason moved them 63 yards.

He was quick, he was calm. He was in control. He led. Esiason completed his first five passes on the drive, and even scrambled for a first down. Cinergy Field caught a whiff of 1988, the Super Bowl year, and inhaled deeply.

In the box, Gunnar wanted to know why the fireworks went off. Esiason explained that was what happened when the Bengals scored a touchdown. Gunnar decided that was "cool."

Boomer plays now so his son can remember what his dad did for a living. At 6, memories dance in and out like fireflies in the dusk, random and fleeting. Some stick, most don't.

"He's starting to know what's going on," Esiason said.

Mostly, Esiason plays to give his work for CF a national voice. He could have retired after last year, but the size of his pulpit would have diminished. Sunday, it only grew.

"That's why I'm playing. We win a game, he's all over TV. Whoever watched the game hopefully now knows what cystic fibrosis is. That's all I really give a damn about, to be honest with you," he said.

After a quarter, the Bengals already had 21 points, and Gunnar's gaze had made the broadcast, his face pressed against the glass, hopeful and new.

At halftime, Esiason waved up to the box. When the game ended, he ran through the tunnel to the dressing room, accompanied by shouts of *Boo-mer! Boo-mer!* And by Gunnar, whom he scooped up from a family friend standing near the dressing room door.

"If you have a child that's suffering from something like he is, it makes it that much more special. It's an unbelievable feeling to share a moment," Esiason said. "The thing is, you wish it could last a lifetime, but it only lasts 30 minutes or so. Some of you are parents," he said. "You know what it's like."

216

What *is* it like? Another question that can't be answered. To lift our kids up above the hurt and sadness that sometimes comes? To make them immune to that? Yes. We all want that.

Boomer Esiason wants what's best for his child. That's all. It's why he's still playing football, mainly. It's why he lives for days such as this, when the cheers sound like '88, only better, because he has someone new to share them with.

What's that feel like?

Hard to say.

Esiason emerged from the dressing room an hour after the game, after all the questions had been answered, all the unknowables probed, all the mysteries made plain. He summoned Gunnar and Gunnar's sister, 5-year-old Sydney. The three walked out and made a quick left.

"Wanna see the field, guys?" Esiason said. He was in the middle, Gunnar to his left, Sydney his right. They held hands. The sharp glare of a still-lit spotlight creased the scene. "There it is," Esiason said.

So much to play for.

Stumbling in an Old Darkness

March 3, 1997

St. Petersburg, Florida—My dad was 14 in 1947, a kid in Shibe Park in Philadelphia the first time Jackie Robinson came to town with the Brooklyn Dodgers. What he remembers about that is Philly manager Ben Chapman during the game, eating watermelon on the dugout steps.

Fans packed the park that day, to see Robinson, but not because they were fascinated by Jackie's skills. They went because they'd never seen a "Negro" in a big-league uniform. They watched him the way a zoo patron might a giraffe.

We say things have changed, and mostly they have. Nobody goes to a baseball game curious about minorities in pinstripes. In fact, sports is often ahead of the game when it comes to racial equality, at least on the field.

But we're still on the short side of understanding. We still struggle with the concept that Jackie Robinson, courageous and sweet, brought to life 50 springs ago. Half a century gone, it's a small hole in our soul that never quite mends.

Deion Sanders brought it home to me. I asked him about Robinson. Contrary to his public posings, Sanders can be a thoughtful spokesman on subjects beyond himself.

"Black players today couldn't endure half the things he did," Sanders said. "That he was able to focus and thrive. That's what makes him a hero."

Then Sanders lost me. He thinks if he were white and doing what he does, he would be more appreciated. He wouldn't have to "pay dearly" for his perceived flamboyance, he said.

My first reaction to that was this: "Deion, you couldn't be more wrong. We would appreciate you more if you weren't doing such a fine job of it all by yourself.

"We figured you didn't need any help. And when you pass us in one of your Mercedes, don't forget to wave."

What would Jackie Robinson think of a man who declares, "The first white man that's able to do what we do, he's going to be on the back of a milk carton, and it ain't going to be because he's lost."

The arrogance is a little heavy. But the point should be taken seriously. I don't pretend to know how an African-American, even one as well-known as Sanders, feels walking into, say, an all-white country club. Neither can I climb into Ken Griffey's head, to see if he wonders why no major-league team wants him for its manager.

Griffey is a Reds coach. He has coached less than many, but more than some. Griffey is universally liked and respected. He compares favorably with Don Baylor, who has taken the Colorado Rockies to the playoffs. So what's the hang-up?

Fifty years later, we grope in the same darkness. "An uncomfortableness," Barry Larkin calls it.

"It's not obvious to everyone," Larkin says. "But minorities as a whole, myself included, come face to face with bigotry. Subtle ways here, subtle ways there."

The common appraisal is that 1947 is a bad memory. Nobody is throwing chicken bones on the infield grass, the way they did at Crosley Field, even into the 1950s, as Joe Nuxhall recalled recently. Things are different. But not entirely.

Fifty years later, it still depends on who's doing the appraising.

Larkin: "In sports, you can transcend the racial barriers, but only while you're playing. When you're between the lines, you don't see black and white. When you get off the field, when you're up in the front office, that's when it becomes an issue again."

We're still stumbling along, dealing with the uncomfortableness. Robinson's legacy is such that we're still trying; his memory should make us want to try harder. "He had the weight of society on his shoulders," Larkin says.

The least we can do is make Robinson's burden worthwhile. Larkin says Robinson "propelled" minorities. Fifty years later, the struggle continues.

Missing Gabe

February 6, 1999

*J*ackie Robinson will go back now and again, just drive by to make sure the rim is still up. When they sold the house in Roselawn a few months after Gabe died, Jackie tried to take the basketball rim with him.

It was the collapsible kind, so when Jackie's son Gabe wanted to work on his dunks, he wouldn't bend the rim. Jackie wanted the memory of that. He took his wrenches and his stepladder, but the bolts would turn only so far.

A young, childless couple had bought the house. They had dreams, too, just as Jackie had, and maybe their dreams involved a son who would grow up tall and athletic the way Gabe did. Maybe he would need a rim that didn't snap when he dunked. Jackie figured that would be OK. He left the rim up, and now he drives by every so often, usually when it's quiet and dark, and he lets his mind rewind.

Jackie and Paulette Robinson live in the northwest suburbs now, in a fine, big house in a newly minted subdivision. Jackie didn't want to leave Roselawn and the memories of his son; the memories were sweet for Paulette, too, but they crushed her.

She would come home from work to find Gabe and his friends gathered in the yard, shooting baskets or hanging out. "OK," she would announce, "does everyone have their homework done?" That would scatter 'em.

Her son Gabe had a way of shutting the front door of that Roselawn house that would rattle the miniblinds in that door's window. He had a way of walking across the hardwood floors— *clomp, clomp, clomp*—in those high-top basketball shoes that make every kid look like he has the feet of a giant.

In the mornings when it rained, he'd miss the bus on purpose, so

220

Paulette would drive him to school. When it was dry, he'd hunch over his cereal and the TV, grunting morning greetings as she kissed the top of his head. Every day, she did that.

But Paulette couldn't bear that now. There were a few months last year, after Gabriel collapsed and died on the basketball court, while playing for Walnut Hills High against Northwest, when she would come home and the silence would shatter her.

The grieving was hard but healthy, she figured. They needed to let it out. But this, this was pure pain. They had to leave.

What they have now, instead of squeaking hardwood floors and blinds that rattle and the clomping of Air Jordans, instead of Gabe, is a wall in the family room filled with mementos of their son's life. A framed No. 22 jersey, pictures of Gabe playing shooting guard for Walnut Hills, letters of condolence from the Ohio legislature. "Gabriel's Corner", they call it. All the time, Paulette will face that corner, look into the memories and talk to her son, who would have been 18 years old today.

"I love you," she'll say. "We miss you very much. I'll see you again."

These are the words of a nightmare. This is the picture of ultimate pain. This is what it is like to see your child die:

"Watching him fall," Jackie says. "What's going on? There was nothing to push him down. Nothing at all. I ran out of the bleachers, to his side. What's going on? His head was going back and forth. His eyes looked strange. I said, 'Come back to us. Don't leave us. Come on back.' Then I knew. He's not coming back. They administered CPR. His breathing started getting labored.

"This is my son. This is real. No, it's not. Yes, it is. Then you see your son take his last breath. You see them put him in the ambulance. I'm in the front, he's in the back. We're driving. They're working on him. Heart stimulation. Nothing. Nothing. I was still praying, but they were saying they couldn't revive him, even before we got to the hospital.

"What? Us? Me? Our family? Why? Oh, God. Why?"

221

Gabriel had a damaged heart. It was diseased in a way no one could tell. He was perfectly healthy. He was 6-foot-2. He could dunk a basketball. Never sick. Then he was gone.

Jackie Robinson says he feels like he's in the world now, but not of it. It's a distinction best appreciated by survivors of tragedy. "I'm like a camera lens looking out at the world, just kind of observing," he says. "I still don't want to believe he's not coming back."

Paulette says a part of her spirit is gone. It was the part that allowed her to laugh easily and joke often. She isn't melancholy, she says. Just quiet.

They are spiritual people, practicing Baptists. "We lean on our faith. We have that hope of being together again," Jackie explains. But they've struggled with the meaning of their son's death.

They have tried to take lessons from it. They've retreated some, into themselves and their faith, seeking logic. But there is no logic in the sudden passing of a 16-year-old child. There is only perspective, to those courageous enough to seek it.

"When something like this happens, you eliminate your worry about anything in this world. There's no anxiety," says Jackie.

Paulette's message is the same. "Press on," she says. Live each moment. Don't hold grudges. Don't be angry. Enjoy your life.

Says Jackie, "You think you're in control of what happens to you. You're not. Live life the best way you can. Treat others right."

He remembers a talk he had with his son, in the car on the way home from basketball practice: "'Gabriel, you know I'm not going to be here with you forever. The body is going to die, but the spirit will live on,' I said. 'You need to realize that and stay in a right relationship with Jesus Christ. That way, we live together forever.' I instilled that in him."

Now Jackie Robinson sits in the family room of his new home, on a couch next to Gabriel's Corner, trying with all he has to take his own advice. The Robinsons have what they call MGMs: Missing Gabriel Moments. The memories crystalize into pain, the longing into despair. They wait for him to come home. They go to Walnut

Hills games, expecting to see him warming up, knocking down three-pointers with that feathery jumpshot of his.

They've had his teammates over to the house. One made the floor creak just as Gabe had.

They've had revelations, strange and troubling and wonderful. After his good games, when the threes fell like rain and the best place in the world to be was at the Walnut Hills gym, inside jersey No. 22, Gabriel would whisper in Paulette's ear, "I did that for you, Mom."

A few weeks ago, one of Gabe's teammates said the same thing to her, never knowing it had been Gabe's special present to his mother.

Not long after Gabe died, Jackie was sitting on the couch when he says he heard his son's voice: "Call Coach. Tell him don't let his heart be troubled."

At the same time Walnut Hills coach Mike Herald sat at home, working on lineups. He was OK until he got to No. 22. His phone rang. It was Jackie Robinson.

"I'd never called him before," Jackie says. "But I did then, 'Don't let your heart be troubled,' I told him."

The Robinsons go to most of the home games. Paulette made a special trip to the Northwest game this year. When Gabe collapsed there last year, on January 30, she wasn't at the game. She still feels guilty.

You make your own peace with tragedy. You make your own deals with your soul and your maker. You do what you can.

The Robinsons have held fast to Gabe's teammates and they to them. "We needed each other," Jackie says. "We still need each other. We don't know how long we're going to need, but we keep on opening ourselves up for each other."

It was in basketball that Gabriel came alive, that his potential bloomed and he saw his life's possibilities.

He began playing when he was 10. He started for Walnut Hills as a freshman. "He was a very serious ballplayer," says Jackie. Before every game, Gabe watched a videotape of Michael Jordan, "Come Fly With Me." When his mother suggested he make his own way and

223

not mimic someone else, Gabe said, "I'm not copying Michael. I'm copying his confidence."

It was what Paulette Robinson loved most about her son's game. His confidence. He was a leader, she says. His teammates liked him, respected him, gravitated to him. There are times now when Jackie will be at a game, and he will whisper to himself, "Pull 'em through, son. Show 'em how it's done."

"I think about sometimes how it could have been," he says.

Today would have been Gabriel's 18th birthday. I spoke to the Robinsons Thursday. A year ago Thursday, they buried their son at Oak Hill Cemetery in Glendale. On Friday night, they watched Walnut Hills play at home against Northwest. Tonight, the annual Walnut Hills alumni game will be played. All proceeds will benefit the Gabriel Robinson Memorial Scholarship Fund.

This week, the Robinsons' emotions are dancing like a kite in the wind. Says Jackie, "We get stronger as we talk about life and the spirit and the soul. We get better."

"We need to cry," says Paulette. "We need to walk."

Jackie drives to Roselawn, easing his white van down the old street, to the house where his son grew into a fine, young man. He'll stop for a bit, to look at the basketball hoop and be alone.

"Did it have to come to this?" Jackie might ask. "What is being learned by this? OK, Lord. You don't have to answer me now. But I'll be waiting."

He'll turn the key, slip the van into drive and ease off at a respectful speed. He might hear Gabe speak to him then; he has in the past, after just such a journey.

"Be strong, Dad," is what Jackie has heard his son say. "Remember what you told me."

The Run of His Life

September 20, 1998

*W*hy do we run?

What are we looking for when we put on the jogging shoes or the three-piece suit or the hard hat? What do we want?

We run through life to prove things to ourselves and to others. We run because everyone else does, and if we don't, we fall behind.

We run to things and away from things, but we never stand still. Life is a race. Maybe we're conditioned to believe that. So we run. Maybe that's it. Or maybe it's as simple as the satisfaction of putting one foot in front of the other, no matter what.

I am running in an Anderson Township park with John Kapoor. I am running slowly enough my feet seem to be treading air. I could walk at the same pace. It's effortless.

John is next to me. He breathes heavily after a few hundred yards. He was sick with a high fever the day before. John has a plastic, form-fitted brace on his right foot that extends above his ankle, to keep the foot pointed straight ahead. His right arm dangles at his side.

Every so often, John veers off course to the right, bumping me as we run. He always apologizes. Every time. His cross country coach at Anderson High, Andy Wolf, says of John's workouts this year, "It's a lot harder for him now. Some days we gauge the workout by how many times he falls down."

We are running around a large field and down a gravel path. John's breathing is labored. I fear for his balance. "Anytime you want to stop, we can," I say.

John doesn't stop. John runs. Down the path, up a hill through the grass, practically sideways, listing to the right, his right side barely working. We finish. Four-tenths of a mile. John runs it by the force of his will.

He was a pretty good distance runner some years ago, before the first tumor appeared in his brain to vandalize his youth. He'd run sixth or seventh man on his junior high team: his identical twin brother Michael was third or fourth. But the difference between them wasn't much.

John always worked hard, always showed up ready to run, always did his best. Five, six miles a day. This has not changed, except the distance, even as one tumor was removed, only to be replaced by another and then a third. Even as John endured surgeries and staph infections and radiation and chemotherapy.

Even now, as the third tumor lives in the left side of his brain, and his parents and his doctors have decided not to remove it surgically. "They've opened his head up so many times," explains his mother, Kathleen. The tumors have all been benign, which is a good thing, if you can consider anything about a brain tumor to be good.

Even now, John runs. One step at a time. One foot in front of the other. Never backward.

The other day, Andy Wolf said to John, "John, as long as you get up as many times as you fall down, you're not behind."

Do you believe people are put here to teach us how to live better? That they are chosen to show us how to run?

Michael, John's older sibling by exactly 10 minutes, said, "John has made me want to persevere more, keep fighting. I won't let anything get me down, because my brother won't."

It started in English class nearly four years ago. John was giving a speech. And then he wasn't. He just stopped, in mid-thought, eyes straight ahead. The book he was holding fell from his hand to the floor.

It happened more than once. Kathleen Kapoor worried, because that is what mothers do. She went to the hardware store and bought a kit to test for radon in their house. She took John to doctors, who suggested he might be epileptic.

They asked questions. Had he suffered any head injuries when he was little? Had he been in a serious car accident?

No and no again. So what is it?

The lapses in speech continued. John saw more doctors. The day before his 13th birthday, John underwent an EEG. A brain scan. Doctors discovered a tumor the size of a pea.

Since then, the Kapoors' emotions have been around the world and back. After the second surgery, a doctor who believed the tumor was malignant said to Kathleen, "Start praying for John."

To love someone with a disability is to own a keener sense of possibilities, limitations, joys, sorrows and perspective. It is at once the best and worst part of your life.

"We thought after that first surgery, he would be fine," Kathleen says. "It has been continuous. You don't ever get used to it."

Says John, sitting across the living room of their home, "I get used to it."

I ask Kathleen if there is light yet.

"We haven't seen it," she says. "We're still hoping and praying it will come."

"We'll see it," Michael says.

"I always believe," John says. "Some people really don't believe."

"No, no," Kathleen says. "We all believe. We all have hope."

This is what John has had to do in the nine months since the latest tumor was discovered: Take chemotherapy, orally and intravenously; learn to write with his left hand; attend physical, speech and occupational therapy.

Try tying your shoes with one hand. Try cutting a steak. Try articulating what is in you brain when your mouth won't let you. John has a 3.6 grade-point at Anderson. He's a member of the National Honor Society. Yet, his speech is bumpy and groggy. He fills his sentences with "likes" and "ums" because his brain can't process his thoughts quickly enough.

Try running the way John runs now, after you've spent your whole life running the way John used to run.

Imagine the frustration, the sadness, the desperation, the dread. John would. If he had the time.

"We're past the dread," Michael says. "John doesn't have bad days."

227

Thanks to John, neither does Michael. With twins, the sharing never stops.

"I'd be a lot different if John wasn't around. His jovial attitude makes me a lot happier," Michael says.

He recalls coming into John's room in the middle of the night when they were small, asking to sleep in the spare bed because he was afraid of kidnappers. He recalls the afternoon Kathleen locked herself out of the house. While she fretted for the safety of her two 4-year-olds, they were in the kitchen, raiding the pantry of bananas and graham crackers.

Michael thinks about his part in all of this: "Sometimes I wonder, since we are twins and we are really alike, if it's something genetic, why him and not me?"

It's not all bad. In fact, very little beyond the physical concerns is bad. The central irony is that the Kapoors have done everything but run from the bump in John's road. As for John, he has run right at it. And never stopped.

"Since the beginning, I thought, 'This is how it's going to be, and that's OK,'" John says.

In the beginning, after the first tumor was found, Vik Kapoor took his third-oldest son to Ellis Island in New York harbor. Vik came to New York from India in 1969. He had an image of America from the books he had read in school. America was "a place where a dream could be realized if you worked hard and smart and rejoiced in other people's success," he says.

Vik had $7 in his pocket. Today, he designs computer chips. He is the dean of the College of Engineering at the University of Toledo. He makes $165,000 a year.

Four years ago, Vik took John to see where Vik had gotten off the boat. He showed his son a register where he had signed his name. He said, "This (disease) is God-given. You have to move on. You can achieve despite difficulties. You have determination and a strong heart."

John says the brace doesn't hurt his foot. We're running again, a little less steadily than before, another four-tenths of a mile from here to there. The brace makes him even more determined to be the runner he once was. "Faster and better," he says.

I trot beside John, slower than before. I'm somewhere between anxiety for him (Will he fall? Am I going too fast?) and worry that if I ask him how he's doing or if I slow to a walk, I'll embarrass him. It's my problem, not his. John finishes the four-tenths of a mile. John runs.

Andy Wolf, the coach Vik Kapoor calls "a father in absentia (Vik and Kathleen are divorced)", says, "He won't give an inch. He won't ask for an inch. You can't find a hound dog more faithful. John keeps running, falling down and getting up."

"What do you hope for him?" I ask Wolf.

"What do I hope? I hope someday I have John's son on my team," Wolf says.

John wants to go to Purdue next year. He wants to be a pharmacist, but there is much to be done before then. John's goal now, what he thinks about as he circles the grass and gravel of the park, is to run in the Queen City Conference Meet October 17. He won't do it unless he feels he's able; he's no charity case.

As Wolf says, "This is not a kid with a problem who wants to be an athlete. This is an athlete who has a problem."

"Are you a hero?" I ask John.

"Now that you mention it, I'm just a regular person," he says.

"An average schmoe," Michael says.

"Yeah."

No true hero assumes he is one. The genuine article practices his heroism the way a monk practices his celibacy. Before John Kapoor could run eight-tenths of a mile with me, twice around the park, a teammate helped him tie his shoes.

We are fortunate there is no cancer of the heart, no cure for optimism, no tumor of the spirit.

We're lucky to have people who remind us of that.

And this is why we run.

229

Praying For Jamie

*M*aumee, Ohio—You wonder what he's thinking, smoothly rocking back and forth in the wooden glider chair in the living room of his parents' home. He's sometimes alert, sometimes vacant. Sometimes here, sometimes there, in and out, smiling, nodding, gazing, drifting. Gliding. Back and forth.

Jamie knows. Everyone says this. He hears you. He knows what you're saying about him. He understands.

Doesn't he watch Seinfeld every week? Doesn't Kramer send him into fits of laughter? Even during the time he spent in Florida, nine months of treatments in a hyperbaric chamber, being force-fed 100 percent oxygen two hours a day to get the neurons moving in his badly damaged brain, Jamie Mercurio still had an awareness.

He'd pinch the nurses who stuffed him into the chamber. Every time.

Same old Jamie. Always a kidder.

It's amazing to hear him laugh. On November 19, 1994, the former point guard for Miami University was driving his new Nissan Altima when he missed a curve on Eastgate Road in Toledo, 10 minutes from his home.

It was 3 in the morning. The car hit a fire hydrant, spun sideways, clipped a tree and rolled down a hill before stopping on its top.

Until then, Jamie had been a basketball player. At least that's how he saw himself, a 6-foot-3 wraith who started 71 games in Oxford, winning team MVP honors as a senior in 1992.

He was never a great player, merely a good one who made others better. Which is ironic, now that everyone else is trying to do the same for him.

He has gone from almost dead to walking with help, from asleep

230

to awake, from helpless to hopeful. He will be back tonight in Millett Hall on the Miami campus, where former teammates and coaches will let him know they haven't forgotten Jamie Mercurio.

Five years ago to the night, he was a senior on the same floor, starting against Ball State. It was a long time ago. His family has lived a thousand lives since then. Pain, sadness, despair. Also hope, perspective, and the peculiar sense of triumph that comes with small achievements.

Jamie has tried so hard. Jim Mercurio calls his son "a stubborn, competitive son-of-a-gun."

In the summers between going to school and playing basketball, Jamie delivered pizzas. He'd show up at the gym afterward, still in his Domino's shirt. He'd have on his Coke-bottle glasses, and he'd be wearing short shorts. What a nerd.

Sometimes, he wouldn't be picked to play. When he was, he'd bomb three-pointers from now until then. They'd say, "Who the hell is that?" and Jamie's buddy and teammate, Jim Paul, would say, "That's Jamie Mercurio. He's on the basketball team."

Now, you ask Jamie about that: "Jamie? You remember that?"

Jamie makes the glider move. He looks at you, then at his dad.

Jim Mercurio prods his son. "Remember those days?" he asks.

Jamie raises his right hand slowly, to pat his father's knee. He looks into his father's eyes and smiles. *Yes*, he nods. He remembers.

"Of course you do, bud," Jim says.

Bad things happen to good people. It's as simple as that. Jim Mercurio and his family never tried to analyze it. Families of tragedy learn to stop asking why. Every now and then, we fall apart. That's why. It's what we do afterward that counts.

You raise three kids in a middle-class suburb of Toledo. Your oldest is a boy. He grows up playing sports. He was a medalist golfer. He'd drive his dad nuts every Sunday, showing up just as their foursome was about to tee off. Jim loved playing golf with Jamie; it was the one sport in which he could compete with his son.

Jamie took a basketball scholarship to Miami. He had two coaches.

231

The second, the volcanic Joby Wright, never knew quite what to make of his point guard. The coach never grasped what was going on behind Jamie's chocolate eyes.

"The team clown," Jim Paul calls him now. "Nothing really fazed him."

Jamie Mercurio was the kind of kid you'd expect a college kid to be. He'd spend the school's meal money lavishly, then blame it on the freshmen. Before games, he'd insert bogus lines in the scouting report, scripting zealous praise for opposing players who never played.

Jerry Peirson, his first coach at Miami, would read Jamie's words to the team, too nervous to catch the joke.

As a junior, Jamie missed three straight free throws at the buzzer, in a tie game against Bowling Green. Even though the Redskins won in overtime, Joby Wright made them practice after the game.

In what came to be known as the "tissue issue," the coach directed a team manager to fetch him a roll of toilet paper during the post-game workout. He tossed the paper to Jamie, explaining to the team why Jamie needed it: "He (soiled) his pants with the game on the line."

When a reporter asked Jamie about the incident, Jamie said, "At least it was Charmin."

He was that kind of kid. And this kind: As a senior in '92, he made eight three-point field goals against North Carolina, in a first-round NCAA Tournament game at Riverfront Coliseum. "North Carolina didn't count on having to stop Jamie," Jim Mercurio says. Maybe the Tar Heels looked at the Redskins point guard and saw the pizza man.

That was the highlight of Jamie's career at Miami. He's second on the school's all-time assists list. He got his degree. He liked working with children. In the summers, he ran the town's recreation program, tooling from playground to playground in a green dune buggy.

He planned to teach in the public schools, and coach. He coached one year of girls junior varsity. He was named girls varsity coach at Anthony Wayne High. The season was a week away when he wrecked.

"There was no pulse in his left wrist," Jim Mercurio says.

He wasn't speeding. He'd had some beer, but hours before. Maybe he fell asleep. Maybe there were deer on the road. Maybe the Nissan's accelerator stuck. The carmaker had had a recall for that problem.

No one knows. Not even Jamie, who has no memory of the night.

They pulled him from the wreck and into the hospital in half an hour. That might have saved him.

What followed was every family's nightmare. Jim and his wife, Debbie, drove eight hours from Washington, D.C., where they were visiting Jim's brother. They cursed God and fate. They couldn't believe their luck. And then they walked into a hospital room that was lit up like the Vegas strip, only it was quiet as a tomb.

Their child slept in a nest of tubes. His existence was monitored by an assortment of electronic beeps and flashes. They forgot all about luck. All they thought was, "Please don't let him die."

"Please, Lord. We'll take him any way we can" is what Jim remembers saying.

Jamie's body was swollen almost beyond recognition. Jim and Debbie identified him by the mole on his nose.

Much later, the attending doctor told them "98 percent" of patients in Jamie's condition don't survive. He spent a month asleep in a coma, then six months in a state rehabilitation facility, where doctors and therapists coaxed the slightest movements from his shattered body. When they'd done all they could, the doctors sent Jamie home.

"What else can we do for him?" Jim asked the doctors.

"Not much," they said.

Clinically, Jamie had just escaped the coma. He couldn't stand, or lift his arms or legs or head. "We had to do something else," Jim says.

A Samaritan arrived, as Samaritans often do. This is something tragedy teaches that is good. A wealthy Toledo family, whose own son had been injured in an auto accident, offered to send Jamie to the Ocean Hyperbaric Center in Lauderdale-by-the-Sea, Fla. They'd pay for it all.

The Mercurios agreed. The trip to Florida would be a desperation shot, a 40-footer at the buzzer. As a treatment, it was...out there. In this country, Michael Jackson is its most famous proponent.

For two hours a day, an hour at a time, Jamie sat in an 8-foot-long sealed "clamshell chamber" while being force-fed pure oxygen. The belief is the oxygen speeds up healing.

Maybe it works, maybe it doesn't. All the Mercurios know is that after nine months, their son was walking, with assistance.

He came home last April, to more months of physical therapy. "He's made good, steady progress," says Jim. "And he's not missing anything. Right, bud?"

Jamie glides, back and forth, without nodding.

The day never ends for Debbie, who does most of the caretaking. It is continuous dawn to dusk. Bathing, shaving, feeding, dressing, bowel movements.

"You learn patience," she says.

"Everything is slow," says Jim. "eating is an hour. That's just the way it is. It's our life. You worth it, bud?"

From somewhere deep, Jamie flashes a Hollywood grin. It is time for him to make a joke. He could always do that. No, he shakes his head. He curls his right hand into his father's.

Jim drops two sections of paper towel beneath Jamie's chin, and begins spooning him some Jell-o. Jamie eats with the family, but his food is pureed. He can't drink without choking, so he takes his liquids through a tube in his stomach.

There are different types of pride, just as there are different kinds of courage. The Mercurios know that now. Braced with the crystalline perspective tragedy brings, they know this more than anything: They've never loved Jamie the way they love him now.

Still, they cry. When the weather is good, Jim will take his 28-year-old son to the back yard. He'll stand behind him. He'll hold Jamie up as Jamie tries to remember how to swing a golf club. "It's terrible, it's awful," Jim says. "But you feel like you have to do something with him. This was something he liked."

In the bad moments, Jim excuses himself and visits his pain in the privacy of his bedroom. Sometimes, pain is a price we pay to feel alive.

You cry deepest for your children. It's why Jim Mercurio would trade a year of his life for a warm Sunday morning in summer, Jamie running from the parking lot to the first tee, spikes in one arm, clubs slung over his shoulder, late as usual.

He can close his eyes and see the kid in the too-short shorts and thick glasses, foolin' 'em all again. Makin' 'em laugh. "Making them better," Jim says.

Jim Mercurio doesn't kid himself about his son's future. He hopes Jamie will walk. "Who knows, five years from now, maybe he'll be talking. They still tell us probably not. But they've said 'probably not' about a lot of things. Right, bud?"

Right. Jamie nods. Rocks and nods. Back and forth.

They're taking him to the Miami game tonight. Jim Paul has organized some sort of tribute to Jamie, some small halftime mention. They plan to award him a "senior blanket" bestowed upon all athletes. Jamie never got his. "He doesn't want anything big," Paul says. "There's a fine line between wanting to support him, and parading him around Millett Hall."

Jamie's family will be there, including Jim's dad, age 81, who never missed a game while Jamie was in Oxford.

You find out what is essential after something like this, and what is noise. Mostly, life is noise. What's essential is usually right there in front of you.

Jim Mercurio takes a corner of the paper towel, dabs Jamie's mouth.

"Jamie's like a guy trying to cross a river, against the current," Jim says. "It's a strong current, the strongest anyone will ever face. But you know what? He's still crossing the river. The current hasn't taken him yet. Isn't that right, Jamie?"

From the place all his own, close and faraway and sadly, hopefully real, Jamie pushes the glider. Back and forth. Silently, like a dream.

10

Home Plate

"My dad never played catch with me. As I launched into adulthood, I grew to recognize that sad fact to be the root of my many and varied deep-seated emotional problems."

—*Paul Daugherty*

Sneaker Wars

August 22, 1997

*T*he kid down the hall needed shoes.

This is what he said. What he meant was, "The perfectly good sneakers I am now wearing are no longer worthy of my feet. I'm slumming, and school starts next week. The only way out of the catastrophe my life is becoming is with a new pair of Penny Hardaway Nikes."

He sags. Did you know this about kids? They sag.

They wear their blue denim or nylon basketball shorts down by the tops of their rear ends. I assume they do this because Penny Hardaway does, or because some rapper does. But I don't know. About kids, who really knows?

The kid down the hall is 11. He dresses in black T-shirts that hang to his knees, so they cover the portion of his rear end that would be covered by his shorts, if he weren't sagging. He is a member of Backward Baseball Hat Wearing Nation. He thinks he knows what he knows.

He said he needed shoes.

"OK," I said. "Get in the car. We'll go to (big discount store filled with reasonably priced sneakers without instantly recognizable logos)." He laughed. "Yeah, dad," he said. "Right."

I am 39. In my youth, there were two types of sneakers. There were Keds, and there were Chucks. Help me here.

There weren't leather sneakers, or sneakers with little pumps built into them or sneakers endorsed by multi-millionaire athletes or sneakers called Air. They weren't fashion statements or marvels of engineering. Why do shoes need pumps?

They were just shoes.

But now that athletes rule the world and sports is all that matters, the only people wearing Keds are octogenarians on cruise ships.

"OK," the kid said. "I'll take the Rodmans."

We are compromising. There are the $180 Penny Hardaway shoes he wants and the $39.99 logo-lorn shoes I want him to have. (As our salesman, Wade, suggests, "Parents have a different set of goals in mind.")

In between are the Rodmans, a pair of red-and-black high tops endorsed by that notable Puritan and All-American boy, Dennis (My Kingdom For Some Lip Gloss) Rodman. The Rodman shoes are heavily discounted because, Wade said, parents are refusing to buy them for their children. Hallelujah.

The kid wanted the Rodmans. Naturally.

"Why do you like them?" I asked.

"They're awesome."

"I told you no Rodmans," I said.

"You told me no Rodman hats."

"I don't like what Rodman represents," I said.

"He's cool."

"No. He's not."

"He's not as bad as Marilyn Manson," the kid said, referring to a rock-n-roller trying to be Alice Cooper 25 years after Alice Cooper was Alice Cooper.

"I don't allow you to wear Marilyn Manson stuff, either," I said. "And please pull up your shorts."

Wade the shoe salesman hears this all day, every day, especially now. Parents everywhere, grim and edgy, taking their offspring shopping for sneakers. I believe it's like going to war.

"I've witnessed some power struggles" is what Wade had to say about that.

As with most things currently connected with professional sports—high salaries, new stadiums, autograph shows—the fans are the ones who ultimately take it in the neck. Buying shoes a kid thinks are "cool" costs you twice as much as it should, mainly because the endorsers have to be paid.

It ain't Nike paying for all that be-like-Mike hype.

I wonder what other parents do. I see kids in good neighborhoods and bad neighborhoods, all wearing Air this or that, and I think: Where does the money come from? If a single mother has three kids, ages 6 through 16, how does she afford to cover six feet in Penny Hardaway sneakers?

The math on that comes to $540. For shoes. Who can afford that? Who should have to? If Nike wants to do kids a favor, sell them cool shoes at a decent price.

"What have you got for under $50?" I asked Wade. He tried not to laugh.

Enduring Memories and the Open

June 11, 1997

Bethesda, Md.—Walking backward 20 years isn't as hard as it sounds. Squinting through the narrow prism of time past, you step off River Road and proceed down the long, slim lane leading to Congressional Country Club. The way is lined with clipped boxwoods, as tidy as memories are messy.

Back 20 years. Back across the scented lawns, through the carnival music of youth, to a place you worked as a waiter for seven summers. To a time when you served people who actually asked for martinis with "a scent of vermouth."

You can go home again. But it helps to have a golf cart.

Most know Congressional Country Club as the site of the U.S. Open. Or, as those gathered here in reverent, burnished droves consider it, the Tiger Woods Invitational of The Week.

Some see it differently.

Some know Congressional as a place where an assistant manager once wanted to fill the baby pool with champagne, as part of a July 4 celebration.

Or as a place where Judge John Sirica retreated each morning to get a rubdown before heading to court to preside over a little shard of history called the Watergate Trial.

Dishwashers and housemen without green cards, running in panic down the halls, pursued by men in suits.

Idle women, lolling on a grassy terrace above the sylvan swimming pools and the magnificent golf course, eating sandwiches with the bread crusts removed.

Dave Stockton, winning the '76 PGA here, as you watched from a tree above the 18th green.

Booker McCoy, the club garbageman, toiling a lifetime in sweat and trash stink, retiring to no great fanfare, dying only weeks later, caught in the crossfire of a liquor store holdup.

And Arthur.

"Died last June," Bill Fisher said Monday.

Bill Fisher, who has worked here since 1961, last June said goodbye to Arthur Brownridge, who had him beat in service time by seven years. Time doesn't actually move at country clubs like this one. Mostly, it sways.

"Nothing changes here," Fisher said to me. "You know that."

Arthur died making drinks, Fisher said. It figured. Arthur worked six days a week here for 42 years. He waited on golfers in the snack bar. In the winter he ran the bowling alley in the club's basement. He tended bar, and on a hot June 22 last year, he collapsed making a bloody Mary.

Arthur hired me in 1972. He taught me the dignity of work and how to keep a job, at least at Congressional. It amounted to three steps:

(1) Give 'em what they want

(2) Keep quiet about it

(3) See steps 1 and 2.

I came back looking for Arthur and the U.S. Open, in that order. The Open showed up.

It's funny where memory takes you sometimes. I remember my own youth through Arthur's words. When I revisit my own blooming summers, Arthur is in the picture, wiping off a table or pouring a beer, keeping his dignity as a few, misguided members make jokes about his African-American heritage.

If we are defined by our experiences, a piece of me remains in 1978, the last year I worked at Congressional. The last time I saw Arthur, he was serving golfers passing through between the front and back nine. Arthur called them all "Mister."

He was too busy to talk. "Come back and see us," was all he said. Now, I wish I had.

They'll begin the 97th Open here Thursday. Somebody will make a memory. Others already have one.

When Bill Fisher went through Arthur Brownridge's personal effects after Art died, he discovered some things: Letters and papers, and the five Bronze Stars Art had earned in World War II.

"Nobody ever knew," Fisher said.

They held a memorial service for Art downtown. Bill Fisher said 100 Congressional members came to say goodbye. Mr. Brownridge died a respected man. The lessons he gave endure, at least in one man's memory.

A Father's Son

*T*his column is two days late, because that is how it works for me on Father's Day. I was away Sunday, as I generally am every Father's Day, with a whole bunch of other fathers, equally rumpled, thrashing about in the toy department of careers.

It's a long-distance joy for me. I am usually at the U.S. Open. Not being a father, only accepting my kids' congratulations over the phone, for the privilege I am missing, again.

You miss a lot of things in this job, a lot of little times lost forever to World Series games, Bengals road trips and the like. My daughter's first steps were taken, as I recall, when I was at a Super Bowl somewhere. After Steve Jones won the Open on Sunday, the first thing he did was gather his kids on the 18th green, and squeeze. It was hard to tell which was the greater prize.

There is this guy I'm thinking of now. Tom Giaccio called me a month ago, to talk about his father. Tony Giaccio was the controller for a local chemical engineering company.

There was nothing special about Tony Giaccio. Also, everything. Tom told me his story. It sounded like sweet notes from a lucky, nurtured childhood. As a father, all Tony Giaccio ever did was care.

"We're going to see one of the best pitchers in baseball" was how Tony set up Tom's first ballgame, a venture to Crosley Field in 1964. Tom and Tony watched Don Drysdale that night. "A Hall of Famer," Tom said Monday.

The family lived in Price Hill. Evenings and weekends, Tony took off the suit and tie and fathered his two sons. They played basketball at the hoop in the backyard. Tony coached Knothole.

Once in the '60s, Tony appeared with two baseballs signed by the entire Reds team. Tom still has one of them, on the mantel in his living room, next to a picture of Tony.

Tony tossed the football. He played a game with Tom they called "Johnny Unitas," after the Hall of Fame quarterback.

"He'd be Unitas and throw me post patterns," Tom recalled. "As long as I wanted, he'd throw."

It is tireless, thankless, rewarding work. It is the best work of all.

"My father taught me two lessons in life," Tom said. "Give your best, and don't ever quit."

Lessons taught best by sports, I think. And by fathers who cherish the glow in their kids' eyes, and only want to keep it there. Sports doesn't have to be an adhesive in all this. But often, it is.

My mother died when I was 8, in November, and what my dad did about that was take me to basketball games. For $5, you got a bus ride and a game ticket.

We rode from Washington to Baltimore to watch the Bullets of Earl Monroe, Gus Johnson and Wes Unseld. When the games were done, we rode back, exchanging unspoken words in the cool, humming darkness.

We had season tickets to the Washington Redskins. My dad hates baseball, but he knew I did not. We'd drive to Philadelphia to watch my team, the Pittsburgh Pirates.

We climbed mountains in North Carolina, we swam in Cape Cod Bay. My dad was never so taken with his own life that he did not yield to mine. This is what fathers do.

I asked Tom Giaccio what it meant to have sports with his father. "Just the fact that we were there participating in something we both enjoyed," he said.

This Sunday, they will run the 7th race at River Downs in tribute to Tony Giaccio and to Tom's uncle, Pete. Tony also worked part time for 40 years at the Downs pari-mutuel window. The 2nd annual Tony and Pete Giaccio Memorial was Tom's idea. Tony died in May 1994.

"He was not only a dad," Tom said. "He was my best friend."

So here's to all the kids whose fathers are there for them, loving them and guiding them and doing the best they can. And to the kids who have no one to offer gifts of love or thanks, and for the hurt they must feel.

The best compliment I ever receive is when someone calls me my father's son.

Happy Father's Day, Dad. Belated, of course. I was at the Open on Sunday. Again.

The Jockstrap

September, 1993

I was 11 when I got my first jockstap. I was terrified.

The first September day of seventh grade at Thomas W. Pyle Jr. High, I was given a pile of books, some forms for my parents to fill out, some get-acquainted slugs on the shoulder from Joe Finch and a list of things I would need to take part in gym class.

White shorts, white T-shirts, white socks, towel fee, athletic supporter.

Athletic supporter?

We fetched it at Bruce's Variety on Bradley Lane in Bethesda, Maryland. Bruce's was an old, dark place of wood-planked floors and many smells. The help at Bruce's killed time by swatting flies and feather-dusting the jigsaw puzzles.

My father and I walked up and down the silent aisles. The jocks were next to the protective cups, hanging from hooks on the wall. My father took particular delight in telling all in the store that we were there "TO BUY MY SON HIS FIRST JOCKSTRAP." It didn't bother him that I wished I was dead. It contributed to his amusement.

DeBlasio, the gym teacher, didn't help. DeBlasio was a frustrated athlete who took his own shortcomings out on the youth of America. DeBlasio like to call all of us "straps," and every day he'd break us into squads and assign some unfortunate son the task of holding jock-check.

This meant the guy had to go down the line of his mates and either pull on the front waistband of your shorts and peer south or, worse, pull up the back of your shorts and check for the dreaded support straps.

If you were caught not wearing your jock, DeBlasio would commence to questioning your manhood in front of the guys. I never could decide which was worse: baring my 11-year-old all to a bunch of kids who weren't my brother, or having DeBlasio expose my pitiful weakness in front of the world.

Either way, DeBlasio was a worm, and I'd love to play a little one-on-one with him right now. I'd hand him his jock.

DeBlasio said I needed the jock for "support." I took this on faith. But I was 11 years old. I was a soprano. The hormones had not yet started their manly dance. They had not yet shimmied south. My need for support was not easily recognizable.

As my father the ex-Marine, All-American wrestler and child of the '40s and '50s (when men were men and women were not), put it: "You don't even have a jock to strap."

There are many milestones on the way to manhood, most of them silly or stupid or misunderstood. This was the first. Over the years, I would wrestle and play baseball competitively. I would swim and jog and commit aerobics and much of the time, I would do it while wearing a jock. It was, and is, the civilized thing to do.

Plus, as someone once said, in an age of confusing roles and rules involving the genders, wearing a jockstrap is just a manly damn thing to do. It is 100 percent cotton macho. It is snug and primal and it remains, along with belching in public and other amusing impolitenesses, a pleasure best enjoyed by men.

Only when you're 11, it's terror unleashed.

I knew guys who didn't know how to wear a jock. They slipped it on over their shorts. I knew guys whose *mothers* took them to buy their jocks. I knew guys who admitted to...wearing a small.

The horror!

What do you do with it? This is what I thought at first. I did with it all the usual things: I wore it on my head. I slipped it over my nose. I hurled rocks with it. In the dark silence of the room I shared with my brother, I quietly tried it on.

It felt like a truss. The thick, elastic waistband grabbed me like a girdle.

And what, exactly, were these two straps doing digging into my butt?

My friend Mike has a son in college now. When the son was a freshman in high school, he played football and wore a jock for the first time. He also wore a cup. The cup was unpleasant and made him dizzy, so in the middle of a game, he took the cup off and set it at the end of the team bench. A freshman cheerleader picked the thing up and, totally without guile, placed it over her nose and announced she was wearing an oxygen mask. Mike's son was never quite the same. Neither, I fear, was the cheerleader.

In high school, we smeared them with Ben-Gay. In college, we gave them to sorority types on scavenger hunts. Now, we just make sure they're washed regularly.

The jock has been around almost 100 years. This is a fact. It was first used by "bicycle jocks" in the 1890s, when their races carried them over cobblestone streets. This is according to Cindy Raines, marketing director of Bike sporting goods.

Bike is the king jockmaker of all time. "We just made our 300 millionth last year," Raines says.

The styles are more varied now. The materials are more sophisticated. More user-friendly. Bike produces jocks and compression shorts made of lycra. You can even buy colored jocks these days. But the mainstay of the business is still the white with the three-inch elastic waistband and the two support straps that girdle your cheeks like a couple of pieces of masking tape.

Lots of professional athletes have gone to the compression shorts, bypassing the traditional jock for a tight-fitting short with added protection sewn into the pouch. If you were wondering.

And maybe some of the old terror has dissipated.

"There used to be that level of intimidation for a kid to go out and buy a jock with his mom," says Mitch Carlin, corporate marketing director for Grid, Inc., another captain of the jock-making industry. "Now there's better education. There's not that fear level.

"I have a 7-year-old nephew. He wears a jock. It's almost like the kids today want to be like the pro athletes."

Not this kid. I was terrified. Maybe that's why I do what I do for a living. Working in the land of the jock has made me strong. No longer jock-a-phobic, I trudge through the land of the millionaire "straps."

Confront your fears, men.

It will set you free.

Cowabunga

May 7, 1990

$\mathcal{T}$he 4-year-old who was christened as Kelly but has come to be known as House Ape owns a wooden Louisville Slugger baseball bat that measures 24 inches long and weighs as much as a full diaper.

It's a handsome bat, made of fine ash, costing much money. It's a symbol of the precious and vital father-son relationship that all fathers and sons must have, lest the fathers be labeled louts and the sons become Charlie Manson.

Baseball is love. I read that somewhere. The Louisville Slugger, then, is a token of my deep and abiding affection for my son.

Kelly uses it to kill bad guys.

"Cowabunga, Dude!" he says, and he nearly gets good wood on the curio in the living room. Something is wrong here.

"Good stroke," I say. "Keep that back elbow up."

But this is not the way it was scripted, not at all. The books said that fathers forge strong bonds with sons through a mutual interest in sports. Baseball was the best, the books said. I read all the books.

There was even one whole book called *Fathers Playing Catch With Sons*. I could do that.

My dad never played catch with me. As I lurched into adulthood, I grew to recognize that sad fact to be the root of my many and varied deep-seated emotional problems.

I make lewd noises in public places and compulsively tear the tags off mattresses. Occasionally, I suck my thumb.

Whenever someone asks me what, exactly, my problem is, I tell them my dad never threw me grounders.

I swore this wouldn't happen with my son. I want to relate, I want to share, I want to bond. I want to catch.

If Kelly is really desperate for something to do, he indulges me.

"Kelly," I say, "let's go out and hit the ball! Let's go play in the yard! What a great day! Let's relate, big guy!"

"I'm watching the Turtles," Kelly says.

Sigh.

Four-year-old boys have lots of interests. Applying peanut butter to the stereo equipment, for instance. Baseball isn't one of them.

We're in the yard. It's one of those freshly-minted mornings in spring that the poets write about. The books said this was a baseball morning. Fathers play catch with sons and form lasting and mutually rewarding relationships on mornings such as this.

Kelly's got the Louisville Slugger. "Choke up," I say, and before he starts to pretend to cry, I slide his hands up the barrel of the bat.

"That's it. Now, line your feet up with your shoulders, Pal. (That's what I call him when we're relating. Pal.) Pal, I was watching the Reds today, and the Cardinals have a guy named Jose Oquendo. This guy,

249

if his stance were any more open, you could fit a truck between his front shoulder and the plate. I don't know how the guy gets any pop at all, Pal. He's got no hip turn, no..."

"I did a burp, Daddy."

He's killin' me.

I persist. There will be no Charlie Mansons in this household, buckwheat.

"Level swing," I say. "Eye on the ball, swing through, elbow..."

"Throw it here, Dude."

Dude?

He calls me Dude. I'm trying to bond here, for goodness sake.

Dude.

Somehow, I think he's missing the point.

Remember the climactic scene in the movie *Field of Dreams*? In the middle of breadbasket nowhere, Ray Kinsella plows under his corn crop to build a baseball field. Shoeless Joe Jackson eventually graces the place but, more essentially, so does Ray's dad.

"Dad?" Ray says. "Wanna have a catch?"

This is the point. A catch.

Kelly says, "I want a Popsicle."

When he gets ahold of one—that is to say, when bat meets ball by accident—I say stuff like "Nice rip, Pal. What a shot."

Baseball stuff. Hip patter between two baseball dudes.

Kelly rips a shot that almost reaches my feet. "Great hit," I say, and I feel we are making definite progress here. "Next time, watch the ball, swing level and..."

"But, Daddy. Splinter's a good guy and Shredder's a bad guy. Michelangelo's a party dude. Can we go to King's Island?"

I won't abandon this special father-son relationship. Even if my son wishes I would. You're never too young to keep the back elbow up.

In a desperate grab at relating, I pitch one more to the 4-year-old who calls me Dude. He sends a line drive past my ear. Really.

What a boy, I say.

"What a shot," he says.

Closing Down Sunday Afternoon

December 24, 1996

*O*n New Year's Eve in 1972, I am 15. It is my birthday. I do what I have done for seven years on Sunday afternoons between September and January. I go to RFK Stadium in Washington, with my dad.

We sit in Section 523, seats 9 and 10. Way up there. In 1972, RFK is only 11 years old. It is already a peeling concrete spaceship. The men's room toilets spill their water onto the floor. By December, the floor freezes.

The Redskins are playing the Dallas Cowboys for the right to go to the Super Bowl. After years of futility, the coach George Allen resurrects a collection of fine old men: Diron Talbert, Verlon Biggs, Jack Pardee, Pat Fischer, Billy Kilmer.

The year before, Allen had taken the Redskins to the playoffs for the first time. Now, they are poised to finish the job.

We make the long walk on the cold day, from the parking lot to the seats. We wonder if Kilmer, the quarterback, has it in him to beat the hated Cowboys. We hope Larry Brown, the battered running back, has knees enough to make it one more game.

They do. "I think that was the year they beat Dallas 28 to whatever," my dad is saying from Florida, where he lives now. "It was December 31, 1972," he says.

I could look it up, but it's not important. Memory has room for only so much. Imagination does the rest, and that's fine.

The Redskins win and all around us, fans drink champagne from paper cups. We know all of them. The two guys in the row in front of us, brothers I think. The guy three rows down, a New York Giants fan who converted a few years back. The little kid and his mom behind us. "Kid's probably a lawyer now," my dad says.

251

It's a little community of Sunday afternoon friendships. You don't really know these people, but you'd have every one of them over for dinner if you could.

It is the memories that mark a place, and the people those memories touch along the way. We had some times in Section 523. Yes, we did. They were the times of our lives.

They closed down RFK Sunday. I watched on TV from the press box at Cinergy Field. I watched at halftime, as they introduced John Riggins and Ron McDole and Sonny Jurgensen, and they were fine pictures for a Sunday afternoon.

I watched again after the game. The Redskins marching band played "Hail to the Redskins" several thousand times, and then, "Auld Lang Syne."

The fans swayed and wept, and I wished I were there, reclaiming a piece of who I used to be, so very long ago.

Because the thing is, they can build all the new places they want. The new stadiums are cash machines, ATMs with JumboTrons. They are pretty places, just as I'm sure the new Bengals stadium will be.

But you can't take memories and hawk them like a club seat. Perhaps 35 years hence, the people sitting in the luxury boxes at the new Redskins stadium in suburban Maryland will tip a glass of chablis at halftime, toasting the good old days.

They can't do that now. There are no memories in money.

"That was probably the best game ever," my dad says. We are back in 1972, swimming the river of time. Upstream, I'm afraid.

"Fourth and 1," he says. Remember 4th-and-1?

"Sure," I say. "Riggins. Super Bowl against Miami. Touchdown."

"Kenny Houston?" he says.

"Seventy-three," I say. "Monday night. Cowboys. He stops Walt Garrison at the goal line. We win."

My dad says, "Those were the days."

He stopped going in '81. Moved to Florida. Between '65 and '81, he missed one game. I stopped in '75, but for the weekends I was home from college.

The memories still visit, though, friendly spirits across the years that pass too quickly.

"You should have gone yesterday," I say. My dad still has rights to his tickets; he sells them to a friend. "You should have made the trip."

"Maybe so," he says.

We build new stadiums now, temples to greed. They're very nice to look at. I sometimes wonder what we're doing.

Remembering the Original

March 9, 1999

*O*n the second of October in 1949, he took the train from the 30th Street Station in Philadelphia to New York City. It was the biggest place he'd ever seen.

He caught the A-Train subway from Penn Station to the Bronx, where at Yankee Stadium, he saw the world stand still for Joe DiMaggio Day. The Yankee Clipper's career was winding down. Graceful to the end, DiMaggio finished the day with a triple. Then, his heel aching with bone spurs, he removed himself from the game. This is how my dad recalls it.

My dad is 66 now. Only today, he feels a little older. We who love sports tend to date ourselves by the accumulated wrinkles of our heroes and the inevitable passing of our idols. Joe D. was 84 when he died Monday. The clock moved a little swifter for those who remembered him.

"You think about special players," my dad is saying. "People who just looked good doing things. Willie Mays had it, too. Maybe Clemente. Those were kinder, gentler times."

DiMaggio was baseball's last original. When he went, something went with him, more precious than long home runs and graceful striding. He had class. It's a term that seems dated now. We don't use it much anymore, either because we've moved on to different descriptives for those who play games or, more likely, we're a little short on jocks who fit the adjective.

He was an elegant man, in a time when we believed that important. Dignity never eluded him. He kept it until the end. Elegance and dignity. Amazing traits, really, given our current appetite for Rodmans and Monicas.

My dad stayed at the Washington Hotel, on 3rd Avenue on the Lower East Side of Manhattan. He doesn't know, but he doubts it's there anymore. In other seasons, he'd take other trains, to the Polo Grounds and Ebbets Field. New York had three teams then, and an endless array of other charms.

He'd walk up and down 6th Avenue, haunting the record shops, hunting Benny Goodman records. "It was a magical time," my dad says. The world stretched before him like a good, long road.

Who didn't think DiMaggio would live forever? Or, at the very least, hoped he would? Those who remember him must feel a little sad today. For him, a little, but mostly for themselves.

My dad loved baseball as a kid. He doesn't watch it now. The game has soured him. Not because there have been no more DiMaggios. Because no one has made the effort.

"DiMaggio, Mays, (Jackie) Robinson, (Duke) Snider," he says. "I recall all these guys being special." (Except, my father noted, Ted Williams, who he says "was a nasty SOB.")

"That's the way they were portrayed to us simple-minded fans by sportswriters who weren't always digging up dirt," my dad says. "There were real heroes in those days. I don't think anybody is a hero anymore."

Nobody is in DiMaggio's league, anyway. It isn't pudding-headed nostalgia that makes us hurt at the Clipper's passing. It is the notion, real enough even to the uninitiated, that we will never see his like

254

again. Grace, dignity and hits in 56 straight games.

On Joe DiMaggio Day, the Yankees loaded Joe down with televisions, a boat and a car. The stuff covered the infield, as my father recalls. One can only imagine DiMaggio's unease at the protracted fuss. My dad doesn't recall that. It was only 50 years ago.

He remembers the era, though, and the youth he spent in it. DiMaggio was part of that. Now it's done.

On October 2, 1949, the last day of the season, the Yankees swept the Boston Red Sox in a doubleheader. Boston came into the day in first place, a game up on New York. The Sox left a game behind. DiMaggio legged out a triple on a bad heel. It's what my dad remembers.

We all were younger then.

Sports Takes a Vacation

July 28, 1993

Montreat, North Carolina—At 5,500 feet, I slide into neutral. Eight hours from the world and a mile above it, I loosen the top button and ease away from the cynicism. It is an easy thing to do in the Blue Ridge Mountains in July. Downy clouds scud the heath balds, and mountain laurel scents the day, a cachet of tranquility. The blueberries are just starting to turn.

If there are people who can make you feel better for having seen them (Sparky Anderson comes to mind) then, too, there are places that offer the same tonic. A bit of feel-good; a brief retreat from the daily gloom; a good, swift kick in the perspective.

I come here, to this warm and dowdy and dull and glowing

anachronism of a place, when I need a good dose of Take It Easy. I come here in the summer to drink from the mountain streams and taste the earth, to be among strangers who wouldn't think not to say hello. I come here to recall what counts. I come when I need to be somewhere where nothing is happening.

Too much in sports is happening. When a ballplayer throws a firecracker into a crowd of fans and scares a 2-year-old child, this is too much.

Sports has fallen off its hobby-horse perch and into something different. Something less.

When a ballplayer dies young of a bad heart, for the crime of playing a game, sports is too much. When a ballplayer squirts a reporter in the face with bleach for no ready reason, sports is too much.

Vince Coleman, the late Reggie Lewis and (supposedly) Bret Saberhagen are not singular culprits. They're just common strains of the current malaise.

Sports is getting so heavy, it's starting to sink. It used to be the corner of life you'd find to seek relief from the rest. Now, it's just like the rest.

I come to Montreat to be apart. Montreat is a place where a few people have been coming for 96 years, and not one of them has left a footprint. Montreat changes at the pace of the local geology. It is as it was 30 years ago, when we first met.

It is a Presbyterian retreat stuck somewhere between the Black Mountain Range and 1920. I can leave the door of my room open all night in Montreat, the cool mountain air wending from window to hallway, and not even think about being looted, maimed or otherwise offended.

The local speed limit is 20. The local speed is considerably less. High excitement is an ice cream cone and a walk along one of Montreat's 30-odd curvy streets, between oaks and beeches and rhododendrons tall enough to choke the sunlight.

In the daytime, you wander or you drive or you hike, but mostly you sit. From the second-floor lobby of the Assembly Inn juts a semicircular porch with rockers and a view of Lake Susan and Lookout Mountain.

No one here cares much about Kevin Mitchell's weight. Or Kevin Mitchell.

Everyone rocks. They all say hello.

For two days and three nights, the must of the place wraps around me like a cocoon. Up here, it's difficult to work up a good seethe about anything.

I travel the Blue Ridge Parkway, atop the spine of old hills, to a place called Craggy Gardens. Where, when I was 5 or 6, my father took me on my first hike and I saw my first deer. I wander up the old trail to the top, way high, above the day, to a hikers' shelter built of chestnut logs in 1935 by the Civilian Conservation Corps. In a beam, I see my initials, carved some three decades before.

At Craggy Gardens, the Catawba rhododendrons go purple-pink in June, blowing up the crag like a five-alarm blaze. They are more beautiful than any home run. In July, the Catawbas are green, exhausted and resting. It is the lilies that bloom now.

I navigate the crest of the mountains, and for three days I pass no judgment and offer no views. Nobody would care.

On the car radio, I hear a preacher rise up against the sins of the Ouija board: "Who knows the future but God?" I listen to "The Bluegrass Gospel Hour." I hear a recipe for green tomato pie.

For good health, I tie a necklace of rhododendron branches. For good luck, there are nuts from a yellow buckeye tree.

For fun, I slide down a smooth and ancient rock slab on a thin sheen of mountain stream water, dropping at a 45-degree angle for 100 feet, into a deep, cold pool. I swim some in the cold, green glaze and let the world wash away from me.

At dusk, I climb Lookout Mountain and reach the top just as the moon comes up. Montreat is below, somewhere. It is quiet and unmoving.

When I leave Thursday morning, back to Bengals and Reds and judgments, I'm reminded what a sportswriter friend once offered about our profession: "This beats working," he said. "But it doesn't beat not working."

Lately, it doesn't beat working. It is working.

I check out of the Assembly Inn with a slump and a sigh.

Everyone smiles. Everyone says hello.

Surprised by Joy

March, 1990

*J*illian has Simian creases. Horizontal lines, running the breadth of her tiny palm, one on each hand, unbroken tracks made by the peculiar genetics that rule her life.

They are what I think of now. It is three months after Jillian's birth, and I remember the words on her chart in the hospital room. "Simian creases."

I remember looking at her palm, no bigger than a cat's paw, the palm of a six-pound baby, then looking at my own. The lines were different.

Your baby is born, the first thing you do in the afterglow is take inventory. Ten fingers? Check. Ten toes? The full complement of ears, eyes and essential moving parts? Check, check, check.

Simian creases?

Jillian was born last October 17, the day of the San Francisco earthquake. You don't have to be hit over the head with the irony.

I remember catching the red-eye flight back from San Francisco, where I was covering the World Series for the *Cincinnati Post*. I missed the birth by some seven hours, but a call from the airport to the maternity ward confirmed that mother and healthy baby were doing fine.

I remember walking from my car to my wife's room, steps lighter than air, a familiar, if lately dormant, warmth spreading over me. You're never closer to your wife than when she brings you a child. You fall in love all over again.

A father again! Our 3-year-old sleeps at a friend's, but he is a boy. This is a girl.

A girl! Daddy's girl.

I walked to Kerry's room, loping down the hall, just floating, whistling the words of Billy Bigelow, in the musical *Carousel*:

"You can have fun with a son, but you gotta be a father to a girl."

I can't remember which doctor in the endless, faceless army of physicians at Good Samaritan Hospital told us our daughter was born with Down Syndrome.

The lines on her palms were a tip-off, but no more than the flat features of her freshly minted face, or her almond-shaped eyes, whose track that first, lost day wandered equally between the soulless gazes of her parents.

"There is a good chance Jillian has Down Syndrome," a doctor said. But we looked in her eyes, and we knew the chance was better than that.

Five weeks later, Jillian would be back in the hospital, a seven-pound waif whiter than pale, connected to life by a nest of monitors and tubes, dying to breathe, and we would pray to God that Down Syndrome was all that was wrong with her.

But now, we were consumed by the grief of anyone who has had something precious taken from him. We had been denied the most passionate event of life, the birth of a healthy child.

I would like to write what that feels like, to describe the sudden, inexplicable loss of joy and the terror that follow so quickly it sucks your breath away, but I can't.

One minute, you are nuzzling a brand-new baby, the next you're fighting life's darkest hurt. No grief runs deeper than that of a parent for his child.

"She's just a baby," I said then, and I said it over and over, a grief mantra. "She's just a little girl."

We laid in the sterile and cheerless glare of Room 507 at Good Sam. Kerry and I cursed God, fate, medical science and the happy coincidence that had been our lives. We tried to talk away the demons, we told each other it was fine to cry. We even said that, somehow, we would make things right.

We didn't know what the hell to do.

Did we do something wrong? Kerry was the model mother-in-waiting. For nine months, she ate nothing stronger than toast. She put nothing into her mouth she couldn't pronounce.

She had sonograms, she stretched and pulled her pregnancy through low-impact aerobics, she ate vitamins. If I made a model car for our son, she stayed out of the room, fearful of glue fumes.

I think of all the women who have babies they don't want, and of all the men who'd rather dance off a building than become fathers.

Babies die in dumpsters, babies are born addicted to cocaine. Babies can be as disposable as diapers. In large cities, so many perfect babies are abandoned, hospitals solicit volunteers who spend their lunch hours nuzzling discarded newborns.

My wife once told me she didn't drink alcohol in college because she wanted to bear healthy children.

That was fifteen years ago.

On the day of Jillian's birth, we really didn't know what to think. We reached for the telephone. The relatives would have to know, so we made the hardest phone calls of our lives.

Jillian was a genetic accident, we said, a bum spin of the chromosomal wheel. She didn't ask to have forty-seven chromosomes per cell, instead of the standard forty-six. It just worked out that way.

Because of Kerry's age at conception (34), Jillian had a one in 465 chance of being born with Down Syndrome. She was one of about 6,000 kids born in the U.S. last year with Down's.

Because of it, she is, at best, mildly mentally retarded. Because of it, she has small ears, which may make hearing difficult. Down's kids carry a whole catalog of deficiencies, not the least of which is a telling,

260

moon-faced physical appearance.

They are likely to have poor eyesight and underactive thyroids. About 40 percent require heart surgery before their fifth birthday. They almost never have children.

Medicine and society have progressed to the point that some adult Down's sufferers now live semi-independently, working at menial jobs for minimum wages.

We have come a long way in our attitudes toward those with Down's. This is what the books say. It is nice, it is hopeful and in the framework of what we're dealing with, it is encouraging. It is not what I envisioned for my daughter.

Jillian is only 3 months old. I can't help feeling her best steps were stolen from her, before she ever got to the dance.

We're dealing with it. That's what Kerry and I say now. Three months after Jillian's birth, the shock is gone. I'd like to say the sorrow is gone, too, along with the rage and the resentment and the fear.

But they remain. My emotions are a balloon in the wind. They groan and bubble and tumble, sometimes all at once. They've never been more raw, more exposed, held more closely to the light.

The night Jillian was born, I pleaded with God to take me into the tenuous and gauzy world of mental retardation. My life was half over. Hers was a sprout in the springtime grass. "Take me," I said.

"Don't do this to my little girl, God. Not to my little girl. Please. Don't do this."

The next day, I swore off religion. How could a just God watch over this? What, exactly, is merciful about retardation?

I wished God a speedy exit from my life. I told Him to go to hell. Three weeks later, I was back in church. Jillian was there, too.

I've rediscovered crying. The deep and essential sobs of the first few days of Jillian's life still make an occasional comeback. They usually hit past midnight, when I'm awake and alone, wandering with my thoughts.

It remains thus. The older Jillian becomes, the easier it gets, but the hurt still comes in unexpected and shocking bolts of terrible clarity.

There are still nights, like one a month or so ago, when I cradled Kerry in my arms in utter helplessness and confusion.

In tears, Kerry had returned from Jillian's 2 a.m. feeding. "I'm not sure I can care for her," she said.

"What?"

"I don't feel right. I don't feel how I'm supposed to feel."

"That's crazy," I said, lying. "I thought she was doing better."

"She'll never be better, Paul."

Things have changed since then. Our baby always accepted us. Now, we have accepted her.

If you met my daughter today, this is who you'd see: a tiny being swaddled in pink, with eyes like saucers, that are threatening to stay the perfect, heartbreak shade of blue.

For someone of just three months, she has lots of straight, brown hair, which we wrap up in a little white bow when we want to make other parents envious.

Her lips are already a deep shade of red. They pout, they pucker for kisses, they bend when she babbles, which is all the time. They make smiles that make me cry.

She is a beautiful child. This is what we hear from friends, family and strangers at the mall. In a culture that glorifies physical appearance, we fear what will happen when her Down's characteristics take over. And they will. Most Down's babies are as beautiful as ours.

I fear for Jillian's health and her happiness, but mostly I fear the day she will look at her face in a mirror and understand that life was not meant to be this way, and she will ask me why.

She is a beautiful little girl with no questions now, a bundle of hope in pink, always pink. In the two months since she was hospitalized for eleven days with bronchiolitis, she has grown from six pounds to nearly ten. We have grown in ways that can't be measured.

Family and friends have diluted our grief with their compassion. One of the joys of Jillian has been to make Kerry and I realize just how much we are loved by those closest to us.

Jillian has broadened our perspective, of course, and I believe that, over time, she will make us feel better about ourselves than we could ever imagine. Already, we like ourselves more for knowing our daughter.

Three months later, we see this, Kerry and I, and we believe that Jillian Phillips Daugherty will teach us more than we will ever teach her.

Once a month, we go to Children's Hospital, to meet with other parents of Down Syndrome infants.

There is a child I'm thinking of now. Elizabeth Doyle turned a year old four days after Christmas. She's a strawberry blonde with a big, beautiful, wide-open face. She's also a miracle, a tribute to the human spirit invincible.

"There were days when the hospital called us and said she's not coming home," says her mother, Joan.

Elizabeth was born with a ventricular septal defect—a hole in a ventricle of her heart. She had open-heart surgery at nine months.

She has also had the chicken pox and a broken leg. For the first six months of her life, Elizabeth was fed through a nasal- gastric tube.

At one time, she was misdiagnosed as having a fatal bone disease. At some point, even imperfections like Down Syndrome become irrelevant to the preserving of life.

"We have this baby who they told us wouldn't live," says Joan Doyle, "and here she is."

Here she is. At night in Jillian's room, I turn the lights down low and hold her in my arms. I love my daughter. It is a deep, aching, melancholy and desperate tie that binds me to Jillian. Someday, she'll know that.

For now, I sing her a song. We dance.

Goodnight, my love.

Pleasant dreams, sleep tight, my love.

May tomorrow be sunny and bright, and bring you closer to me.

Jillian goes to early-intervention classes, aimed mainly at developing her motor skills. Like most Down's babies, she has low muscle tone. For lack of a better word, Jillian is floppy.

At home, we roll up a beach towel, lay it beneath her shoulders and beseech her to lift her head. When she does, which is often, it strengthens her neck.

We rub her down. Down's babies sometimes have an aversion to touch, so we spend twenty minutes every day massaging Jillian's body, rubbing deeply the palms of her hands and soles of her feet. Maybe this helps her, but no more than it does us.

We dangle plastic toys from her stroller, and mobiles from her crib. We have her hold a bristly ball. We try to remember that children with Down Syndrome are much more like other children than unlike them.

In vacant moments, we think of shopping. Can we take her shopping, her mom wonders? If malls are the New World, then Kerry is Columbus. She'd love nothing more than to introduce her daughter to the womanly world of accounts receivable.

Kerry and Jillian. The girls. What about shopping?

I see girls, too. Sixteen and 17-year-old girls with their dates, handsome and lovely, draped in innocence and cymbidium orchids. Will they ever look so happy again?

I see a teenage girl late on the night of her prom, a wispy and fragile halo under the front porch light, wrapped in the shoulders of her young man's cologne.

I wonder if some enchanted evening, my daughter will know the smell of cologne.

We are adjusting our expectations for Jillian, but not our goals. We want her to be productive, respected and fulfilled. We don't care if she can be a singer. We just want her to be able to sing.

Jillian's condition is a big deal to us. The last thing we want is for it to be a big deal to her.

Happiness doesn't have to be tethered to physical and mental perfection. Dreaming is everyone's right. We want Jillian to be happy. We want her to have the courage to dream. That's all.

We're still trying to make the mental turn from curse to blessing, still trying to muster the spiritual resolve to beat back our own fears, still hoping the desperate hope that it really is gonna be okay. We have our own syndrome.

I still wonder sometimes if the fog of pain is lifting, or simply gathering silently for a lifetime encore.

But happily, I don't dwell on it so much anymore.

Someone once said that having a baby with Down Syndrome is like planning a dream vacation to Paris, then mistakenly catching a plane to Amsterdam. The joy's still there. It's just different.

Jillian is a joy. She is a treasure, a miracle and the prize of our lives. And she breaks our hearts every day.

We have a little game we play, my daughter and I. I lie her on her back on the floor of her room, a quilt beneath her. The first sound she made was a soft, cooing "Aa-oooh." That was more than a month ago, and I can still remember my amazement.

You mean Down's babies actually talk? Well, of course they do.

Jillian and I have clung to that first sound, though, even as she has become infinitely more verbal. She's into advanced cooing now.

"Aa-oooh, Jillie," I say.

Her room is tender as a dream. A sliver of moon seeps into the hallway, a clean and luminous testament to the miracle of a child.

Here's to you, my little baby. May tomorrow be sunny and bright.

"Aa-oooh," she says.

A Father's Special Gift

December 26, 1988

*O*n Christmas night in 1967, my father and I took a bus from Washington to Baltimore to watch the Baltimore Bullets play the St. Louis Hawks.

This was back when the National Basketball Association was a shot-and-beer league. It was before marketing strategies and David Stern and Jack Nicholson, back when gyms were gyms and not Domes. Back when pro basketball was Guys Night Out. In 1967, the NBA was a weekend alternative to bowling or poker. It was not the yuppie fascination it is now.

I was 9 years old. My father was 33. My mother would have been 31, if she hadn't died.

Your mother dies when you're 9, what do you know? You come home one day from fourth grade, the door is locked. The door is never locked.

The phone is ringing, no one answers. You put your ear to the door. Nothing. Your mother is always home, only this time, she's not. You're in fourth grade. You're only 9 years old. You don't know. You wait by the door.

Your father comes soon enough. Too soon for a weekday, and his face is red. He sits you down, he hugs the breath out of you and tells you your mother is dead. What do you know?

We started by watching the games on TV. The 1967 Bullets had Kevin Loughery, Bob Ferry, Wes Unseld, Gus "Honeycomb" Johnson, Jack Marin and, if memory serves, a rookie from someplace called Winston-Salem State in North Carolina.

His name was Earl Monroe. He dribbled the ball behind his back. Other than Elgin Baylor and Oscar Robertson, who did that?

He called himself The Pearl. In 1967, when self-promotion was not quite the rage among athletes it is now, when egos and contracts weren't quite so large, this was a great, raw leap of audacity. A rookie calling himself The Pearl.

The Bullets had The Pearl and a deal by which hoop-starved D.C. people could get to a game without breaking their wallets, or having to pay a South Baltimore street kid 50 cents to "watch" their car during the game.

The Bullets dispatched buses to the D.C. suburbs. For $5 or so, you got a round-trip bus ride and a ticket to the game.

We had a tree that Christmas, my father and I. We had presents, more than ever before, and cards. The Christmas cards and the sympathy cards all sort of ran together, scattered atop the TV and in the window shades, but the nights were too soft, too aching, too tender. We really didn't know what to make of the world.

My father suggested the bus. He wanted, I'm sure now, somewhere to escape the silence of home. He wanted to make his little boy happy on a cruel Christmas night. He wanted something to cheer about.

It picked us up at a shopping center in Langley Park, a roustabout, working-class Washington suburb. Little pink houses.

This was a great adventure, this trip after dark on a bus. Not a school bus, but a Greyhound!

My father sat real close to me in the seat that night, closer than he ever would. We talked about things.

A boy who is 9 and in the fourth grade wants to know how Earl "The Pearl" Monroe can dribble the basketball behind his back without having it bounce off his heel. He wants to know if Wes Unseld is the strongest man in the world, and if he can have a big popcorn at the game. He wants to know when his mother is coming home.

They'd call it father-son bonding now. We didn't know what to call it. It was equal parts love and desperation, faith and hopelessness. It was a mysterious trip in a dark bus. It was all we had.

Sports can work like this sometimes. You have only to cut through what seems to matter—money and drugs and greed and winning—to get to what makes sports eternal, to see why its forever beauty will survive its current storms.

Sports is as human an endeavor as we attempt. As much as we try to make it something greater, something bigger than life, it is no more than our reflection. It's love in the ruins of a Christmas night, 21 years ago. Sports is special because it's us.

My dad lives in Florida now. He's 56. He has been remarried now for almost 20 years, to a woman I now call my mother. Everyone at Christmas should have as much to be thankful for.

The Bullets moved to Washington, the Hawks to Atlanta. Gus Johnson died a few years ago, of cancer. Honeycomb was a power forward before there were power forwards. He shattered backboards by accident, before it was fashionable. The last fight was the only one he ever lost.

I talked to my father Sunday, but not about 1967. Time passes, so we talk silently about 1967 now. It's gone everywhere but in our hearts. Occasionally, one of us will make some small mention of The Pearl—What's he doing now, Dad?—or of Christmas night, 1967. When all we really had was each other. And a bus ride to Baltimore.